Judith Henry Wall

$\mathcal{F}$amily $\mathcal{S}$ecrets

A Novel

SIMON & SCHUSTER

New York   London   Toronto   Sydney

Simon & Schuster
Rockefeller Center
1230 Avenue of the Americas
New York, NY 10020

Designed by Karolina Harris

Manufactured in the United States of America

ISBN 978-0-7394-8673-3

With profound gratitude to
Laura Zeller
Dr. Jim Wall
Dr. Robert Rankin
Dr. Kenneth Stokes

Acknowledgments

I AM grateful to Amanda Murray, my talented and perceptive editor, and Philippa Brophy, my agent and friend of many years.

And I am indebted to Daranna Bradley, JoAnna Wall, and Joan Atterbury for their help and encouragement.

Family Secrets

Eagles Nest, Colorado

*A*s was her custom, Myrna had deliberately kept her visitor waiting for half an hour—a practice that established hierarchy. And the visitor would have had plenty of time to admire and be intimidated by her office with its sleek décor and the view from a spacious deck that jutted out over a veritable abyss and took one's breath away.

The man was on the deck when she entered the room, his hands on the railing, the wind lifting his longish hair as he took in the breathtaking view of Colorado's Elkhead Mountains. She watched him for a time, imagining the firm, youthful body beneath the well-tailored sport coat, and found herself regretting the vast difference in their ages. Not that she would have tried to seduce him, but a little sexual tension was to a business meeting what seasoning was to food; it made the experience more pleasant.

Of course, there had been a time in her life when a pleasant business encounter sometimes led to other things. It had been years, however, since she'd had a man in her arms and life, and probably she never would again. She'd always assumed that a time would arrive when she stopped having sexual thoughts, but they still came unbidden. In the night, they came. Or sometimes in the presence of an appealing man.

She cleared away such thoughts with a shake of her head and crossed the room to the open French doors. "Mr. Farris?"

He turned and smiled. His teeth were white and perfect. "You have the most incredible home I have ever seen," he said.

She accepted his compliment with a nod, then headed toward her desk with Mr. Farris following. She was still tall and erect and carried herself in a manner that belied her age, but she knew that he saw her as a person made all but genderless by advancing years.

Even if he were willing, she had too much pride.

Once they both were seated on their respective sides of her large, highly polished, and absolutely bare desk, he handed her a thick manila folder.

She placed it in front of her and folded her hands on top of it. "Tell me what's inside."

"Basically I discovered nothing about any family member that would cause insurmountable problems in your son's upcoming gubernatorial campaign," he said with his elbows resting on the arms of his chair, his body leaning slightly forward. "Other than Randall's DUIs, your children and their spouses and your grandchildren have been extremely circumspect in conducting their personal lives."

He waited for her to comment. When she remained silent, he said, "Your son has already acknowledged his DUIs in previous campaigns, and they seem to have been written off by voters as youthful indiscretions. His long-standing second marriage to the daughter of a noted architect is certainly in his favor. And Randall has an impressive military record, has been a reasonably effective congressman during his three terms, and is popular with the media."

Again he paused. When she didn't comment, he drew in his breath and slowly let it out.

She suppressed the smile that was playing with her lips. He was either feeling intimidation or frustration. Or both. *Poor baby.*

"As for your own background," he said with a bit of a stammer, "it is a bit more problematic. While it's not unheard of for birth records to be destroyed in courthouse fires and for an individual to apply for and receive a new birth certificate based on affidavits from relatives, baptismal and school records, and the like, the only documentation provided when you applied for a new birth certificate was an affidavit signed by two 'cousins' who have no paper trail at all, which could make one wonder if these two individuals ever existed."

He squared his shoulders as though expecting her to refute his statement. When she did not, he continued, "And this most likely fraudulent birth certificate is the only sort of documentation I was able to find on you until your second marriage. In fact, the first two decades of your life are devoid of any verifiable information. This absence of a paper trail is unusual at best, and if I were the suspicious sort, I would wonder if you hadn't created a new identity for yourself in young adulthood. According to the brief bio used by your company, you came from a mining family and were raised in Montana, but it would help if I knew something about your parents and your childhood."

"That was a very difficult time in my life," she said, "and I prefer not to make it public."

He regarded her, his head tilted to one side, as though he was trying to decide how insistent he should be. "Ordinarily," he said, "the media might not take much interest in the widowed mother of a potential candidate for high office. Since you are not the usual candidate's mother, however, there will likely be some snooping. Actually I predict there will be a great deal of snooping."

"It's your job to see that such 'snooping' goes no place," she said.

"Yes, of course." He leaned forward and placed his hands on the desk. "As a diversionary tactic, I suggest we clandestinely hire someone to write an 'unauthorized' biography on your life that will put forth a version of your difficult childhood and young adulthood that you can live with. The book will highlight your courage in overcoming adversity, your dedication to your family, your contributions to the mining industry, your generous support of numerous worthy philanthropies, and your incredible success in building one of the nation's largest family-owned companies from the ground up. However, the biography should also include a few salacious and apparently embarrassing details that in reality only serve to make you more interesting and colorful and make the book more believable but will cause no real damage to you or your family's reputation. You will make a public show of trying—unsuccessfully, of course—to stop publication of the book, which guarantees that it will be widely read and be used as a seemingly valid source of information for journalists."

She wanted to tell him no. Up to this point, she had led an exceedingly private life. But ironically the last decades of her life were a lead-up to one very public moment that would be played out in front of the Capitol in Washington, D.C. The governor's chair was but a stepping-stone to the presidency.

"The book is an intriguing idea," she said. "I will read your report and get back to you."

ONE

$\mathcal{V}$ANESSA tried to look interested while her sister Ellie fretted about the lack of eligible men in her life and expressed her irritation over the fading of the "permanent" eyeliner for which she had paid five hundred dollars and while her other sister, Georgiana, tried to decide if she should have her hair straightened and whether she should "invest" in an iPod.

Vanessa glanced in their mother's direction, ready to roll her eyes as an editorial comment on her sisters' lack of maturity, but Penelope was absently toying with the stem of her wineglass, her mind seemingly elsewhere.

Vanessa reached for her own glass and took a sip of the pricey Pinot Noir that Ellie had insisted on ordering. Ellie also had insisted that they eat at this trendy French restaurant with its hot new chef. As an associate editor at the fashion magazine *Stiletto*, Ellie considered herself an authority on anything remotely connected to style and the good life. And it was their mother's sixtieth birthday, she had pointed out. Of course, Ellie was single, as was Georgiana, who made a ridiculous amount of money as a hand and foot model. They had no one to take care of but themselves; whereas Vanessa had two daughters in need of orthodontia, a husband who after fourteen years of marriage was still trying to find himself, and a suburban home that they couldn't afford to maintain.

As though sensing her older sister's disinterest, Ellie wound down her tales of woe with the assertion that what this city needed was a major incursion of heterosexual men, then lifted her glass. "Here's to our glamorous mother on her very special birthday," she said.

Vanessa studied their mother's face and its somewhat detached smile. Glamorous. Yes, she was that. Maybe even a bit too glamorous considering she had been widowed for less than a year. Penelope Wentworth was trim, unlined, elegantly attired, and could probably pass for her daughters' older sister.

People often told Vanessa that she looked like her mother. And while she was tall and had her mother's thick, dark hair, she had not inherited Penelope's brown eyes, high cheekbones, or her olive complexion. Like her sisters, Vanessa had their father's fair skin and blue eyes. Ellie and Georgiana also had their father's thick, reddish blond hair, but Ellie's hair was sleek and straight, while Georgiana's hair was a mass of unruly curls. Vanessa had always thought that her sisters' hair reflected their personalities. Ellie was a control freak, and Georgiana was scatterbrained. Ellie's outfit du jour was always meticulously planned. Georgiana rolled out of bed and started grabbing but somehow managed a charmingly bohemian look.

They had not celebrated their mother's fifty-ninth birthday. A year ago their father had been close to death. A horrible time. The worst of Vanessa's life. Thinking about it brought the all too familiar ache to her chest. God, how she missed him. Her father had been her hero. The dearest man she'd ever known. The man against whom she compared all others. Her husband, Scott, had never come close to measuring up. Not that she didn't love him; she just wished he was more ambitious. And more thoughtful. But maybe Scott felt the same way about her.

After dinner they sauntered along, heading for the apartment on Park Avenue where their mother now lived alone and that the sisters still referred to as "home." They had gathered there before dinner and were returning for birthday cake, champagne, and the opening of gifts. It was a wonderful summer evening with the sidewalk full of Friday-night strollers on their way to and from restaurants or simply enjoying the sights and sounds of this Upper East Side neighborhood.

After more than a decade of living in northern New Jersey and navigating her life from behind the wheel of an SUV, Vanessa still thought of herself as a New Yorker and probably always would. And while she sometimes complained because her mother—and her sisters, too—seldom came to visit her and her family in New Jersey, they did give her an excuse to come into the city.

The eighth-floor apartment was spacious by New York standards and filled with a diverse mix of furniture, artwork, and clutter that their parents had collected over the years or was left over from the days when the apartment had been the home of Penelope's parents. The sisters cleared magazines, books, and a potted plant from the coffee table. Georgiana placed six candles—one for each decade of their mother's life—in the cake. Ellie uncorked a bottle of champagne, and Vanessa placed a stack of presents in front of Penelope.

They sang "Happy Birthday" and watched their mother blow out the candles, then exchanged knowing glances as she opened the several smaller presents—perfume, bath oil, the latest book by one of her favorite authors—that were but a prelude to their very special gift for her very special birthday. They had hired an artist to paint a portrait of their parents based on one of the many photographs taken at their thirty-fifth wedding anniversary. Vanessa had tears in her eyes as she watched her mother remove the wrapping. Her sisters' eyes were also glistening. They had conferred long and hard over the gift, debating which photograph to use, locating just the right artist to paint a portrait of their beloved parents, selecting the perfect frame. The results were stunning. Penelope and Matthew Wentworth looked wonderfully happy and very much in love. Vanessa had grown up assuming that she, too, would one day marry a fine-looking, considerate, witty man like her father and have the same sort of loving, respectful marriage her parents had had.

Not that she and Scott had a bad marriage. It was just that they didn't adore one another the way her parents had. Scott never looked at her the way her father was looking at her mother in that anniversary picture.

Vanessa held her breath while Mother pulled away the last of the wrappings and regarded the painting. "Oh, my," she said softly, her fingertips touching the face of their father. "What a dear, beautiful man he was."

"You were such a handsome couple," Vanessa noted as she dug in her purse for a tissue. "Everyone said so. And so devoted. And I never once heard you guys say a cross word to one another."

"I was always so proud of my great-looking parents," Ellie chimed in.

Penelope dabbed at her eyes, then rose from the sofa to give each of them a hug. "Your father was a wonderful man," she said, "and, oh, how he did love his darling daughters. You girls were the light of his life."

When she sat down again, it was not on the sofa but

in the wing chair, which Vanessa had always thought of as her mother's throne. Daddy had preferred the comfort of the well-worn easy chair and ottoman. Vanessa closed her eyes, remembering evenings in this room. She and her sisters sprawled here and there doing their homework. Their parents in their places with reading glasses parked on their noses. Their parents were both writers. Their father worked for a major news service, and their mother wrote magazine articles. Both had deadlines to meet. They proofread each other's work. Even if the television was on, they were reading or editing or proofing.

"We thought the portrait would look fabulous over the mantel," Ellie said, her voice almost childlike in her delight and pride. The portrait had been Ellie's idea. Vanessa and Georgiana had thought a special piece of jewelry would be appropriate, but they had immediately acquiesced when Ellie told them about her idea.

When Penelope did not respond to her suggestion about where to hang the picture, Ellie added, "That picture has faded over the years."

Vanessa glanced up at the courtly ballroom scene. Yes, the picture had definitely faded. As had the wallpaper, drapes, and upholstery. The room was overflowing with furniture, bric-a-brac, framed photographs, stacks of newspapers and books and magazines. Through an arched opening was the dining room—with its scarred table and cluttered china cabinet—where the family used to gather for dinner. Lively gatherings. Good times that were gone forever.

Vanessa waited with her sisters for their mother to say yes, that over the mantel would be a perfect place for the portrait. *Had Mother not heard Ellie?* Vanessa exchanged worried glances with her sisters.

When Penelope finally spoke, her words had nothing

to do with the wonderful birthday present that now lay seemingly forgotten on the coffee table. "I've been going through your father's things," she said.

They watched as their mother rose, went to the handsome mahogany secretary that had once been their grandmother's, and returned with a yellowing envelope, which she handed to Vanessa. "I found this in a Bible that belonged to your daddy's Miss Vera."

The envelope was addressed to Miss Vera Wentworth, the spinster lady who had raised their orphaned father. There was no return address, but the postmark indicated that the letter was mailed in Deer Lodge, Montana, almost sixty-one years ago.

Vanessa pulled out a single sheet of lined notebook paper and read the brief, pencil-written message:

> Dear Aunt Vera,
>
> Thank you for taking in my baby. Please tell him only that his mother died when he was born and that you were never told her name or anything about her.
>
> God's blessing on you both.
>
> Sincerely,
> Hattie

A shiver went up and down Vanessa's spine. *Her father's mother had given him away.* How strange to learn something so elemental about her father's life that he himself had never known. For his entire life he believed himself to have been orphaned at birth. He'd been raised on a farm outside a small town in West Virginia by an elderly woman who died when Ellie was just a baby and Georgiana had not yet been born.

Vanessa had clear memories of the gaunt old woman

with frizzy gray hair, spectacles resting on her nose, her face a road map of lines and creases. She remembered Sunday dinners at the round table in the farmhouse's austere kitchen listening while Vera and Daddy discussed crops and pigs and the weather and who'd died since he'd last visited the rural community. She always called him by both his first and middle names—Matthew Wade. He called her Miss Vera. She had raised Matthew Wade to believe that his father had died in a mining accident before he was born and his unmarried mother had died giving him birth and that Vera had been asked to care for the baby until a permanent home could be found for him. But after only a few weeks, she realized that God expected her to raise him and began legal proceedings to adopt him.

Vanessa looked again at the postmark on the envelope. Her father would have been little more than a week old when it was written.

Once again the living room was filled with silence. Vanessa became aware of the street sounds eight floors below. A distant siren. Squealing tires. Horns honking. Laughter.

"I thought about putting the letter back in the Bible or maybe just throwing it away," Penelope admitted. "But the woman who wrote it *is* your grandmother."

"She's probably dead by now," Ellie pointed out.

"Maybe," Penelope said with a shrug. "Or maybe not."

"So what do you think we should do about the letter?" Vanessa asked.

"That's up to you girls," Penelope said.

"I think we should take a trip to Montana and look for her," Georgiana announced with an emphatic shake of her curly mop. "That's what Daddy would have expected us to do."

"I'll bet the single men in Montana are all straight as arrows," Ellie observed in a wistful voice.

"We can't just go traipsing off to Montana looking for an old woman named Hattie," Vanessa pointed out.

"Why not?" Georgiana demanded with a wave of a perfectly manicured hand. "Lots of people who were adopted find their birth parents. I don't see why we can't find our birth grandmother. I'm sure there are Web sites that explain how to search for long-lost relatives."

"Well, I have a family to look after," Vanessa reminded them. A family that should have been here with her tonight, but the girls had been invited to a slumber party, and, as was usually the case, Scott had some reason not to accompany her into Manhattan. Tonight he'd claimed that his throat was sore when she knew that he really wanted to watch a baseball game. And what she really wanted was for just her and her sisters to watch their mother unwrap the portrait and witness her delight from the gift itself and from her daughters' thoughtfulness.

Their mother's reaction had been tepid. Not one of delight. Vanessa took a deep breath fighting against a wave of disappointment. Bitter disappointment. And even anger.

The mysterious letter and its envelope now sat on the coffee table next to the portrait. Why had her mother chosen to show it to them on her birthday?

Now that Vanessa thought about it, Mother had seemed preoccupied all evening. And when Vanessa had used the bathroom before they left for the restaurant, she noticed a stack of cardboard boxes in her parents' bedroom. The top box was opened, and she recognized various items of her father's clothing folded inside. Vanessa picked up his favorite cardigan and buried her face in it. Of course, she didn't expect her mother to hang on to her father's clothes forever. Probably seeing them still hanging there in his closet made her sad. The clothes would be sent to some charity, which was the correct thing to do.

But the thought made Vanessa momentarily ill. She felt as though her father's memory were being erased.

Vanessa had not looked in her father's study, but she wondered if her mother had also been going through the desk, file cabinets, and bookcases deciding what should be kept and what should be disposed of. That's why she'd come across Vera's Bible and the letter hidden away among its pages.

But why this sudden rush of activity after living among Daddy's things for the last year? Vanessa took comfort in them. His presence still permeated every corner of the apartment.

Then a disturbing thought crossed her mind.

"You aren't planning to sell the apartment, are you?" Vanessa asked her mother. After she'd spoken the words, she realized that they had sounded accusatory. Ellie and Georgiana both looked startled that she would ask such a thing.

Penelope shook her head. "No, but I am planning to rent it."

"Rent it! Why would you do that?" Georgiana asked, puzzlement in her voice.

"Because I don't want to live here anymore," Penelope said with a small shrug, "and rentals being what they are in this part of town, the apartment will provide a nice income for me."

"I don't understand," Vanessa said. "Why don't you want to live here anymore? It's our home."

"It *was* your home," Penelope corrected. "It's where your father and I raised our three daughters, but you girls live elsewhere now, and as much as I loved your father, I don't want to spend the rest of my life living with his ghost. You girls are welcome to whatever you want of all this stuff," she said with an airy wave of her hand apparently indicating the entire contents of the living room and the rooms beyond. "I plan to get rid of the rest. The painters and carpet layers are scheduled next month. And I guess I'll have to do something about the antiquated kitchen."

Her mother didn't want to keep anything? Vanessa was stunned.

"I know my decision comes as a surprise to you girls," Penelope continued, "but I wanted to wait until I was absolutely sure before I said anything. And I wanted the three of you together when I told you about my plans."

"Where will you live?" Ellie asked, her voice quivering.

Penelope's arms were resting on the arms of the chair. Her chin was high, her gaze distant. A tiny smile was playing with her lips. "I plan to live in a lovely old farmhouse in the south of France," she said.

"France!" Ellie and Vanessa exclaimed in unison.

"You can't be serious," Georgiana said. "Why would you want to live in France?"

"Because I've lived my entire life in this city and would like to live someplace else before I die," Penelope said, then added with a girlish shrug, "and because it makes be happy to be there."

"How could you know that?" Vanessa demanded, not even trying to keep the disapproval from her voice. "You've never been to France before."

"Oh, but I have," Penelope said with an enigmatic smile that would have done the *Mona Lisa* proud. "I was there just last week."

Vanessa exchanged glances with her sisters. Their mother was losing her mind. She could not possibly have gone to France on her own and without any of them even knowing about it.

"You must be thinking of Montreal," Vanessa suggested.

"No, my dear, I was thinking of France. A small village in Provence. It's called Château de Roc.

TWO

*E*LLIE waited until the elevator door slid closed before announcing, "Mother has met a man."

"That's absurd," Vanessa snapped.

Ellie felt a wave of irritation at her older sister. Vanessa could be such a know-it-all. "You're right," she said, her voice dripping with sarcasm. "Mother just woke up one morning and out of the blue decided to get rid of everything she owned and leave behind her daughters and granddaughters and friends of a lifetime and move half a world away from the only city she's ever lived in."

"She probably met him online," Georgiana said with a sigh.

"How disgusting for you even to think such a thing," Vanessa told her sisters with her shoulders square, her chin high, her voice filled with indignation. "Sixty-year-old widows still grieving for the love of their life don't violate their dead husband's memory by going online to find a man to run off with."

Then Vanessa burst into tears.

Ellie and Georgiana immediately put their arms

around her and tried to soothe. "Come on, Nessa, it's not the end of the world," Ellie said.

As the elevator door opened, Ellie thought about suggesting they find a quiet bar and discuss this surprising turn in their lives, but she had other plans for the rest of the evening. And Georgiana would be heading for the club where her nerdy musician boyfriend was playing. Besides, while a part of Ellie would like her mother to be the keeper of the family shrine for the rest of her days, she could understand how even a sixty-year-old woman might want something more in her life.

On the sidewalk in front of the building the sisters hugged each other, then Georgiana headed for the subway entrance and Ellie stepped to the curb to hail a cab. "You want a ride to Grand Central?" she asked Vanessa.

Vanessa shook her head. "No, I think I left my cell phone in the apartment," she said over her shoulder as she headed back toward the building entrance. "I'll call you tomorrow."

Oh dear, Ellie thought. Now Vanessa's going to go give poor Mother the third degree. Momentarily she thought about following Vanessa and acting as an intermediary or whatever. But when a cab pulled up to the curb, she got in.

"JoJo's on Lafayette," she told the driver, and went about the business of transforming herself, removing her chic Marc Jacobs jacket to reveal a strapless, red-satin bustier, using hair spray to give her hair a more tousled look, adding a heavy coat of glossy red lipstick and an ample dusting of blush.

Growing up, Ellie had assumed that she would someday fall deeply in love with a man as kind and loving as her father had been and have children with him. But throughout the third decade of her life she'd seen what marriage and motherhood had done to her older sister, who used to be beautiful and loads of fun. Now Vanessa was a worried, frazzled mother of two and the wife of a nice-enough-but-somewhat-ineffectual man who claimed to be marketing business property online but didn't seem to be contributing much to the household budget. Ellie found herself wondering if she really wanted to share her domicile with anyone—male or female, adult or child, two-legged or four-legged.

But something began happening to her about the time she turned thirty. She wasn't sure if it was hormonal or societal or just plain insanity, but she started taking notice of babies. *Really* noticing them. Wherever she came upon babies—in restaurants, on the street, in a park, on the subway—she couldn't take her eyes off them. Babies were like magnets. Ellie felt an almost worshipful reverence for them and found that she adored baby toes, baby shoulders, baby thighs. She wanted to be a mother. She could actually *feel* the emptiness of her uterus.

Just about the time she started going nuts over babies, she began noticing something about the babies' fathers, who were delighted to show off their offspring and who were the sort of earnest, wholesome-yet-sexy-in-a-sweet-vulnerable-way kind of guy she'd been looking for. Maybe fatherhood turned inconsiderate, self-centered, egotistical men into decent guys who sincerely loved their wives and children. Maybe a girl just had to take a man on faith no matter how much of a jerk he appeared to be and hope for the best.

The problem was the straight guys in her day-to-day life were few and far between. Ellie's domain was the world of fashion, and most of the men she worked with—fashion designers, graphic artists, hairdressers, makeup artists, photographers, and the like—were gay. Actually, she preferred the company of gay men, but they weren't much good when a girl was horny. Or when she wanted to get married and have a baby.

By the time the cab had reached its destination, Ellie had completely transformed her look from stylish career woman into sex kitten on the prowl. JoJo's had been described in the *Village Voice* as a hot singles nightspot for the overthirty crowd. Ellie had been to many such nightclubs since beginning her quest and hated them all. Hated putting herself on display. Hated wearing attire that had nothing to do with the sleek, fashionable woman she really was. Hated the blatant, over-the-top flirting. Hated the entire scene. And kept vowing that she wasn't going that route ever again. But a friend of a friend had set her up with an "all but divorced" guy named Boone—Ellie wasn't sure if that was his first name or his last name. Apparently JoJo's had been Boone's suggestion. She'd told the friend of a friend to tell Boone that she'd be wearing a red dress and a white gardenia in her hair.

The gardenia!

She paid the cabbie, then fished the fake flower out of her Chloé leather tote and clipped it over her right ear as she made her way through the milling crowd on the sidewalk.

She left the tote with the hatcheck girl, then waited for her eyes to adjust to the dim light and the pulsating strobes. The music was deafening. The dance floor was a gyrating, arm-waving mass of humanity. Ellie closed her eyes and allowed the music to take her. Her body began to sway. Her arms floated over her head. *Please let Boone show up. And please let him be thoughtful and kind and attractive and smart and not looking for a one-night stand but for a woman to cherish and spend the rest of his life with and make a baby with.*

Georgiana sat alone at a small round table just outside the spotlight illuminating Trisha Bell, a plump, middle-aged singer who'd had a huge hit decades ago. "My One True

Love" was still being sung at weddings and was familiar to most adults of a certain age. The bar on Houston in the West Village was packed with older tourists for whom the name Trisha Bell had some meaning. A band of six was accompanying her with Georgiana's boyfriend, Freddy, on the electric guitar.

The waiter appeared with a vodka tonic. Compliments of Freddy, he told her. Before she could tell him to bring water instead, the waiter was gone.

She'd had a glass of wine at the restaurant and champagne with the birthday cake. To avoid fluid retention in her hands and feet, she never drank anything alcoholic or ate salty food forty-eight hours before a photographic shoot, and she had a shoot scheduled first thing Monday morning.

And to make sure her feet exhibited no marks or redness, she wore only soft moccasins for twelve hours before a shoot. She also had weekly manicures and pedicures performed by Dr. Lou, an elderly Chinese podiatrist who'd been recommended by the modeling agency as the best in the business. Per Dr. Lou's instructions, Georgiana buffed her nails and rubbed cocoa butter into her hands and feet several times a day and avoided shoes that might put undue pressure on any part of the foot. Dr. Lou told her that the longest any hand and/or foot model—even those who religiously followed his instructions—could expect to be successful was the early thirties, after which time the skin started to coarsen, veins became more prominent, and ridges began to appear in the nails. And don't get pregnant, he warned. "Pregnant bery, bery bad for hands and feet. Make hands and feet puffy."

Georgiana's plan had been to save half of the money she made so that by the time she was thirty she could carry herself over a lean year or two while she became established as a prominent creator of art photography but now worried that might not be a feasible expectation. Not that she wasn't making a significant amount of money, but it took so damned much just to get by.

Georgiana had really been into photography during high school and never went anyplace without a camera. At NYU she'd been a fine arts major with an emphasis in photography until the hand and foot thing came along out of the blue. A woman on the subway told her that she had beautiful hands and asked if she'd ever thought of being a hand model. The very next day Georgiana began calling agencies. It turned out that her feet were beautiful, too.

Now that she was busy with her modeling career, she had little time for pursuing the art of photography, but she couldn't pass by a photographic gallery without going inside. And she was always looking at the world through an imaginary lens framing imaginary pictures. She was a purist using only black-and-white film and developing it herself and was no more tempted by digital technology than a painter would be.

Even now as she sat at the tiny nightclub table, she imagined how she would photograph Trisha Bell in the smoke-filled column of light. Then her attention moved to the shadows. To Freddy's barely illuminated form. Every sinew of his body was concentrating on the music. It didn't matter that he was playing sappy ballads from the sixties and seventies. His job was to make music, and just as Georgiana had a fascination for images captured with a camera—from the faded snapshots she'd come across in shoeboxes and albums at junk stores to Ansel Adams landscapes in pricey galleries—Freddy had a passion for all music from hillbilly to classical. She knew that her sisters didn't understand why she hung in there with a guy whose occupation required him to make music into the wee small hours of the morning and who didn't care diddly-squat about clothes and money and impressing people unless it was with his virtuosity. But Freddy was sweet and lovable, and their relationship was as comfortable as her favorite pair of bedroom slippers. And that counted for a lot, she told herself. Except sometimes she wished he were as good with words as he was with melodies.

Georgiana took just a tiny sip of the drink, which tasted wonderfully crisp and cool, and thought of the hundreds of nights she'd spent sitting at a table or standing backstage as she watched Freddy play his guitar with whatever trio or combo or group of which he was currently a member.

When they'd first started hanging out together, Freddy was the best-looking, smartest, most popular boy in the tenth grade. No one from those days would even recognize him now, what with the long hair, piercings, tattoos, and the scrawny body that he'd acquired after he'd left home and no longer ate meals regularly. She'd had other boyfriends off and on over the years, but she hadn't gone out with anyone else for almost two years, long enough that it irritated her when one of her sisters asked if she was "still seeing Freddy."

Trisha Bell was singing a ballad about a convict escaping from prison so he could see his dying wife one last time. It was hokey as hell, but Georgiana found herself dabbing her eyes with the tiny, stiff paper napkin that came with her drink. After the convict had been shot dead by the sheriff's men and the song ended to loud applause, Trisha threw kisses, made her exit, and the lights came up. Freddy blinked a few times, then came over to the table.

"Hi, doll," he said, leaning over to give her a kiss. A very nice kiss. He sat next to her and she pushed the drink toward him. He removed the straw and downed it in one gulp. "You staying for the next set, aren't you?"

She shook her head. She wanted to tell him that she

was upset. That her Mother had not shed a single tear when she'd seen the portrait and was getting rid of all the family possessions and moving to France. And that even though she had defended their mother's right to make such a drastic change in her life, it was disturbing to realize the home of their childhood would be lost to her and her sisters—and shocking to think of their mother with a man other than their father.

"What did you think of that last arrangement?" Freddy asked. "I talked Trisha into letting me update some of her stuff. The old girl still has a great set of pipes, but she's stuck in the dark ages when it comes to music."

"Do you love me?" Georgiana asked.

He reared back in his chair a bit and scrutinized her. "Silly girl," he said, punching her arm. "You're my one and only."

Then he took a second look and realized he had not provided the correct response to her query. "You are my one true love, Georgiana Wentworth, and always will be." He took her hands in his and kissed first one palm and then the other.

THREE

VANESSA rang the doorbell, then inserted her key into the lock. "It's Vanessa," she called out as she stepped inside. "I forgot my cell phone."

"I'm on the phone," her mother's voice called from her bedroom.

Vanessa reached into her purse for her cell phone and waited with it in hand. Her mother was laughing. Girlish laughter.

Vanessa considered moving closer to the open bedroom door and eavesdropping a bit but resisted the urge, going instead to the kitchen for a drink of water. Then she went back to the living room and perched on a sofa arm.

Finally her mother appeared. "Oh, are you still here?" she said, her face a bit flushed. "I see that you found your phone." Then she paused and regarded her oldest daughter's face. "But that's not really why you came back, is it?"

"I came back because I'm in shock," Vanessa acknowledged.

"And the reason you're in shock is because ... ?" Penelope asked as she headed for the wing chair.

"Because I assumed you'd always be here in our family home," Vanessa said with a wave of her hand indicating the entirety of the apartment, "being my sisters' and my mother and Lily and Beth's grandmother."

"Do you really think that my moving out of this apartment means I'm relinquishing my position as mother and grandmother?" Penelope asked, her head tilted to one side.

"Well, you certainly seem to be changing your priorities. Ellie and Georgiana both think you've met a man—probably some guy you found online."

"I did read several articles about online dating services and actually roamed around some of the sites," Penelope acknowledged, "but I met Jean Claude walking down Madison Avenue. It was a cold, windy day, and he looked lost. I asked if I could help. He was searching for the quilt store. He said he wanted to buy a genuine American quilt to take home to his sister. He bought a quilt. We had dinner. There were numerous transatlantic e-mails and phone calls. He made a return trip to New York."

Penelope paused, a soft, remembering kind of smile playing with her lips. "And then he sent me a plane ticket. I suppose I should have let you and your sisters know right away what was going on, but first I wanted to keep the secret all to myself—to savor and enjoy. Then I worried that you girls wouldn't approve, and I can tell by the expression on your face that, at least when it comes to my oldest daughter, I was correct in that regard."

"How can you be with someone else so soon after Daddy's death?" Vanessa said, rising from her perch. She began to pace, the cell phone still in her hand.

"So, would you feel all right about my being with 'someone else' if I'd waited another year?" Penelope asked, using a calm, reasonable tone of voice that Vanessa found infuriating.

"Or how about five years?" Penelope continued. "Or ten? I don't consider myself old, Vanessa, but I don't have so many good years left that I have the luxury of wasting them."

"Did you know before Daddy died that you'd marry again?" Vanessa demanded, still pacing. She felt like an attorney in a courtroom interrogating a witness. She paused beside the coffee table to stare down at the birthday-present portrait. She wondered what would happen to it. It certainly wasn't going to accompany her mother to France. Maybe she'd put it over her own mantel, Vanessa thought, except she wasn't sure she wanted it. The portrait was about forever and ever, and maybe there was no such thing.

"Who said anything about marriage?" her mother asked with a shrug. "I don't want to be Jean Claude's wife, but if we get along and both stay healthy, I would like to have a nice long relationship with him. He inherited a farm with a charming house that has a lovely view from the terrace. We plan to grow roses and vegetables and keep dogs and cats and chickens. I will write some, but not as much as before. Jean Claude loves to cook, and I love to drink wine while I watch him cook."

"I will rephrase my question," Vanessa said in a testy tone. "Did you know before Daddy died that you would enter into another relationship should the opportunity present itself?"

"Before your father left to cover the war in Bosnia, we discussed the possibility of his getting killed." Penelope's voice was calm, her body relaxed. "Several journalists already had lost their lives, and he said that he would expect me to get on with my life if that happened to him. We had the same conversation and came to the same conclusion before he left to cover the war in Afghanistan. He expressed that same sentiment again when he first became ill."

Her mother's composure irritated Vanessa. She wanted

her to be ashamed. To show some contrition. "You and Daddy were my role models. I've never known anyone who had a happier marriage than you guys."

Penelope's expression grew thoughtful as she absently played with a strand of her silky, dark hair. "It was a good marriage," she agreed, "probably better than most, but it was not perfect, Vanessa. Your father and I had our differences and came close to divorce on two different occasions. Maybe we didn't do you girls a favor by never letting you see the undercurrents."

Wordlessly, Vanessa stood and walked down the hall to the bathroom. She closed the door and leaned against it.

Her parents had come close to divorce. *Twice.*

How could that be? She had held her parents' marriage up as her ideal and carried a deep sense of failure that she had not managed to have the same sort of marriage. Except maybe she had such an idealized notion of marriage that no man could ever have measured up to it.

She glanced at her watch. She needed to get herself back to New Jersey, and it was getting late, the trains running further and further apart. She had an early meeting in the morning. And in spite of her written instructions on the kitchen counter, she doubted if Scott had put the trash container in the alley for tomorrow morning's pickup or checked over Lily's math assignment. The girls would have done a half-ass job cleaning up the kitchen. And no one would have taken the dry clothes from the dryer and folded them, nor would they have moved the wet clothes from the washer to the dryer and put in another load. But she could not make herself move. Her body was frozen in place while an avalanche of thoughts went tumbling through her mind. She allowed one especially poignant memory to perk to the surface.

The last months of his life, her father would have bad

days and not-so-bad days and an occasional reasonably good day. Vanessa was focusing on one of the latter. A Sunday. As soon as she arrived at the apartment, he announced that he wanted to go to the park. Just the two of them.

The two-block walk to the park entrance left Daddy exhausted, so they climbed into one of the horse-drawn carriages. Their family had always taken advantage of their residence's proximity to Central Park, but this was the first time she and her father had ever ridden in one of the carriages.

It was a glorious summer day with just enough of a breeze to keep it from being hot and to move puffy, little clouds across a vividly blue sky. It was the sort of day that made people comment on how great it was to be alive. Vanessa knew that it might well be her father's last visit to the park and was overwhelmed with suffocating sadness. Her shoulders began to shake as she fought to keep the tears from coming.

Daddy took her in his arms. "My darling, Vanessa," he said, and planted a kiss on her forehead. "You were our firstborn and taught me how to be a father and have always been so very special to me. I know how difficult this is for you, but this is the way of things, honey. I would have preferred to have another decade or two, but children are supposed to bury their parents."

Vanessa wanted to jump out of the carriage and run away from his words and any responsibility on her part to acknowledge her father's impending death. She withdrew from his embrace, rubbed away her tears with the back of her hand, and said in a voice that came out gruff, "Don't talk like that."

He leaned back and lifted his face to the sun. "I've had a most satisfactory life thanks to your mother and you girls. And to Miss Vera Wentworth, who for some reason

known only to her took in a nameless foundling in the sixth
decade of her life and managed to live long enough to get him
raised. I married the woman I loved and I have loved being a
father. And I've been a pretty good journalist and finally got
my book done after a decade of procrastination. So I have no
quarrel with the Fates, and I don't want you to either."

But Vanessa did want to quarrel with the Fates or with
God or whatever power in the universe it was that gave her
father a terminal illness. She wanted to curse and scream at
all of them. And beg. Make bargains. Anything that would let
her keep her father for a while longer.

"I think it's going to be harder for you than your
sisters and mother," her father said. "You always seemed to
think that if you just worked hard enough and were a good
enough girl, everything would turn out okay."

They were passing by the open-air Delacorte Theater
where they attended plays in the summertime. Her father
reached for her hand. "So many good memories," he said.

Vanessa nodded, then used her free hand to wipe away
the tears.

When the ride ended, he was too weak to walk back.
Vanessa hailed a taxi.

Little more than a week later, he entered a coma from
which he never returned. And now, almost a year later, her remaining parent had decided to relinquish her mothering role
and raise chickens in France with some man who was probably a gigolo.

Her mother was tapping on the bathroom door asking if she was all right. Vanessa didn't want to give her the
satisfaction of an answer, but she mumbled a bit and turned
on the faucet.

When she finally emerged from the bathroom, she
went into her parents' bedroom and removed her father's

cardigan sweater from the open box and stuffed it in a plastic bag.

Her mother was standing by the open French doors.

"Okay, so you want a man in your life," Vanessa said, "but couldn't you at least find one who lives here in the city?"

Penelope turned. "I feel young again, Vanessa. I know that's difficult for you to understand. I am embarking on a great adventure. Maybe it will be a disaster, and maybe not. But I am thrilled at the prospect of living in France with a delightful man who also wants to make the most of the rest of his life. And there are telephones and e-mail and airplanes, you know. We shall talk and send messages often and visit back and forth. I'll be able to help with plane tickets when I get the apartment rented, and I expect you and your sisters to come at least once a year, and I'd like my granddaughters to spend next summer with me. In fact, I insist that my grand-daughters spend next summer with me and subsequent sum-mers as well. I want them to learn French and perhaps attend a French university when the time comes."

"That's bribery," Vanessa accused.

Penelope cocked her head to one side. "Perhaps, but you will allow your daughters to come because the experience will enrich their lives. And you and your sisters will come as well."

"Perhaps," Vanessa said, parroting her mother's word. Then she walked over to the desk and picked up the well-worn Bible that had belonged to the woman who had raised her father. "Where did you find it?"

"In a box with Vera's papers that I found on the top shelf of the closet in your father's office."

"Could I have the box?"

Penelope shrugged and led the way down the hall-way, which was covered with pictures of generations of her mother's family. Vanessa's grandparents had moved into the apartment when the building was brand-new. She and her parents moved here when her grandparents moved to Florida. That was when Vanessa was just a toddler.

She was shocked at the disarray in her father's study and realized what a formidable task her mother had undertaken. How could a man's professional life be reduced to a mess like this? For years, her father had covered wars, political upheavals, and natural disasters all over the globe. Now his files filled bulging trash bags that were piled in one corner, and boxes were stacked two and three high wherever there was room for them.

"He said he didn't want anyone going through his first drafts and false starts and planned to get rid of all this himself after he finished his book," Penelope explained, "but he didn't have the strength or the will to undertake the task."

"You're just throwing it all away? Without even going through it?"

"It is what he asked me to do, Vanessa," she said in her this-is-not-negotiable voice.

She watched while her mother moved boxes around, finally unearthing a sturdy carton with the word EGGS written on the side.

"I remember helping Miss Vera gather eggs," Vanessa said.

"Yes, your father used to take you with him when he visited her."

"And I went with Daddy to her funeral." Actually it had been just a graveside service on a really cold day. Vanessa held her daddy's hand as they made their way across the frozen ground toward a casket waiting by a precisely dug hole. Someone had produced a blanket to drape around her shoulders.

Penelope nodded. "Ellie had strep throat, so I didn't

try to go. Your dad and I argued about whether or not you should accompany him. I thought you were too young."

"Daddy cried," Vanessa recalled.

"He loved his Miss Vera and was very grateful to her."

"Did you like her?"

"I didn't know her very well," Penelope said. "She was a painfully shy woman and seemed very uncomfortable when I was there. She kept apologizing because she didn't have a dining room, and we had to eat in the kitchen. I think she thought that because I was a 'city girl' I looked down on her. Your father finally gave up trying to get her to come visit us."

Vanessa put Vera's Bible in the plastic bag with her father's sweater and placed the bag on top of the box's yellowing contents, then stooped to pick it up.

"Can you manage it on the train?" Penelope asked.

"I think so. Good night, Mother."

"Could I give you a hug?"

Vanessa shook her head and headed back up the hallway. Penelope did not follow her.

Vanessa took a cab to the station. The train ride seemed longer than usual.

She continued to nurse her anger. Did her mother's decision to leave the country and abdicate the throne of motherhood mean she didn't love her family as much as they thought she did? Would the day arrive in Vanessa's own life when she wanted to fly away and live just for herself?

She was too exhausted to come up with any answers and tried to concentrate instead on her schedule for tomorrow at the private women's college where she was the overworked development officer. She had to make a day trip to Philadelphia to call on a prominent alumna and propose that she make a major gift to the college, then make it back to campus for a meeting with the senior-class officers to discuss their class gift. And she was behind on correspondence. Behind on returning phone calls and e-mails. Behind on visiting prospective donors.

When the train arrived at her station, she got off and carried the box with Vera Wentworth's papers across the dimly lit parking lot to her SUV.

Scott had asked her to buy something on the way home. *Milk? Bread?* She couldn't remember. She stopped at a convenience store and bought both. When she got home, two unopened gallons of milk were in the refrigerator and loaves of both white and whole wheat were in the bread box. Then she remembered. It was orange juice he'd wanted her to buy.

Vanessa emptied the dishwasher and wiped off the counters. The Formica was coming loose around the sink. And the cupboards needed painting. The entire room needed painting. The whole house inside and out.

She put Vera's box on a shelf in the basement and her father's sweater on a shelf in her closet.

Scott woke when she came to bed.

"Nice evening?" he mumbled.

"It was okay," she said. "Did Lily finish her book report?"

"Uh-huh."

"Scott?"

"Mmmm?"

"My mother is having an affair with a Frenchman and is planning to move to France. Maybe I should feel happy for her, but the truth of the matter is I am very angry." The only sound from Scott's side of the bed was a soft snore.

Vanessa rolled away from him. And to think I once loved him more than anything, she thought. Of course, she still loved him. A great deal. He was her husband and the father of her children.

She had never thought of untidiness as being much of a character flaw until she married Scott. How much effort did it take for him to hang up a towel or put his dirty clothes in the hamper or put the milk carton back in the refrigerator or close a drawer? And Lily and Beth were becoming more like him every day.

Scott used to make jokes at social gatherings about his obsessive-compulsive wife. He especially loved describing how she used Q-tips to get rid of the grunge around the faucet in the kitchen sink. That had been when they still lived in the city and hung out with their Penn State friends who'd landed jobs in New York or were going to grad school at NYU or Columbia. Now they seldom went to social gatherings, but they still had grunge around the kitchen faucet. Mostly she ignored it, reminding herself that Scott was now in charge of the kitchen.

Vanessa glanced at the clock. She needed to sleep to be at her best tomorrow when she talked to Miss Clara Proctor, president of the class of 1958 and author of the column *Fin, Feathers, and Fur*, one of the longest-running syndicated newspaper columns in the country. The college wanted to honor Miss Proctor by naming the proposed reflecting pool in front of the library after her, provided, of course, that she make a sizable donation to the project. Such pitches were delicate. People were offended when she asked for too much or not enough. Or because she'd asked someone else first. Or they hadn't received sufficent recognition for their last gift.

Vanessa thought almost daily about finding some other line of work, but she was vested in the college's pension plan and her daughters could attend there tuition-free. Of course, Beth and Lily would probably want to attend some other college—one with boys on campus. And with that thought, she forced her mind to call a halt to the tumbling avalanche of thoughts and concentrated on falling asleep.

At JoJo's, Ellie danced on her own through several numbers and was beginning to think she'd been stood up. She debated whether she should just leave or try to find a seat at the bar when suddenly there was a man behind her, his hands on her waist, his mouth close to her ear. "You must be Ellie," he said.

Ellie had a smile in place before she turned around.

He was older than she had expected and a bit thick about the middle but otherwise attractive. Tall. A good head of hair. Clean-shaven. Nice jawline.

Boone picked up the beat of the music and began to dance. Ellie would have preferred having a couple of drinks and getting acquainted, but Boone obviously loved to dance and moved well for a guy his size. Ellie reconnected with the music for a time, but tiredness began to get the best of her. It had been a stressful day. A cover story for the November edition for which she'd hired one of the top fashion writers in the city was poorly written, inaccurate, and unusable. And Mother's birthday celebration had turned into a major disappointment. Ellie had been so excited about the portrait. Vanessa and Georgiana, too. God, what a downer Mother's reaction had been. And then she up and announces that she's leaving the country. Which caught them all by surprise and sure raised Vanessa's ire. Ellie didn't want her to move away any more than Vanessa did, but it wasn't as if their mother were elderly and demented. She could do whatever she wanted to do, and there wasn't anything her daughters could do to stop her. Then there had been that business with the letter in the Bible, which was just too weird. And even if the woman who wrote the letter was still alive, finding her would be next to impossible.

With her smile as vivacious as she could manage, Ellie nodded in the direction of the bar. "I need a drink," she mouthed over the music.

She wondered just how old Boone was and if he was successful at whatever he did and why he and his wife were getting a divorce and if he had kids, when not so long ago her first wonderings about a man would have to do with how he was between the sheets.

FOUR

*T*HERE'S iced tea and sandwich fixings in the kitchen,"
Penelope announced when Vanessa arrived.

Ellie and Georgiana had already arrived and were
inspecting the contents of the refrigerator. Vanessa hadn't
seen or talked to her sisters since the birthday gathering last
month. Penelope had summoned her daughters to the apartment to decide which things they wanted. The items they
selected were to be removed from the premises before the end
of the month, when the remaining contents would be turned
over to an auction house.

Penelope stuck her head in the kitchen to announce
that she had errands to run and they should take all the time
they needed. "Should there be any arguments over who gets
what, I suggest you draw cards," Penelope said over her shoulder. "There's a deck of playing cards in the top right-hand
drawer of the secretary."

With their mother gone, the only sound in the small
kitchen was the drip of the faucet. Vanessa made a turkey
sandwich but realized she had no appetite and took only

a few bites. She opened the refrigerator and pulled out an opened bottle of Chablis. "I don't know about you guys, but I need something alcoholic before we undertake this task."

They downed the wine and found an unopened bottle in the pantry. Wineglasses in hand, they wandered around aimlessly, discussing memories they associated with various items. So much stuff. Stacks of framed diplomas and honor-roll certificates. Boxes of photograph albums and scrapbooks. A box of old phonograph records. Boxes of dishes and of pots and pans. Boxes of sheets and towels. Not to mention all that furniture, some of it dating back to their grandparents' tenure in the apartment. And the books. Hundreds of books.

"It makes me angry that she's making us do this," Vanessa said, picking up a chipped bookend on which a bronzed baby shoe had been mounted. Her own, she thought. But maybe not.

"Come on, Vanessa," Ellie said. "It's something we would have had to do eventually. We're just doing it sooner rather than later."

"What a morbid thing to say!" Georgiana chastised.

They selected mostly small things—family pictures, vases, lamps, objets d'art—and argued frequently.

No one claimed the silver-anniversary portrait of their parents. Georgiana took it just so it would have a home.

After Penelope had turned over the apartment to the painters and carpet layers, she stayed with Vanessa for two weeks, spoiling her granddaughters, making frequent trips into the city to wind down her affairs and be wined and dined by various friends wanting to wish her *bon voyage* and *bon chance*.

"And just what do your friends think about this abrupt change in your life?" Vanessa wanted to know.

"Some of them think I'm crazy," Penelope said with a shrug. "Others are green with envy."

The night before her departure, Penelope rented a suite at the St. Regis and had a slumber party for her daughters and granddaughters. She treated them to dinner at the Four Seasons, during which, at Penelope's insistence, Beth and Lily had their first sip of champagne.

"I really think that this Jean Claude person should have come to fetch you and meet your family," Ellie said. "How do we know you haven't made him up?"

"You don't," Penelope said, offering Ellie a radiant smile. "Maybe I'm really going to enter a convent and spend the rest of my life scrubbing and praying."

Vanessa had never seen her mother look happier, which seemed so unfair. Her father was dead, and her mother was blushing like a bride.

The next day, they all piled in Vanessa's SUV for the drive to the airport. After the hugs and kisses and tears, they watched as Penelope headed toward security. "Be happy," Ellie called after her.

"Call as soon as you get there," Georgiana added.

Vanessa just waved.

Ellie and Georgiana took a bus back into the city. The drive home for Vanessa and her daughters was quiet. Even Beth and Lily seemed to realize that they were all going to have to renegotiate who they all were to each other with their grandmother gone. Penelope had always been the head of the family, Vanessa realized. Always. Even when Daddy was alive.

The revelation was a bit startling. Had her father liked it that way? Or had there been a river of resentment running just beneath his calm demeanor? The way Scott resented her.

She dropped Beth and Lily off at volleyball practice,

then drove on home. Scott was mowing the lawn. His shirt was off, his body glistening with sweat. He was getting a paunch, Vanessa realized.

On weekends, she was supposed to cook the evening meals and had planned to do something quick for their dinner—omelets maybe or scrounge around for leftovers. But when the girls were invited to have dinner and spend the night with a friend, she decided on salmon and scalloped potatoes instead. And set the table in the dining room complete with candles and wineglasses.

Scott paused on his way upstairs to shower, a puzzled look on his face. "Is it our anniversary or something?" he asked, his forehead wrinkling with concern.

"No, I'm just feeling a bit melancholy and decided that a nice evening with my husband would be the best cure."

"You know that the Yankees game starts at seven?" he queried a bit fearfully.

She could ask him to record the game and watch it after dinner. But what Vanessa really had in mind was the two of them lingering over dinner, then ending up in bed. She could, of course, insist, but that would cast a pall over the proceedings.

Dinner was served on the coffee table in the family room. She watched part of the game with him, then went upstairs to bed. Probably, Vanessa rationalized, she was too exhausted from the emotion of the day to enjoy sex.

When Scott came up to bed, she was still awake though. He tiptoed across the darkened room to the bathroom. She listened while he brushed his teeth and used the toilet. He got in bed gingerly in an obvious effort not to disturb her. "I'm not asleep," she said.

"You're feeling blue about your mother leaving, aren't you?" he asked.

Vanessa was startled by the tears that immediately came to her eyes. A sob erupted from her chest. Vanessa couldn't remember the last time she'd cried, but she was about to cry now.

"Ah, baby, don't be sad," he said, taking her in his arms and stroking her back. It had been a long time since Vanessa had experienced tenderness. It made her cry all the harder. Then suddenly she was reaching for him with a need so deep it startled her.

Ellie had hoped Boone would spend the night, but he got up after sex, pulled on his clothes, kissed her forehead, and left, claiming he had an early-morning flight. Last time his excuse was an early-morning meeting. And the time before that. More and more, he just wanted to "drop by for a drink." No dinner. No movie. No evening stroll.

Ellie eventually realized that Boone had gone back to his wife. He never answered his cell phone in the evening, and she had gone from seeing him three or four times a week to once or twice and only on weeknights, which meant he was telling his wife that he had to work late at the office or was having a dinner meeting with clients. The whole situation was pointless, but she could not bring herself to break it off. Which made her feel stupid and cheap. But obviously, Boone didn't love his wife if he was screwing around on her. So why did he go back to her? Cynthia was her name. His children's names were Terrence and Beverly.

Maybe his wife was rich. Or maybe she was such a nice person and such a good mother to his children that Boone could not bring himself to divorce her. On that depressing thought, Ellie promised herself that she was absolutely not going to answer her phone the next time he called.

Tomorrow she would check the sperm bank listings in the yellow pages.

But did she really want to do that—have a baby on her own?

Ellie wasn't sure. She wanted the whole package—husband, kids, a house in the suburbs—but maybe a fatherless kid was better than no kid at all.

She clutched her middle and curled around her empty uterus. She was at midcycle. Tonight would have been a good night to get pregnant. How many more good nights to get pregnant did she have left before menopause set in?

She did the arithmetic in her head. Some women went through menopause in their late thirties or early forties. She could have fewer than one hundred nights left when a man could make her pregnant.

Maybe she should just go off the pill and let nature take its course—with Boone or some other man. If she did that, she'd never tell the man. It would be her baby alone.

She thought of the hundred or so ova lined up down there waiting for their chance to amount to something. She prayed that at least one of them would be successful.

Freddy was on the road with Trisha Bell's comeback tour and back in town just for the night. Georgiana insisted that he had to wear a coat and tie and take her to a classy restaurant where they could linger over dinner and wine. And, no, they could not go to some nightclub to listen to this or that band afterward. She wanted his undivided attention for the entire evening. After dinner, they would go to her apartment and light candles and make beautiful love. It was the seventh anniversary of their first date, and Georgiana planned to make an occasion out of it.

She had spent the afternoon hanging up the dozens of garments scattered about her small residence and making her cluttered apartment presentable. Then she put out candles. Lots of candles.

Freddy's apartment was uncluttered. Other than musical and acoustical equipment, he was a man of few possessions. She and Freddy had tried living together but come to realize that to do that successfully they would need a larger residence in which there were three domains—his space, her space, and a common area that was the responsibility of a third party to clean.

They met for before-dinner cocktails at a bar in the Village. Georgiana's heart melted as Freddy weaved his way across the room. He was almost on time and was wearing a navy blazer left over from high school Glee Club days with the school emblem still sewed to the pocket and a pair of brand-new jeans. He was carrying a teddy bear equipped with a backpack and wearing a HAPPY ANNIVERSARY banner across his chest.

"You look adorable," she said as they embraced.

"Adorable? I was trying for suave and sophisticated."

"That, too."

He took in the plunging neckline of her dress. "And you look like a woman in need of ravishment. You sure we have to eat dinner first?"

"I'm sure," she said, then she nibbled his ear.

She sat down and cuddled the bear in her lap while she opened its backpack. Inside was a gold charm bracelet. "Oh my gosh, Freddy, this must have cost a fortune."

"I had to get gold for my golden girl."

Georgiana scooted close to him on the banquette and examined the charms. There was a treble clef for his music, a camera for her talent, the Statue of Liberty for their city, and a heart for their love. Georgiana got tears in her eyes.

Freddy possessed the one quality in a man that she found the most appealing.

He was sweet.

Her sisters had made it obvious over the years that they wondered why in the world she hung in there with Freddy. And maybe, Georgiana realized, at some point in the future her biological clock would kick in, as Ellie's now had, and she would have to find some responsible man with a 401(k) and health insurance to plant the seed of motherhood in her womb. And unless this stalwart man was willing to cook, clean, launder, and carpool while she strived to become a photographer of artistic renown, she would have to stop being a slob and turn into a responsible, tidy, efficient lady. She would have to become her sister Vanessa, who was uptight, frazzled, and no longer in love with the man she had married, although she would never admit that to anyone, including herself.

Georgiana had a hard enough time imagining a messy, self-indulgent person such as herself ever being a mother, but Freddy the musician as a father was beyond comprehension.

By the time Georgiana was unlocking the door to her apartment, she and Freddy were tugging at each other's clothes. They staggered across the room leaving garments and shoes in their wake.

FIVE

*V*ANESSA drove slowly down Main Street, surprised at how much of the sleepy little West Virginia town looked familiar even though the last time she'd visited Pikesville she'd been only six years old. The trees that lined the street were considerably larger, but the drugstore where she drank cherry phosphates sitting on a high barstool was still there. Old men still lingered on benches in front of stores.

On the outskirts of town she turned west onto the Clarksburg highway. Then all she had to do was drive. Vera's farm was the last property on the right before the river bridge.

Vanessa knew that some of Vera's land had been sold to pay for her father's college education and that he had inherited and then sold the remainder of the farm. But Vanessa had always assumed the house was still there. She'd planned to knock on the door and explain that her father had grown up there and ask if she could walk around the property and hoped the present owners would even invite her inside the clapboard farmhouse.

But the land where the farm was supposed to be was occupied by a sprawling truck stop.

She drove around the perimeter, passing rows of parked rigs, looking for some sort of landmark—a section of fence, a familiar tree, building foundations. But there was no sign that generations of Wentworths had once lived on this land.

Vanessa wondered if her father would have sold the farm on which he had been raised if he'd known it was to be razed. Maybe he felt less attached to it because he believed himself to be an orphan and his forebears had lived someplace else. Except, if the letter from Vera's Bible was what it seemed, her father had Wentworth blood in his veins—unless the word *aunt* was an honorary designation. But it seemed more likely that a woman in her fifties would accept responsibility for raising a child if she and the child shared family ties.

Vera had apparently honored Hattie's request that the child never know anything about her, a request that seemed terribly unfair to both Vera and the child. But maybe Hattie had good reason to make such a stipulation, and Vera adhered to it because it was in Matthew's best interest.

Vanessa had carefully gone through the box with Vera's papers. According to her birth certificate, Vera had been born in Hancock County and her parents' names were John Robert Wentworth and Mary Wilma Oliver Wentworth. The box also held Vera's high school diploma, various certificates and ribbons awarded at the county fair for everything from a reserve champion sow to fruit preserves, death certificates for her parents, and a document showing that she had purchased a burial plot. A tin that had once held chocolate-covered cherries now held several loose photographs of nameless people in dated clothing. Also in the tin was a pink hair ribbon, a dance program in which a boy named William had signed every line, and a yellowed newspaper clipping dated August 12, 1918. It was an obituary for PFC William Joseph Washburn, age nineteen, who had been killed by enemy fire during the Second Battle of the Marne.

And there was an album devoted to documenting the life of Matthew Wade Wentworth, beginning with a picture of him as an infant propped up on a pillow and ending with him as a young man with five-year-old Vanessa standing on the front step of the farmhouse that no longer existed. Intermingled with the photographs were his baptismal certificate, report cards, and newspaper clippings chronicling his exploits as a high school baseball player, along with a clipping announcing his graduation with honors from the West Virginia University.

Vanessa had invited her sisters to accompany her to this rural, northeastern corner of West Virginia—just for a couple of days, then they could catch a bus or train back to New York and she would drive on to Lynchburg, Virginia, to attend a meeting of private-college development officers being held on the campus of the women's college there. She thought her sisters would jump at the chance to get out of the city for a time and enjoy the scenery and fall foliage and see the town where their father grew up. Although Ellie and Georgiana both thought it was a wonderful idea for Vanessa to search for information about the mysterious Hattie, they had both declined her invitation.

Vanessa had already made contacts in the town. During a telephone conversation with the secretary at the church where Vera Wentworth had been a lifelong member, Vanessa learned that the pastor who presided over the church during the last two decades of Vera's life still lived in the community. And the county agricultural agent had given her the name of a retired farmer who once owned the property adjoining the Wentworth farm.

She filled up her vehicle at the truck stop and used the restroom before driving back to town. She had no trouble locating the Queen Charlotte Bed and Breakfast, where she had a reservation. After she'd checked in, she asked for directions to the Golden Age Retirement Home.

The retirement home director led Vanessa down a corridor to the Reverend Reuel Ruston's room. The aged clergyman was dozing in his recliner.

The woman gently shook him. "You have a visitor, Reverend. This nice lady drove all the way from New Jersey just to talk to you." She adjusted his chair so he was more upright and pulled a side chair over for Vanessa.

It took the old man a few minutes to process that information and open a window to the past. Vera Wentworth? Yes, of course, he remembered her. And the boy. Matthew was his name. "So Matthew Wentworth is your father," he said.

Vanessa explained that her father had died more than a year ago and accepted the reverend's condolences. Then she listened while the old man recalled how Vera and her boy were always there in the third pew on the right every Sunday until Matthew went off to college. "I've never seen a youngster with better manners," the minister added.

Reverend Ruston recalled how, after Matthew left for college, Vera stopped coming to church and became a bit of a recluse. "I think she missed the boy. I'd always heard that she'd been a loner before she adopted Matthew, and with him gone I reckon she just slipped back into her old ways."

Vanessa explained that she was interested in tracking down her father's birth mother and wondered if he knew anything about the circumstances of his birth and subsequent adoption. She told him about the letter written to "Aunt

Vera," by someone named Hattie, which made her think her father's birth mother could have been a relative of Vera's.

"Your father was around nine or ten when my wife and I arrived in Pikesville," the elderly minister said, leaning back in his chair. "And Vera Wentworth wasn't much of a talker. I knew that she'd inherited the farm from her father and had raised the boy since he was a newborn. If my predecessor at Bethany Lutheran had anything to do with placing the boy with Vera, I never knew about it, but let me tell you, young lady, it was a blessing to Vera and the boy that they got paired up. He received a good upbringing, and Vera had someone to fuss over."

Vanessa explained that she had come with her father to Vera's funeral. "I don't remember much about the service except that my daddy cried and it was really cold."

Reverend Ruston couldn't recall Vera's funeral. So many folks he'd buried over the years. Hundreds, maybe more than a thousand. Some of them he knew well and others he didn't know at all.

Vanessa ate dinner at a small café on Main Street, drawing several stares from the locals while she ate her solitary meal.

On the way back to the bed-and-breakfast, she stopped at a convenience store. She'd wanted to buy a *New York Times* but had to settle for a *USA Today*, which she read after bathing in a tub with clawed feet and crawling into a canopied bed with eyelet curtains and a mountain of fluffy pillows.

She had a hard time falling asleep. The old house creaked around her, and the canopied bed was distracting. It was a bed more suitable for couples on their honeymoon or celebrating a special anniversary. She felt a bit stupid about coming to this town at all. She'd thought it would be an interesting excursion for her and Ellie and Georgiana, and the three of them hadn't been together since their mother had left for France more than two months ago. Georgiana had come to Lily's birthday party, but Ellie was in charge of a special edition on affordable fashion and couldn't get away. Or at least that was what she said. Vanessa had been in Manhattan on business last month, but only Ellie was free for lunch. In her usual business suit, Vanessa felt matronly next to her fashionable sister in her spike heels and perfectly accessorized outfit. All Ellie could talk about was her latest boyfriend. A guy named Boone. His divorce was proving to be lengthy and wouldn't be final for some time, Ellie explained, but something in her tone made Vanessa wonder if the man was on the up-and-up. Ellie admitted that he had not yet mentioned marriage, and she didn't know if he would be willing to father another child or two since he already had two by his first wife. She was still feeling her way with him, Ellie explained. By the time Vanessa could get a word in edgewise and mention the possibility of a sisterly trip to West Virginia in search of their roots, Ellie was already glancing at her watch. "Next month is just impossible," she said, "but I'll be anxious to hear what you find out."

Georgiana had seemed more interested in making the trip, but her hands and feet were booked for photo shoots on the days that Vanessa planned to be gone.

Vanessa hadn't realized just how instrumental their mother had been in keeping her and her sisters connected. Without their mother acting as facilitator, the three of them were already drifting apart.

Penelope sent infrequent e-mails addressed to her three daughters but made a point to call each of them every week. She always sounded relaxed and happy. "I've gained a couple of pounds and don't even care," she'd admitted to Vanessa. Mostly she asked questions—about her granddaughters and son-in-law, about Vanessa's latest projects at work, about the weather in New York and if she'd spoken to her sisters recently. Vanessa couldn't bring herself to inquire about details of her mother's life. She could hear the sullenness in her own voice and was sure her mother did, too. "How long are you going to punish me for being happy?" Penelope had asked during her last call.

"Don't be silly," Vanessa snapped. "I'm just tired."

And she had been. Tiredness was a condition of her life.

She hadn't told her mother about her plan to visit West Virginia. At that point, she wasn't even sure that she would really go. It meant she would be away from home four days instead of the two it would take to attend the conference in Virginia, and she would return to even greater mayhem at home. But the mystery of her father's birth had piqued her interest and put her in the mood for a sentimental journey. And maybe a break in her hectic routine would be restful.

But it wasn't restful enough for her to fall asleep in the canopied bed. She turned on the lamp and read herself to sleep.

The next morning, she took flowers to the cemetery.

Vera Wentworth had been buried alongside her parents with four generations of the family nearby. Vanessa put the flowers on Vera's grave and said, "I wish I could have known you better. Thank you for raising my father. He thought the world of you."

Her words brought tears to her eyes, and she had to fish a tissue from her purse to blow her nose.

From the cemetery, she sought out the elderly farmer whose land had abutted Vera's. Judson Mallory was ninety-two, wheelchairbound, and now lived in a trailer home with his widowed daughter, Felicia. His memory had failed years ago, but Felicia agreed to tell Vanessa what she remembered about the Wentworth family. A small, pretty woman with wiry gray hair, Felicia explained that she and Matthew were the same age and had grown up together. She seemed genuinely sorry to hear that Matthew had "passed on."

"You must be putting together a family tree," Felicia commented as she filled a kettle with water.

"Not exactly," Vanessa said. Then she explained how the letter her mother had found in Vera Wentworth's Bible sparked her interest in family ties.

Vanessa waited while the woman wheeled her father into his bedroom for a nap. When she returned, Felicia poured the boiling water into a blue teapot. "Were you the little girl that Matthew brought to Miss Vera's interment?" she asked as she took two mugs and a sugar bowl down from the cupboard.

Vanessa nodded.

"Terrible weather for a burial. I felt so sorry for you with your bare little legs. I sent my husband to the car for a blanket to put around you."

"And I've remembered that kindness all these years," Vanessa said.

Felicia put a plate of cookies on the table and filled two heavy, white mugs with tea.

Felicia picked up her mug with both hands, as though she were warming them, and got a thoughtful, remembering expression on her face. "Vera was a woman past fifty when she took in your father," she began. "The story goes that one Sunday morning, the minister announced from the pulpit that Vera had taken in a foundling and asked for donations of clothing and a crib. Vera always called him Matthew Wade, but at school he was always just 'Matthew.' If I have the Wentworth family history correct, there was a terrible depression in the late 1800s, and Vera's father and his brother went to work in the mines up in the Northern Panhandle. Lots of men from these parts did that to keep family farms afloat. The brother was killed in a mining accident. Mr. Wentworth married a Hancock County girl, and Vera was born up there. When Mr. Wentworth's father died and he inherited the farm, he moved back to Pikesville with his wife and Vera, who was a grown-up woman by then. Both of her parents died before I was born and before Matthew came into Vera's life."

"Did Vera have any siblings?" Vanessa asked.

"Yes, she did," Felicia said with a nod of her gray head. There was a framed photograph of Vera's parents and her as a young woman and a young boy of about nine or ten on the mantel. I remember her saying the boy was her brother and that there had been bad blood between her father and her brother, and Vera hadn't seen him for years. When I told my mother about that picture, she said that Vera's father had been a mean, cantankerous old man that no one liked and she could see how he might have run off a son. Isn't that sad? I wonder if he ever regretted being that way."

Felicia paused to take a sip of tea before continuing. "My mother always thought that Matthew's birth mother must have been a relative of Vera's, possibly the daughter of her long-lost brother. Why else would anyone give a baby to a woman of Vera's age, especially one who'd never had children of her own? Course, Matthew could have been the baby of some local girl from around here who'd gotten herself in trouble and her parents kicked her out—folks did that back then—and for some reason only known to the doctor or midwife who delivered him or maybe the mother herself, Miss Vera was asked to take him in. And maybe that made some sense. Other folks had children of their own to raise, and Miss Vera, being a spinster lady, had only herself to look after. She wasn't rich by any stretch of the imagination, but she was better off than most folks in these parts, especially back then," Felicia said as she refilled Vanessa's mug.

Felicia rambled on a bit more telling how she and Matthew had ridden the school bus together and been in the same grade at school. "He was hands down the smartest one in our grade. That boy always had his nose in a book, and he was a good baseball player. It always seemed peculiar to me how a really smart boy could be such a good baseball player."

While eating another solitary dinner at the Main Street Café and later while trying to fall asleep in the canopied bed, Vanessa struggled to figure out some way in which the information she had gleaned that day could help her discover the identity of her father's mother.

But did it really matter whether she ever found out the reason why her father ended up being raised by a spinster aunt? Was it going to give her any meaningful insights into her own on-the-surface-reasonably-good-but-deep-down-not-so-happy existence on this planet? Or provide some understanding as to why she loved but often did not like her own sisters? Or help her figure out why her mother—the woman who married the smart, athletic boy that Miss Vera Wentworth had raised and dearly loved—had not been totally devastated when he died? Not that Vanessa would have wanted her mother to spend the rest of her life consumed by grief, but she'd never broken down, never been inconsolable.

Of course, Vanessa fully realized that if Scott died, she would be sad, especially for her daughters, but not inconsolable. She would sincerely grieve, then get about the business of remaking her life. But even with this acknowledgment, she could not forgive her mother and maybe never would.

Six

$\mathcal{N}$AVIGATING the narrow, steep path with its tight switch-backs was somewhat harder than it used to be, but Myrna still made her way down the incline each day to her mailbox. The daily climb up and down her mountain kept her body and mind strong and sound and confident.

For almost twenty-five years she had been making the trek—ever since she'd built her home in the Elkhead Mountains in Colorado's Park Range. Eagles Nest she called her home, a totally unconventional, light-filled dwelling anchored firmly into solid rock on the mountain's southwest face with spacious decks cantilevering breathtakingly outward. Myrna had conceived the design herself, imagining what Frank Lloyd Wright would have done if asked to design a house tucked high against the side of a mountain. Then she had hired the best architects and engineers to execute her vision. Constructing the private road that wound its way up the mountain was almost as expensive as the house itself. Always a private person, she'd originally used Eagles Nest as a weekend retreat, but as she became ever more prominent in the business world and ever more wealthy, she was uncomfortable with the attention such success garnered and began to spend most of her time here, ruling her family and her business empire from her lofty dwelling.

Fall was in the air, and she paused to zip her jacket before carefully making her way downward, always keeping a hand firmly on the iron railing bolted to the stone face of the mountain. She stopped frequently to admire the view and take great inhales of the invigorating mountain air. Physicians had told her for years that there was no cure for the asthma brought on by all the coal dust she had breathed as a child, but they were wrong. The mountain air had cured her. She felt invincible as she made her way down her very own mountain and planned the day that lay ahead.

The first thing on her agenda was preparing her remarks for a meeting of her company officers this afternoon. The men and women who managed her empire, including two of her four children, came six times a year to pay homage and give their reports and either bask in her praise or cower under her displeasure. As always, when she strolled into the room, she would be wearing a black pants suit custom-made for her by a London tailor who came twice a year to Eagles Nest to show her his sketches and fabric samples and check her measurements, which were always the same. He marveled at that. And her posture. She had promised herself that the day she could no longer stand erect was the day she would turn the reins of her business empire over to her younger son or one of her daughters.

She had other plans for her older son.

As Myrna descended, she considered the remarks with which she would open the meeting, pausing for a time to watch a red-tailed hawk circling high in the sky, the master of his world. She knew how that felt.

When she reached the bottom, she unlocked the gate in the security fence and continued down the path another twenty yards to the large metal mailbox. She inserted a key into the lock and placed the mail and newspapers in a backpack and secured it on her back. When there was too much mail for the backpack, Willy, her longtime "girl Friday," would drive down to fetch the rest.

Climbing up the path was easier on her knees than coming down, but it required more frequent pauses to catch her breath.

Once she had reached her house, Myrna headed for her office, where a carafe of freshly made strong, black coffee and a freshly baked whole-wheat muffin loaded with nuts and berries and still warm from the oven were waiting for her.

She unloaded the backpack on her desk, stacking the newspapers and then sorting the mail and placing the envelopes in the precise order in which they would be opened and read. That done, she seated herself in her high-backed desk chair, poured coffee into her favorite mug, enjoyed that first delightful sip, and took the first bite of the warm muffin. Then she expressed her contentment with a sigh and allowed herself to think how far she had come in her life. A story of rags to riches were she ever to tell it, something she had no intention of doing.

Her name had been Hattie back during the rags part of her life. Such an old-fashioned name. One never heard it anymore. But for years after she had renamed herself, hearing or seeing the name Hattie would make her heart skip a beat.

But gradually the name retreated into the deep recesses of her mind, and Myrna would go for years not thinking of that time in her life in any significant way. Not that she didn't have good Hattie memories, but they ended when her brother died.

Patrick was his name. *Dear little Patrick.*

Myrna closed her eyes. She could see Patrick sitting beside her in front of the unpainted shack where they'd both been born—the shack where she'd spent the first sixteen years of her life.

Usually she would not have allowed her mind to probe any deeper into a memory. She would shut it off and get on with the business of her present life. But thoughts of Patrick and the good years she'd spent in that meager dwelling lured her back to that other time. She remembered how she and Patrick would sit on the front step waiting for Papa to come trudging up the road with the other miners, all of them carrying a black lunch pail, all of them grimy with coal dust, their shoulders stooped with exhaustion after a day underground hacking coal out of Mr. Sedgwick's mine.

And Myrna remembered how, as soon as she spotted Papa, she would run to him and take his lunch pail in one hand and grab his calloused, grimy hand with the other. Patrick, who'd been born with a clubfoot and walked with a decided limp, would wait for them, then hobble around back where Papa would strip himself down to his underclothes and wash himself clean at the pump and Mama would pat him dry with a towel. Hattie could tell from the look on Mama's face that she liked doing this for him. She would cluck like a mother hen about how tired he must be and what he needed was a nice hot dinner.

Whenever Hattie saw her father's bare back, she always wondered about the strange marks that crisscrossed it, but knew it was something she wasn't supposed to ask about.

When Papa was dry, he'd put on a clean shirt and a clean pair of overalls and carry Patrick into the kitchen. And Mama would put his coal-blackened clothes to soak in the washtub on the back stoop.

Dinner was usually something from a pot—stew or soup or boiled potatoes with mustard greens—served with corn bread or biscuits. Over dinner her parents often talked about money, always in worried tones. They were trying to save enough money to pay for an operation on Patrick's misshapen foot so that he could walk and run like other children. And Papa wanted to trade in the old Ford for a truck so they could move to Alaska, where a man could earn a fair wage and a family could still get good free land from the government. He didn't want to be a miner for the rest of his life. His dream was a dairy farm. But he would settle for any sort of farming or ranching so he could spend his days in the open and not underground. But Mama said that the winters in Alaska were even colder and longer than they were in Montana. What if summer wasn't long enough for her to grow a decent garden up there?

"And what about West Virginia?" Mama would often ask. "The winters are mild there. I wish you'd make things right with your father so we can move there. If you don't make up with him, he'll leave that farm to your sister when he dies. Seems to me you're cutting off your nose to spite your face."

Hattie knew there was "bad blood" between her papa and his father because Papa would get a scowl on his face whenever her mother said something about West Virginia.

Hattie didn't want to move someplace that would make her papa unhappy, but she was on her mother's side when it came to Alaska. It was plenty cold enough in Montana, and she couldn't imagine living someplace that was even colder.

But Papa would insist that if the family moved anyplace, it would be Alaska. He spoke the word *Alaska* like the preacher said *Jesus*. It was a word full of hope.

And besides, Papa pointed out, often as not the grasshoppers ate Mama's garden, and sometimes windstorms ripped the plants right out of the ground and even blew away some of Mama's chickens. And Mama would ask what made him think there weren't windstorms and grasshoppers in Alaska.

Hattie helped her mother in the garden, carrying buckets of water and picking worms off the tomato plants. Unfortunately the plants that grew best were beets and turnips, the only two vegetables that Hattie didn't like. Mama would preserve beans, corn, and tomatoes and store the jars away in the root cellar along with the potatoes, carrots, beets, onions, and turnips. But the cellar was always empty before the next year's garden started producing, and Mama would have to use money saved for Patrick's operation to buy food. When Hattie's shoes got too small for her feet, Mama would cut away some of the leather so they wouldn't pinch her toes. And Mama would let the seams out on Hattie's winter coat and leggings so she could wear them another year.

Each year that went by and Patrick was still hobbling around, Hattie could tell that her brother's deformity weighed ever more heavily on her parents. No matter how thrifty they were and how carefully they saved, it seemed as if something would happen that kept them from having enough money for that operation.

One day her father received a letter from his sister in West Virginia informing him of the death of their mother and that, according to her last wishes, she would be sending him the solid-gold pocket watch that had once belonged to their maternal grandfather. And sure enough, a week or so later a package arrived with the pocket watch. Papa sold it and with the money he got for the watch, there was almost enough for Patrick's operation. But the old Ford stopped running, and he had to use the money to buy a newer old Ford.

One summer evening when Hattie was twelve years old and Patrick had just turned six, when she skipped down the road to meet her papa coming home from the mine and carry his lunch pail the rest of the way, he seemed especially happy to see her. He gave her a great big smile, his teeth white against his coal-blackened skin, and ruffled her hair, asking, "How's my big girl?" as he always did.

"Just fine," she answered as she always did.

"I hope your mama has a big pot of something good to eat cooking on the stove, because I'm hungry enough to eat a bear."

"Just turnip greens and beets and yesterday's corn bread," Hattie announced, as she took his lunch pail and fell in beside him.

"My favorite meal."

"No, it's not," Hattie scoffed. "Nobody with their head on straight likes turnip greens and beets and stale corn bread, specially when there's no molasses for the corn bread."

Papa smiled again. "Well, maybe you're right, but if you think of all the folks that have to make do with less, it will make that food taste a whole lot better. And if you clean up your plate, maybe we can drive to town after dinner for an ice cream cone."

Hattie was so astonished she stopped in her tracks. *Ice cream cones* when she knew that her mama was worried sick about not having enough food stored for the winter and was fearful that they were never going to have enough money to get poor Patrick's foot operated on and he would have to spend the rest of his life as a cripple.

She looked up at her father's face. His blue eyes seemed brighter than usual—as if candles were burning behind them. And he seemed bigger and taller than he had been just this morning when he'd trudged off to the mine. His shoulders weren't hunched over, his head not bent forward.

"The ice cream cones are a secret," her father told her with a wink, "just between you and me. And just thinking about that secret is going to make those greens and beets taste like the best thing you have ever tasted in your entire life, better than whatever ole FDR and his family are eating tonight in the White House in Washington, D.C. Those greens and beets are going to taste so good that you'll clean up your plate without your mama reminding you and maybe you'll even ask for seconds."

When they reached the porch, Papa leaned down and grabbed Patrick's freckled, smiling face in both of his hands and gave him a great big kiss, leaving a ring of coal dust around his mouth. Then Papa picked Patrick up and clutched him to his chest, getting coal dust all over Patrick's clothes, and tears started rolling down Papa's face, leaving tracks on his blackened cheeks. Hattie was confused. Just seconds ago Papa had winked at her. "Are you sad, Papa?" she asked.

He shook his head. "Just sentimental."

"What's that mean?"

"It means I'm thinking of the happy day when our Patrick has two good feet to stand on, but at the same time I'm sad because it's taking so long."

Mama was in the backyard pumping water wearing her usual worried frown. Mama looked pretty when she smiled, but she frowned a whole lot more than she smiled. Hattie could smell the turnip greens cooking in the kitchen and wanted to hold her nose but knew that would make Mama mad.

Hattie sat with Patrick on the back stoop and watched their papa's evening cleanup ritual that would soon end with the advent of cold weather. Then Papa would have to wash up in the kitchen, and no matter how careful he was, he would get coal dust all over everything.

But tonight was nice and warm. Maybe it was the nice weather that was making Papa act silly. He was trying to tickle Mama's ribs and acting as if he'd forgotten how to un-button his shirt. Mama's worried face went away for a time, and she actually laughed a little. "Hattie and I sure are look-ing forward to our turnip greens and beets, aren't we, Hattie girl?" Papa asked with a wink in her direction.

Hattie nodded and wondered if a nod counted as a lie.

Patrick regarded his sister with a puzzled look. He knew that she didn't like either vegetable.

"Hattie, I just don't know what's gotten into your father," Mama said. "If I didn't know better, I'd think he stopped at a tavern and had himself a great big glass of beer that went straight to his head and is making him act as silly as an organ-grinder's monkey."

"Yes, ma'am," Hattie said, wondering why her mother would tell her such a thing. There wasn't a tavern on the way home from the mine, just a bunch of shanty houses each with a vegetable garden out back like the one they lived in. Some-times grown-ups acted downright stupid. Next thing you know Mama and Papa would be kissing.

And sure enough, when he finished washing himself and without even drying first, Papa grabbed Mama and twirled her around, then planted a great big kiss right on her mouth. Patrick giggled and covered his eyes.

After dinner, Mama and Papa went for a walk, leaving Hattie to watch Patrick. She helped him build a road in the dirt for the wooden truck that Papa had made for him.

Mama and Papa were gone for what seemed like a

long time, and Hattie wondered if he'd forgotten about the ice cream cones. She and Patrick had lined their dirt road with rocks and twig trees by the time they got back. Papa had his arm around Mama's shoulders, and her face was a strange mixture of happy and sad, and her eyes all red and puffy as if she'd been crying. Before Hattie had a chance to ask if Mama was okay, Papa was loading them in the new old Ford. He asked Hattie which flavor of ice cream she wanted.

All the way to town she tried to decide what flavor she would have. She loved going in the drugstore with its beautiful marble soda fountain. A mirror covered the wall behind the counter, and in front of the counter were tall stools where people sat to drink their sodas or eat their ice cream. The last time she'd had an ice cream cone was way last summer on Patrick's birthday. She'd chosen strawberry because pink was her favorite color. But maybe this time she would ask for chocolate.

Hattie was disappointed when they didn't sit on the tall stools. Papa insisted they carry their ice cream cones to the park across the street where an old man was playing his fiddle and lots of folks had gathered around to listen.

The benches were full so they sat on the grass to eat their ice cream and listen to the music. When the fiddler played "God Bless America," everyone stood up and sang along. Some of the ladies cried, and some of the men looked close to tears themselves. And Hattie knew why. The Japanese had bombed Pearl Harbor and now the country was at war, and men from Coal Town had joined the army and were off training to be soldiers so they could go fight the Nazis and Japanese on the other side of the world. But since the coal that came out of Mr. Sedgwick's mine fueled the ships that took soldiers and tanks and guns across the ocean, the miners who dug the coal out of the ground were needed right where they were, and her papa wouldn't have to go off and fight the war.

But when everyone sat down again, Papa put his arm around Hattie's shoulders and told her that he was leaving and would be gone for an entire year. Mr. Sedgwick had bought a chromium mine in Alaska that had closed down a number of years back, but now America needed chromium armor plates for tanks and battleships. And all the miners in Alaska were already working in other mines, and new miners were needed to get the mine opened up and producing, so Mr. Sedgwick was giving a bonus to any of his miners who would go up there and work for a year. That bonus would be enough for Patrick's operation.

Hattie wanted her brother to have his operation more than anything, but she couldn't imagine her father being gone for an entire year and began to cry. "Can't you even come home for Christmas?" she asked.

Papa shook his head. "But there will be store-bought presents under the tree this year."

The fiddler started playing again, and Hattie tried not to cry while Papa hummed along to "When the Red, Red Robin Comes Bob, Bob, Bobbin' Along." When the song ended, Papa called out to the fiddler asking if he would play a special song for his family, and the man said that he would if Papa would sing the words. And Papa went to stand beside the fiddler, and he looked right at Mama and Patrick and Hattie and wished them an early Merry Christmas and promised he would be thinking about them come Christmas morning. And then he sang:

> It came upon the midnight clear,
> That glorious song of old.
> From angels bending near the earth
> To touch their harps of gold.

All these years later, sitting in her magnificent mountaintop home, the woman who was once named Hattie remembered sitting on the grass beside her weeping mother and her crippled little brother while her handsome father sang Hattie's favorite Christmas song in his best church voice. She was so proud of him she thought her heart was going to burst wide open. It was a moment of pure love, the sort of which does not come often in a lifetime, the sort of which one buries away because remembering is too painful.

SEVEN

HE weatherman had promised beautiful, unseasonably warm fall weather for the last weekend in October. Vanessa called her sisters midweek to ask if they would be free for a family outing in Central Park on Sunday and considered it somewhat of a minor miracle that both had agreed to come. Even so, she'd half-expected one of them to cancel. Or for the weatherman to have been wrong about his forecast.

But the weather was perfect, and the three of them—together for the first time since their mother had left for France—were sitting at a picnic table under a large oak tree at the edge of Central Park's Great Lawn watching Lily and Beth, who had shed their jackets and were turning cartwheels while covertly ogling three boys tossing a Frisbee about.

The balmy weather had brought out sun worshippers, who were lying on blankets that dotted the vast grassy meadow or simply stretched out on the grass. The rooftops of the museums and hotels along Fifth Avenue were visible over treetops aglow with fall foliage. A beautiful scene.

Vanessa had planned for them to lunch on hot dogs

purchased from street vendors, but Ellie had showed up with a large wicker picnic basket from which she had already produced a bottle of wine and corkscrew.

"I'm not ready for my nieces to be boy crazy," she remarked as she opened the bottle and poured wine into three wineglasses.

"You and me both," Vanessa acknowledged as she watched her daughters show off for the boys while pretending not to be aware of them. And the boys' voices became increasingly louder as they laughed and called out to each other, and their antics became increasingly more outrageous as they dove for and leaped after the Frisbee, all in an obvious effort to impress the two cartwheeling girls.

"Good God, Lily is growing boobs!" Georgiana wailed. "Isn't she too young for that?"

"No younger than you were when yours sprouted," Vanessa pointed out, then took a sip of her wine, which was exquisite, of course. She complimented Ellie on her choice while continuing to study the antics and physiques of her daughters. The curves were definitely coming, especially on Lily, who was older by eleven months. And when had they started showing off for boys? Pretty soon she was going to have full-blown teenagers on her hands.

Vanessa couldn't decide if life was going by too quickly or too slowly. Lily and Beth were growing up too fast, and sometimes she even yearned for another baby. But at the same time, she longed for the day when the worries and upsets of childrearing would be behind her. Maybe then she and Scott would have a saner life and a better marriage. Or drift apart and go their separate ways. She felt almost indifferent as to which outcome awaited her.

"I'm sorry Scott didn't come," Georgiana said. "I haven't seen him in forever."

"He had a restless night and woke up not feeling well," Vanessa said. Actually, she hadn't pushed the issue when Scott had remained in bed this morning, preferring that he not come along if he was going to sit around popping pills and feeling sorry for himself. "So when are you going to tell us about your trip to West Virginia?" Georgiana asked, setting down her wineglass and pulling a nail buffer from her backpack.

"Yeah," Ellie chimed in as she fished a wedge of cheese from the basket. "I thought we'd have a full report the minute you got back."

Vanessa shrugged. "I'm busy. You guys are busy. I didn't want to tell it twice over the phone. And our social secretary moved to France."

"All of which means you're pissed because we didn't go with you," Ellie observed.

"Somewhat," Vanessa allowed.

"Georgiana wasn't born until after Daddy's Miss Vera died," Ellie pointed out. "And I was too young to remember her. It wouldn't have been a trip down memory lane for us like it was for you."

"Yeah, it was silly of me to think you and Georgiana might want to see the town where our father spent his boyhood," Vanessa said with a shrug and forced nonchalance.

Georgiana scooted closer to Vanessa and put an arm around her shoulders. "I'm sorry, honey. If I'd realized the trip meant so much to you, I would have declined the photo shoot. Come on, Nessa," she cajoled. "We really would like to hear all about it, wouldn't we, Ellie?"

Ellie drew an X across her chest. "Cross my heart."

Vanessa focused her attention on two squirrels scampering about in a game of chase. "I thought the West Virginia trip would be a fun thing for us to do together," she said, allowing a bit of wistfulness to slip into her voice. "Do you realize that this is the first time in more than three months that the three of us have been together? And, yes, we are all so very busy, but somehow we managed before Mother left. Maybe she moved to the other side of the world to force us to forge onward on our own."

"Or maybe she moved away for exactly the reasons she gave," Georgiana said as she buffed the nails on her right hand. "She's a widowed lady who met a nice man and wanted to explore new vistas while she's still young enough to make the most of it. Now, unless you're going to punish us for not going with you to West Virginia, I wish you would tell us what you found out."

"I was kind of excited driving down there, wondering what I would find," Vanessa acknowledged. "But like Ellie said when Mother showed us that letter, the mysterious Hattie is probably dead by now. And even if she's still alive, maybe she doesn't want to be found. After all, she knew where her child was the whole time he was growing up and apparently never came looking for him."

"Maybe she promised Vera that she wouldn't do that," Georgiana said. "Maybe that was part of their bargain. Maybe she even begged Vera to let her have her child back, but Vera refused."

"In that letter she asked Vera to tell Daddy that she was dead," Ellie pointed out as she offered Vanessa a slice of cheese.

"She could have changed her mind," Vanessa noted.

"I suppose," Ellie conceded, "but even if Hattie is dead, it would be kind of interesting to know something about her—like what sort of a person she was and why she gave away her baby."

"Come on, Nessa," Georgiana begged, pausing in

her buffing long enough to plant a kiss on Vanessa's cheek. "Pretty please, tell us what you found out."

Vanessa nibbled on the cheese. "Not much," she admitted, "especially considering the cost in money and time, two commodities that are definitely in short supply in my life. I now know that Vera was born in Hancock County in the West Virginia Panhandle and she didn't move to Pikesville until she was a grown woman."

"Well, that's very important information," Georgiana said as she inspected her nails. "Even if Hattie is dead, some of her relatives might still live in Hancock County and could tell us about her."

"I suppose that's a possibility," Vanessa allowed, "but it all happened so long ago, and I don't know if Vera's father had siblings other than the brother who died in a mine accident, and I don't know if her mother had any siblings. But, unless Hattie was using the term *aunt* in an honorary way, Hattie would have been the daughter of a sibling of Vera's. Apparently Vera did have a younger brother, but even if Hattie was born a Wentworth, she could have married and have had an entirely different name by the time Daddy was born. Nevertheless, I went to one of those people-search Web sites and searched for Hattie Wentworth. Unfortunately, there are an amazing number of women with that name. And what does it all really matter anyway? We've lived our lives up to this point not knowing anything about Daddy's pedigree."

Vanessa took another sip of wine and nibble of cheese. She could almost feel the wine loosening her tongue. It was a beautiful day, and she didn't want to be surly when she was actually pleased to finally be with her sisters and that her plans for the day had worked out. And maybe they needed to know that finding their father's birth mother was in all likelihood an insurmountable task.

"If Daddy was born out of wedlock," she continued, "quite possibly Hattie's circumstances and her tender years would have made it difficult for her to raise her own child, and she decided—or was forced by her parents—to give him away. If she was married when Daddy was born, perhaps her husband had died in a mining accident like Vera's uncle had been. Or her husband could have been in the military and killed right before the Second World War ended. Widowed and far from home, Hattie might have asked her aunt Vera to take the baby off her hands. But then, we don't really know if Daddy was born in Deer Lodge. The closest thing he had to a birth certificate was a document that said he was adopted by Vera Louise Wentworth in Brooke County, West Virginia. Maybe Hattie gave up her baby because she was ill. She might have arranged for her baby's adoption on her deathbed."

Ellie put her hands up in surrender. "Okay. I get it."

But Vanessa wasn't finished. "There's another possibility. Hattie might have been raped and decided she wanted to have the baby but could not bring herself to raise a child who would be a constant reminder of the worst thing that had ever happened to her."

"Well, on that grim note, I think I'll go see if my nieces are ready for lunch." Ellie swung first one leg and then the other over the bench. Once she was on her feet, however, she just stood there staring.

Vanessa turned to see what had captured her attention. A man was approaching—a tall, broad-shouldered man wearing freshly pressed jeans and an expensive-looking tweed sports coat.

"Oh my God!" Ellie squealed. "He came! He actually came!" And she went racing in the man's direction.

"Boone, I take it," Georgiana said, reaching for her

wineglass. "I thought she had gone a bit overboard on the fancy picnic fixings. Now we know why."

"I thought he'd gone back to his wife," Vanessa said.

"Maybe it didn't work out," Georgiana speculated.

Together Vanessa and Georgiana got to their feet and stood waiting to meet the man. Ellie was clinging to his hand and dancing along at his side. Her cheeks were flushed, her eyes sparkling.

"Boone, these are my sisters—Vanessa and Georgiana."

"At long last," he said with a smile. "I've heard so much about you both." He extended his hand first to Vanessa. "You must be Vanessa, the sister who lives in New Jersey and has two daughters. And Georgiana is the model," he said as he took Georgiana's hand in both of his.

Boone was a bit soft about the middle but otherwise attractive, Vanessa decided. He had nice skin, and his smile revealed a perfect set of very white teeth.

Ellie waved Lily and Beth over and introduced them to Boone, then, keeping up a continuous stream of chatter directed toward him, busied herself spreading a tablecloth and laying out the picnic fare. "Do you like pâté?" she asked him. "I bought this at a little French deli in my neighborhood that has the best pâté imaginable—it's made with goose liver and truffles."

Behind Ellie's back Lily and Beth were making faces. *Goose liver and truffles?* Vanessa gave her daughters a threatening look, then moved to sit between them. Together they watched while Ellie named each delicacy she pulled out of the basket—mushrooms stuffed with crabmeat; artichoke potato salad; a second salad made with black beans, cabbage, and dates; smoked-turkey-and-apple sandwiches on herbed beer bread; and Kahlúa gingerbread with key-lime curd.

Even if her daughters only picked at their lunch, Vanessa found the food delicious but had lost her appetite. The man with whom Ellie had probably convinced herself that she was madly in love and that he loved her in return and was going to marry her and make her pregnant could not take his eyes off Georgiana.

To Lily and Beth, Boone hardly said a word, asking them only how old they were. He did ask Vanessa if she liked living in New Jersey and how long she had been a development officer. But he had an endless stream of questions for Georgiana. Did she live near Ellie? Did she get to spend much time with her nieces? Did she enjoy live theater? Did she belong to a health club? Was she a sports fan? What was her favorite nightspot? How long had she been a hand and foot model? He complimented her on her beautiful hands, adding that the rest of her was beautiful, too, and he loved her magnificent hair.

Ellie was so in seventh heaven over Boone's showing up to meet her family that she sat smiling beside him, frequently stroking his arm or patting his shoulder. She didn't even notice that he was trying to make time with her younger sister.

Vanessa and Georgiana carefully avoided eye contact.

Boone left first, announcing that he was going to take his kids out to dinner and a movie. Ellie had obviously thought they would be spending the evening together and did her best not to look crestfallen. Vanessa and Georgiana helped Ellie pack up the remains of the picnic lunch and tidy up. Before heading home, Vanessa gave Ellie and the basket a ride back to her apartment building.

Once they had dropped off Ellie, Beth announced from the backseat, "I don't like Ellie's boyfriend."

"I don't either," Vanessa admitted, then immediately regretted her words. Ellie might very well marry the man, and she didn't want to have gone on record with her daughters as disliking him. "But then, I hardly know him," she amended. "He may prove to be very nice when and if we get to know him better."

"He acted like he's more in love with Georgiana than he is with Ellie," Lily observed.

"Maybe he was just being friendly," Vanessa said.

Lily folded her arms across her developing chest and told her mother all in a huff, "Well, he sure wasn't being friendly with you and Beth and me."

"Are you going to tell Ellie that we don't like him?" Beth asked her mother.

"Probably not. If he's not the right person for her, she needs to figure that out on her own."

"Well, if Beth goes gaga over some weirdo, *I'm* going to tell her that the guy is a weirdo," Lily announced in a firm voice, "and I expect her to do the same for me."

"I hope they don't get married," Beth added.

"But if they do, will Beth and I be in the wedding?" Lily wanted to know.

"I have no idea," Vanessa said as she drove into the Lincoln Tunnel.

"Are Ellie and the Boone man having sex?" Beth asked.

Vanessa wanted to tell her that the question was improper. That girls her age weren't supposed to be speculating about whether their aunt was having sex with her boyfriend. But she sighed and said, "Yes, I suppose they are."

EIGHT

$\mathcal{S}$COTT'S car was not in the garage.

Vanessa looked for a note in the kitchen.

The kitchen was just as she had left it with no cupboard doors or drawers left open and no dirty dishes on the counter, which meant he hadn't eaten lunch here. She wondered if he was feeling worse and had gone to an urgent care clinic. But if that were the case, he would have called on her cell phone or left a note.

Maybe he'd been faking his illness and skipped the picnic so he could play golf and planned to beat them home.

They had soup and sandwiches for dinner, after which the girls tackled their homework, their books and notebooks spread out on the kitchen table. Vanessa went into the family room to call Scott's cell phone number. When the leave-a-message voice answered, Vanessa said, "Hi, honey. Just wondering when you'll be home."

When she returned to the kitchen, Lily said, "I'm worried about Daddy."

"He probably started feeling better and decided to

play poker with his golfing buddies and forgot to leave a note," Vanessa speculated, then announced that she was heading upstairs to take a bath.

Scott's cell phone was on his bureau.

His note was on Vanessa's bedside table. She stared at the envelope for a long time. Scott never put notes in envelopes, and he'd never left a note on the bedside table. Just in the kitchen. Notes telling her that someone had called or that the girls were at a friend's house.

Her hand was shaking when she finally reached for it.

> Dearest Vanessa,
>   I've needed to get away for some time now. I'll call you in a few days and let you know how to reach me.
>   For now, just tell the girls I had a chance to sell some property out of state.
>
> Scott

Vanessa sank onto the bed. *Needed to get away?*

Where could he have gone? They hadn't had a fight. They'd even had sex last night. Not great sex. They only had that on the rare nights they had a weekend away from the girls and were staying in a hotel. A hotel room offered an aura of romance about it that facilitated great sex. Or sometimes they rose to the occasion when both girls were spending the night with friends and they opened a bottle of wine. Otherwise, sex had long been reduced to a routine, each knowing exactly what was needed to make it satisfying.

But last night was one step up from routine. Sweeter. His kisses more tender. But in the night he was restless. He got up several times and had even gone downstairs once. She asked him if he was okay.

"Just an upset stomach," he'd responded.

Had he gone downstairs to call a girlfriend?

Scott had plenty of time to wander while she was at work and the girls were at school. Maybe he'd met a bored housewife at the supermarket.

But if he was having an affair, wouldn't she have had a clue? Lipstick on a collar? A change in his routine? More frequent haircuts and more interest in shaving?

She couldn't think of a thing that was different. Everything had been the same yesterday as it had been the day before that and the day before that pretty much for years now. He had business cards showing that he was a realtor, but his sales had been few and far between.

But men didn't just up and leave unless they had someone waiting in the wings. Vanessa looked around the bedroom that she had shared with him since Lily was a baby and she was pregnant with Beth. They had moved to New Jersey with such high hopes. She already was working at the college, and he had been hired as a loan officer by a bank in Paterson. But he hated the bank job—for almost five years he hated it—until finally he opened a store that sold and serviced computers, an endeavor he struggled with for almost three years but at which he never made a profit. By the time he got his realtor's license, he seemed to have lost whatever ambition he once had. Under the guise of working at home, he played a lot of computer games. And he played pickup basketball at a nearby recreation center. And golf whenever he got the chance. But he also did most of the grocery shopping and cooking and carpooling, which certainly made life more manageable for her. But they struggled financially, and more and more he only did whatever chores she specifically requested that he do and often not even those. Still, she had never thought of their marriage as troubled.

But Scott had *needed to get away for some time now.*

She knew that he wasn't happy, but then neither was she. Happiness was the stuff of moments. The rest of the time one simply put one foot in front of the other and did what needed to be done.

In the park today, however, she had admitted to herself the possibility that she and Scott might drift apart after the girls were grown. He would find someone else. Men always did. And she might, too. An interesting man with whom she could go out to dinner and take an occasional trip and share enjoyable sex would be nice. But that was someday and not while she and Scott still had two daughters to raise.

Lily and Beth would be devastated if their parents got a divorce.

Divorce. The very word made her shudder. No, they absolutely could not do that to their children. Scott would come home, and they would work through whatever their differences were.

So what would they change?

At that thought, tears welled in her eyes, and sobs swelled in her chest. How did two people fall in love all over again?

Georgiana called the next morning. "Did I wake you? I wanted to catch you before you headed off to work."

Vanessa wanted to snap at her that she hadn't been able to sleep and had been up for hours. That she had two daughters to roust out of bed and get off to school and needed to get herself ready for work. And that this morning was a particularly trying morning because her husband had left and her life was falling apart. But she wasn't ready to tell her baby sister or anyone else what was happening to her.

"So, what's going on with you?" she asked in what she hoped was a normal-sounding voice as she tucked the phone under her chin and began setting bowls, cereal boxes, and the milk carton on the kitchen table.

"I've got some ideas about how to proceed with the search for Hattie and wondered if we could have lunch later in the week," Georgiana told her. "I could even come out to the college, if you like, and we can eat someplace near the campus."

Vanessa closed her eyes and drew in her breath. Searching for Hattie was the furthest thing from her mind.

"It occurred to me," Georgiana continued, "that since Mother is planning on Lily and Beth spending next summer in France, that would be the perfect time for you and Ellie and me to go to Montana. I've been waiting for something to inspire me to get back into photography, and I thought maybe I could take pictures during our trip."

Vanessa sank into a chair. "You've caught me at a bad time."

"Are you sick or something?"

"Just a headache. And Scott is away on a business trip. And I need to get the girls up and fed and take them to school."

"I thought Scott wasn't feeling well," Georgiana said.

"He's not, but he went anyway."

"You want me to come look after things until you feel better?"

Her sister's offer brought tears to Vanessa's eyes. "Thanks, honey. That's sweet of you. I'll feel better after coffee and a couple of aspirin. I'll call you in a few days. Okay?"

"Okay, but do you care if I nose around the Internet?"

"Be my guest. I'll be anxious to hear what you find

out," Vanessa said, trying to sound a bit more chipper. She hadn't lied. She was sick. Sick at heart.

And now she was starting to feel anger. And fear. What if Scott never came back? How in the hell was she going to manage on her own?

She was already overwhelmed, and if Scott was out of the picture, everything would be up to her. He wasn't the greatest husband in the world, but he was a good father.

"One more thing," Georgiana said tentatively. "I really need to tell you something."

Vanessa squelched a sigh and rubbed her forehead instead.

"Nessa, are you still there?"

"Yeah. I'm still here."

"That Boone guy that Ellie's seeing called me after the picnic. He wanted to come over."

. Vanessa felt a wave of weariness wash through her body. *Not now,* she wanted to say. *I've got major problems of my own.* "What did you tell him?"

"I told him to go to hell. But what about Ellie? She needs to know that the guy's a jerk. But if I'm the one to tell her, I'm afraid she'll blame me somehow. You know, 'kill the messenger.' I thought maybe if you could talk to her and let her know that I didn't encourage him in any way. I didn't, Nessa. You were there. You know that I didn't. You know that I wouldn't do something like that. Actually the man made my flesh crawl—trying to come on to me while Ellie's knocking herself out to be nice to him. We can't let her get hooked up with a lowlife like that. He'll break her heart. She's always telling me that I need to find a guy more up-scale than Freddy. I know that Freddy has his faults, but he's loyal. As for the creepy Mr. Boone, I doubt if there's a loyal bone in his body."

"Look, Georgiana, I really can't deal with this right now. I'll call you in a day or two."

"What kind of sick are you? You don't sound so good. Are you sure you don't want me to come out?"

For a heartbeat or two, Vanessa considered calling in sick and accepting Georgiana's offer. She could break down and cry in her baby sister's arms. But she had to get Lily and Beth to school and was scheduled to meet with the college president and the department heads this morning to present her plan for the upcoming Reach for Excellence Fund Drive.

"I really appreciate the offer, but I'm fine," Vanessa insisted. "I'll call you later in the week. I promise."

Beth was already in the bathroom. Vanessa sat on the side of Lily's bed and smoothed her hair. "Wake up, baby."

"Just five more minutes," Lily murmured, her eyes still closed.

Lily had dark, thick hair from her mother and grandmother. She also had Penelope's wonderful cheekbones, brown eyes, and olive complexion. With her long legs and lean body, Lily was on her way to being sleek and elegant, whereas younger sister Beth was blond, on the plump side, dimpled, and cute. "Sorry, honey. It's time to get up," Vanessa said, planting a kiss on her daughter's forehead.

Lily's eyes fluttered open. "Is Daddy back yet?"

"He called from Richmond after you were in bed," Vanessa lied. "He drove down to meet with a prospective client and had car trouble. He may be stuck there for a few days."

Georgiana sat there for a time staring at the telephone. All was not well in New Jersey. And unless Vanessa had lost her job or one of the girls was sick or had run away, the problem was probably marital. Scott was a nice guy, but he and Vanessa had never seemed like the perfect match. Nessa was uptight like Ellie, and Scott was laid-back.

She called Freddy on his cell phone. He was in California. Trisha Bell and her band were playing a two-week gig at a nightclub in Santa Monica.

"Yeah," he answered, his voice groggy.

"Do you love me?"

"You called in the middle of the night to ask if I love you when you already know the answer?" he mumbled.

"It's not the middle of the night," she said. Of course, Freddy never got up before early afternoon. She tried to remember if it was earlier or later in California. "Do you think we should get married?"

"Whatever you want, baby. Now, can I please go back to sleep?"

"Do you have sex with other women?"

"What brought that on?" he muttered.

"According to a survey taken by Ellie's magazine, thirty-two percent of married men have cheated on their wife, forty-six percent of engaged men have cheated on their fiancée, and fifty-nine percent of unmarried and unengaged men with a steady girlfriend cheat on her."

"And you think I'm one of the fifty-nine percent guys?" Freddy demanded. "What the hell happened to trust? And what about the female side of the equation? What percentage of women cheat on their husband or boyfriend?"

She hung up.

Now why had she done that? Georgiana asked herself as she poured a glass of orange juice.

But she knew why, and it had nothing to do with Freddy. That a man her own sister had fallen in love with and thought was in love with her and maybe even wanted to marry her and make babies with her was putting the make on Ellie's own sister had given Georgiana pause. As had the survey published in Ellie's magazine. Of course, it had not been a scientific survey, and only two hundred men between the ages of eighteen and forty had been interviewed, but the results were enough to make a girl wish she were a lesbian.

Freddy wasn't the type to play around. But how could she know for sure?

Georgiana thought about pulling on some clothes and heading to her neighborhood coffee shop for a latte and muffin.

But instead she went to her computer.

She typed "Deer Lodge, Montana" on the search line. Less than a half hour later, her heart was pounding. "Oh my gosh!" she said, and reached for the phone.

NINE

$\mathcal{A}$FTER the picnic, Ellie had done some laundry, dined on leftover food from the picnic basket, then checked her calendar for the upcoming week, which included fashion shows on Wednesday and Thursday, and on Friday she was to be interviewed on a local television show about the latest trends in women's fashions.

She decided on an outfit and accessories for each day, including a fabulous Tracy Reese outfit for the TV interview, then tidied up the apartment, changed the sheets, took a shower, and put on a silk peignoir set. Boone had said nothing about stopping by after he did whatever he was doing with his kids, but she had let him know that she would be at home this evening.

She wondered if he was really doing something with his kids.

Or maybe it was his kids *and* his wife with whom he was spending the evening. Marlene was the wife's name. Maybe Boone and Marlene had tucked the kids in bed and were now having sex while she was sitting here in a slinky peignoir and gown for which she had spent a fortune at Barneys. Boone insisted that his reconciliation with his wife was not working out, and he was apartment hunting.

Just in case Boone did show up, she lit candles, put a really nice Chablis on ice, and curled up on the sofa to watch *Casablanca* for the umpteenth time.

The movie made her cry. Unrequited love always did. But at least the two star-crossed lovers would never fall out of love. Never see each other grow old. Never disappoint one another.

She wasn't in love with Boone. Not yet. She had promised herself that she wasn't going to allow herself to fall in love with another man until she was absolutely certain they had a future together.

She changed into a pair of well-worn pajamas and took two over-the-counter sleeping pills, slid between the freshly laundered sheets, and waited to fall asleep. But she kept thinking about Boone and wondering where he was. She had been thrilled out of her gourd that he'd come to the picnic. His presence there meant something. She was certain of that. And whenever they had sex, he told her how good they were together and how much he loved making love with her.

But sometimes she worried that Boone was not a truthful man.

And that made her wonder if she really wanted him or any other man messing up her domicile and her life. Maybe she should forget all about motherhood and continue living her focused and quite satisfying life.

After a restless night, Ellie woke early and decided to head to the office and get a few things done before the phone started ringing.

With her promotion to associate editor, she had moved from a cubicle into a real office. It was smallish but had a wonderful view of the Chrysler Building, and she had redecorated it, of course. Her desk was built-in and made with cheap-looking fake wood, but she'd had it recovered with a handsome laminate that looked like Moroccan leather. And she'd found an elegant camelback love seat with claw-feet at a used-furniture store in the East Village and had had it upholstered in distressed black leather. The coffee table was an authentic Hans Wegner that she'd spotted in an antique store near Vanessa's house in Jersey.

She'd spent more decorating her small office than decorating her three-room apartment, but more people saw the office and she spent more time here than at her apartment. And she always got a thrill when she walked into the room, which—like her name on the magazine masthead—was a tangible sign of her success.

Working on a top-tier fashion magazine was a heady experience, and Ellie had never minded the hard work and late hours. Once a month, when she had the latest edition in her hands, she took great satisfaction in knowing that she and her colleagues had pulled off yet another miracle and took great pleasure in knowing that all over the English-speaking world and beyond, stylish women would enjoy the fantastic magazine that she had played an important role in creating and find inspiration and useful advice on its pages.

She had come to the magazine as a journalist and missed the pleasure that came from creating a carefully re-searched, creatively crafted piece. And while she now did only incidental writing—cover copy, cutlines for photographs, and the like—she had learned a great deal about the craft of writing from the hundreds of articles she had assigned and edited. Ellie's job was to smooth, cut, rearrange, and sometimes ask for more information. She had to decide when a piece was lacking if it was salvageable and how that might be accomplished. When a particularly challenging or interesting topic came along, she sometimes wished she could write it herself instead of deciding which of the magazine's stable of free-lancers—or "contributing editors" as they were listed on the masthead—would get the assignment. But with her promotion, she had no time for writing.

Of course, if she ever rose to "editor in chief," she would have her own monthly column and become a recognized arbiter of style and a real force in the fashion world. Such women did not go around with a baby on their hip and a diaper bag over their shoulder even if the diaper bag had a designer label.

Ellie had reached a point in her life when she had to decide what her ultimate goal should be. Editor in chief or motherhood? Of course, in theory, she was supposed to be able to do both. But were there enough hours in the day to do justice to both?

With that thought, she stashed her Marc Jacobs handbag in the bottom drawer of her desk, logged on to her computer, checked her calendar for the week, answered the most important of her e-mails, then began editing an article on a Peruvian footwear designer and manufacturer. Ellie had paused to look through some of the photographs supplied by the designer when the phone rang. The operator asked if she would hold for a conference call. Soon Georgiana's voice said, "Ellie, Nessa, are you both there?"

Ellie pressed the speaker button and replaced the receiver. "I'm here," Ellie responded, wondering what was so important that Georgiana had placed a conference call. After all, they had just seen each other yesterday.

"Me, too," Vanessa said. "What's going on? My secretary called me out of a meeting in the president's office to take the call."

"I had to talk to you both at the same time," Georgiana said, excitement evident her voice. "I just discovered that female convicts in Montana used to be incarcerated at a prison in Deer Lodge. The prison originally was built to hold just male prisoners, but they had to have some place for women so they put up a wooden building for females inside the prison walls."

Ellie waited for Georgiana to say more. When she didn't, Ellie asked, "That's it? That's why you made a conference call?"

"That letter from Daddy's birth mother had a Deer Lodge, Montana, postmark," Vanessa reminded Ellie in a voice that sounded weary. And distracted.

"Well, just because the town had a prison doesn't mean that Hattie was ever incarcerated there," Ellie pointed out as she resumed her perusal of the Peruvian photographs. The boots were absolutely stunning. And quite expensive. But already she knew she had to have a pair.

"If Hattie was in prison when Daddy was born, it would explain why she gave him away," Georgiana pointed out. "Maybe her parents had disowned her or were dead, and Hattie decided that she wanted to have a relative raise the child rather than having him end up in an orphanage or with a total stranger."

"She may have something, Ellie," Vanessa said, sounding a bit more interested. But tired. Definitely tired. Ellie was going to ask her if she felt all right when Vanessa added, "I need to get back to my meeting. We'll have to talk about this some other time."

"Hattie also could have been an ordinary, *un*incarcerated young woman—an unmarried schoolteacher or a waitress or even a schoolgirl—who ended up pregnant," Ellie added as she continued her examination of the photographs, which included handbags along with the boots and shoes. "Back then, there was such a stigma against unwed mothers that most girls either had a backstreet abortion or gave the baby up for adoption. Maybe in addition to a prison, there was one of those places in Deer Lodge where girls went to have babies in secret."

"Perhaps, but I don't think we can just rule out the possibility that the prison had something to do with Hattie's situation," Georgiana said. "Apparently Deer Lodge was just a small town back then, and the prison would have been the town's major industry. The women's prison is in Billings now. I just talked to a woman in the warden's office there, and she said that any existing records from the Deer Lodge prison would be in the state archives in Helena. So I called the number she gave me, and a very nice woman named Janet said that, yes, what remained of the Deer Lodge records were stored there. But she said it wouldn't be a big deal to go through them since very few women were incarcerated back then. In fact, only seventeen female inmates were at Deer Lodge the year that Daddy was born. So I asked Janet if maybe she could look and see if any of them were named Hattie. She called me back to say that one of the female inmates was named Henrietta, and that she was pretty sure that Hattie could be a nickname for Henrietta."

Ellie put down the photographs. The Hattie story had just got more interesting.

There could be a story here, she decided. Of course, with no fashion angle it wasn't anything that *Stiletto* could use. But maybe one of the traditional women's magazines would be interested. She envisioned a bonding story about three sisters who were drifting apart until they took this journey into their beloved late father's past.

"Well, it may be something we want to pursue," Ellie

said. "You've been awfully quiet, Vanessa. What do you think about Georgiana's discovery?"

"Maybe it really doesn't matter who Hattie was and why she gave Daddy away," Vanessa said. "It was a long time ago, and as we keep saying, she's probably dead by now anyway."

"But what if she's not?" Georgiana insisted. "She's probably wondered about the baby she gave away all of her life—I know that I would if I'd given away a baby—and now as she approaches the end of her life, she might be really grateful to find out that her baby grew up to be a good, kind man and had three daughters who loved him very much, so much that they wanted to find his birth mother and thank her for making sure he had a good home."

"Perhaps," Vanessa said. "But I *must* go. Maybe we can talk about this some other time."

TEN

$\mathcal{G}$EORGIANA listened to the click from Vanessa's phone. "What's going on with Nessa?" she asked Ellie, slumping in her chair. She'd been so excited when she'd discovered that a woman who was possibly *their* Hattie had once been incarcerated in Deer Lodge, Montana. But obviously Vanessa was not interested.

"I'm not sure," Ellie allowed. "She sounded tired, and maybe you just caught her at a bad time."

Something in Ellie's voice made Georgiana ask, "Do you know something I don't know?"

"Maybe."

"Explain please."

There was a pause before Ellie said, "Well, it may be nothing, but I saw Scott in town a couple of weeks ago. We were doing a photo shoot down in the Financial District. I ran into a coffee shop and was waiting in line to buy something mostly so I could use the bathroom and realized that he was sitting at a table in the back corner with a woman."

"Did you talk to him?"

"No, I was in a hurry to get back to the shoot and didn't have time for introductions and chitchat."

"So what are you implying?"

"Oh, I don't know," Ellie said, wishing she hadn't mentioned the incident. "They seemed to be kind of deep in conversation. But no touching or anything inappropriate. It was just so surprising to see Scott in Manhattan without Vanessa and the girls. And then he wasn't with them at the park yesterday when Vanessa had said that they all were coming."

"What did the woman look like?"

"Early thirties. Attractive. Shoulder-length brown hair. She was wearing a navy pants suit with a white blouse. Probably she worked in the neighborhood. There was a box on the table."

"What sort of box?"

"Just a brown cardboard box," Ellie said.

"You don't think Nessa and Scott are having problems, do you?" Georgiana asked. "She didn't sound like herself on the phone."

"Maybe Lily and Beth have been acting out or one of them is having trouble in school."

"Oh, God," Georgiana gasped, "I hope Nessa hasn't found a lump in her breast or something awful like that."

"No. She'd tell us if it was something like that. You know, that day in the coffee shop—at first I thought the man at the corner table was some guy who looked like Scott. He seemed younger and more engaging. I'd thought about having a private moment with Scott yesterday in the park and asking him about it. But then he didn't come. He never seems to show up at family gatherings anymore. I can't remember the last time I saw him."

"At Daddy's memorial service," Georgiana said.

. . .

When the meeting in the president's office finally ended, Vanessa hurried back to her office and went through her phone messages.

Scott had not called.

She sat staring out the window for a time at the students strolling across the campus with autumn leaves blowing about and squirrels scampering. It was just the sort of scene found in the college's recruitment bulletins. And in the annual reports she sent to donors.

Finally she sighed and pulled out her sack lunch.

She'd hardly slept at all last night and was so exhausted she felt ill. Staying awake during the weekly meeting of the President's Council had been painful. Just being at the weekly meeting of the President's Council had been painful. Even after that strange conference call with her sisters, it took all her concentration to keep from nodding off.

Her stomach was growling with emptiness, but she could not bring herself to take a bite of the smashed peanut-butter sandwich. She glanced at her watch. It was evening in France. She thought about calling her mother, but she wasn't ready for that. Not yet. Maybe Scott would come back home. Maybe he really did need time to think.

She hadn't eaten any breakfast and was beginning to feel light-headed. She forced herself to take a bite of the sandwich and managed swallow it with the help of a sip of water.

Then she took another bite.

The girls were going to want to know how long their father was going to be away and why he wasn't answering his cell phone. She would tell them that he'd forgotten it. But she had no answer as to how long he would be away. She wondered if she should admit that all was not well or keep up the pretense.

She wanted to be mad at Scott for putting her through this, but she was too afraid to be mad. She had been less than content with their life for a long time now, but she'd never stopped to think what life would be like if he left her. If they *divorced*.

They didn't have enough money to lead separate lives. They would have to sell the house. And arrange for shared custody. There would be days and nights when she wouldn't see her daughters, when she wouldn't be able to make sure that they were dressed appropriately and wouldn't always know where they were and whom they were with and what they were doing.

In the night she had looked back over her entire marriage in an attempt to reach some sort of understanding as to why this had happened. Was it her failure or Scott's? Maybe she should have been more sympathetic when his computer business failed. She hadn't said, "I told you so," but he knew she was thinking it. She had wanted him to stay at the bank and earn a regular paycheck.

Maybe he would come back home on his own. If he did, she would be more encouraging and help him regain his self-confidence. He'd always been involved in the girls' school and athletic endeavors. Maybe he could be a schoolteacher or a coach.

But this other voice was bouncing around ideas in her head. She wasn't happy with her lot either. Her job was stressful and demanding and no damned fun. She had to suck up to people she didn't particularly admire.

She had never liked her job and never would. But she was vested in the college's pension plan and had health insurance for herself and her family, and while she didn't get summers off, she was able to cut back and have more free time. And there was always that free tuition for her daughters. If she and Scott were divorced, Lily and Beth might have no choice but to attend there.

She choked down the rest of her sandwich, answered the rest of her e-mails, then wrote a presidential letter thanking a recent graduate who had made a two-hundred-dollar donation to the drama department. *I especially recall your sterling performance as Katharina in* The Taming of the Shrew . . .

The ring of the phone made her jump. *Please let it be Scott,* she begged the Fates. *Please.*

It wasn't.

The president was in the midst of signing the stack of donor thank-you letters Vanessa had left with her this morning. "This letter to Margaret and Fred Stinson—shouldn't you have mentioned their daughter's recent engagement?" she asked.

"It was their niece Cynthia Stinson who got engaged," Vanessa pointed out. "Margaret and Fred's daughter is named Beverly."

"Oh, yes. The rather large girl on the field hockey team."

"That's the one. Cynthia plays softball."

She hung up and turned to her computer. Ten donor thank-you letters, she promised herself. Then she needed to make a few phone calls. There was a reception at four for the new members of the Alumnae Council, but with Scott gone, she would have to leave early to pick up the girls.

She finished the letter to the library donor and started another.

Dear Dr. and Mrs. Martin:

Thank you so very much for your generous five-hundred-dollar gift to the Hamilton Hall Renovation Project. It is because of loyal supporters such as yourselves that we are able to provide a superior education for talented young women like your granddaughter . . .

She stopped to reach for a tissue. The tears in her eyes were blurring the words on the screen.

She drove around the block to make sure Scott's car wasn't waiting in line to pick up Beth and Lily. At precisely three thirty, the door opened and a river of girls in white blouses, navy sweaters, and navy pleated shirts, each with a backpack slung over one shoulder emerged.

Her heart turned over as she watched her beautiful, healthy daughters racing toward the car, hair flying, and Lily's shirttail half-out.

Beth opened the door and stuck her head inside. "Isn't Dad back from his trip yet?" she demanded.

"Not yet," Vanessa told her.

Lily's head came in beside her sister's. "Can we go to the mall with Jenny and her mom?" she asked breathlessly.

"*Pleeeze*," Beth begged. "Jenny wants us to help her decide what dress to buy for her cousin's wedding. She's going to be the candlelighter."

"What about homework?" Vanessa dutifully asked.

"We'll do it right after dinner," Lily promised. "No television or time on the computer until it's done."

Jenny's mother waved from her SUV. "I'll have them home by dinnertime," she called.

Vanessa gave them each money for a snack. She considered going back to the office and writing some more letters, but she thought of the empty refrigerator at home and headed for the grocery.

Wandering aimlessly up and down the aisles, she tried

to visualize what was in the pantry and refrigerator but ended up randomly grabbing this or that. Grocery shopping was no longer her province. Nor was the day-in-and-day-out preparation of meals. Or transporting the girls to and from school and to their after-school activities.

How in the world was she going to manage with Scott gone?

But he wasn't gone, she told herself. He was just away. He would come back, and they would talk. They would work things out.

After a complete circuit of the grocery she had only a loaf of bread, ketchup, popcorn, and orange juice in the basket. *Dinner,* she told herself. *Get something for dinner. And for the rest of the week.*

As she headed home, driving down tree-lined streets past well-kept houses and lawns, she wondered how long it would be before their neighbors began to complain about the dead oak in their front yard and the peeling paint on their house. She and Scott had bought the house as a fixer-upper and had only got partway down their list of repairs and renovations. The house still needed new windows. The floors still needed refinishing. The oven was still in need of a functioning thermostat. The garage door still was on its last legs.

As she turned the corner and her neglected home came into view, she realized someone was sitting on the front step. Two someones.

Her sisters. Ellie and Georgiana were sitting on her front step.

They stood as she turned into the driveway. And Vanessa felt the resolve that had kept her afloat throughout the long day flowing from her body. Somehow she remembered to put her foot on the brake. To put the car into park.

She put her head against the steering wheel and felt her body go limp. She was aware of her sisters opening the car door, pulling her out, hugging her, then supporting her as the three of them walked toward the house.

"How did you know?" Vanessa asked between sobs. "How did you know?"

ELEVEN

*F*OR days, the memory of her father singing "It Came Upon the Midnight Clear" in the park had continued to come unbidden to Myrna's mind. Such a bittersweet memory. The last truly happy memory of her childhood. The remembering came with a price, dragging from the deep recesses of her mind the darker times that came after that day.

Usually she was able to squelch these girlhood remembrances when they threatened to erupt. She hadn't been that girl eating an ice cream cone in the park for more years than she wanted to count. Her parents had been dead for so long that she was probably the only living person who had any memory of them. They had been poor people, and the poor leave no legacy. And when she was gone, they would be truly dead and completely forgotten for all time.

She had known two things growing up—she would do anything to keep from being poor and she would live only for herself. Children robbed their parents of options, and she wanted nothing to stand in the way of success. Fatherhood had brought her papa an early death.

But the time came when Myrna realized she needed children to carry on the empire she was creating. And what an empire it turned out to be. Not just mining. She owned an oil company with its own fleet of tankers. She owned hotels, shopping malls, a chain of grocery stores, and a company that manufactured and exported munitions throughout the world.

It was more than a commercial empire, however, that she wanted to leave behind. She wanted to be remembered as the founder of a great American family. She wanted her progeny to be not just captains of industry but also statesmen and ambassadors. She wanted one of her children to be elected president of the United States. Her oldest son was a congressman and, according to plan, would soon announce that he was entering the race for governor of Colorado. The governorship would be his stepping-stone to the White House. If he should fail, her other son would step up to the line. She would do whatever needed to be done to make one of her two sons the most powerful man in the world. A man whose name would endure as long as history was being written. A man whose mother would be remembered as a powerful person in her own right, a mother who had paved the way for her son the way Joseph Kennedy had done for JFK. And when a son of hers took the oath of office on the Capitol steps for all the world to see, she would be there with him. It would be the culminating event of her lifetime. Erasing all evidence of her past had been the first step in fulfilling that dream.

Her past now existed only in her memory. Remembrances of those other times had flitted through her brain from time to time, but of late she had been preoccupied by them. Which she found disturbing.

• • •

Hattie's father had left for Alaska shortly after they ate ice cream cones in the park. He had made her mother promise to write often even though she had only gone as far as the seventh grade and writing was difficult for her.

Papa had tried to schedule Patrick's operation before he departed but had to leave that for Mama to take care of. Poor Mama, who'd never driven anyplace except Coal Town on her own, left twelve-year-old Hattie with a neighbor lady and drove to Billings with Patrick in the backseat with a pillow and a blanket and his wooden truck.

The neighbor lady, Mrs. Simpson, was elderly, skinny, didn't hear well, and had whiskers on her chin. Hattie knew her from church but had never been in her house, which had a parlor with upholstered chairs for when the preacher came. Mama had instructed Hattie to weed Mrs. Simpson's garden, which she did. And she washed the windows and scrubbed the floors without being asked.

And when she wasn't doing chores, Hattie carried a book to the front porch and read as long as the light was good, looking up every time a vehicle drove by, hoping it was Mama and Patrick returning from Billings.

Finally the evening of the fourth day at Mrs. Simpson's house, the old Ford pulled up out front, and Hattie went racing across the yard.

Only Mama was in the car.

"Where's Patrick?" Hattie asked.

Mama buried her face in her hands.

Hattie sensed Mrs. Simpson coming up behind her. The women's old, veined hand reached out and opened the car door. She took hold of Mama's arm, pulled her out, and put her arms around her.

Hattie grabbed her mother's sleeve. "Where's Patrick?" she demanded.

Mama withdrew from Mrs. Simpson's embrace and put her arms around Hattie. "We've lost him, honey," she sobbed. "We've lost our sweet little boy."

Hattie knew what her mother meant, but she didn't want to believe it. All she could do was say, "No," over and over.

Mrs. Simpson put a hand on Hattie's shoulder. "Your little brother is with the angels."

They went into the house and sat at Mrs. Simpson's kitchen table. And Hattie listened while Mama explained about Patrick. The doctor said his heart sounded just fine before the operation, but it had something wrong that couldn't be heard with a stethoscope. The doctor fixed his foot, but they couldn't get him to wake up after the operation.

When Mrs. Simpson asked about a funeral for Patrick, Mama explained that it had taken most of Papa's bonus money for the operation, and she didn't have enough left to pay for an undertaker to bring Patrick's body to Coal Town in a hearse, and the people at the hospital said it was against the law for her to bring him home in a car. Patrick had been buried in Billings in a corner of the cemetery set aside for the poor. Then Mama put her hands on the table and stood. "We'd best be getting home, Hattie."

Patrick's chair was in its usual place at the table. Patrick's toys were in a cardboard box in the corner of the kitchen.

"Where's the wooden truck Papa made for Patrick?" Hattie asked.

"I buried it with him," Mama answered, then sank into a chair and threw her head back and began making a sound unlike Hattie had ever heard before, a sound so hopeless and full of pain that she wondered if her mother was going to die, too.

Hattie put her hands over her ears. "No, Mama, no," she sobbed. When Mama didn't stop, Hattie put her hands over her mother's mouth and pushed with all her might to keep that terrible sound from coming out.

Mama went limp and gradually her arms came around Hattie's body and her head rested on Hattie's shoulder. Then Hattie felt her take a deep breath and lift her head. "I bet you are hungry," she said.

Mrs. Simpson had sent food with them. Hattie set the table and Mama put out the sandwiches and fried chicken. But they both just sat there not eating and looking at nothing. Finally Mama got out a tablet and sharpened a pencil with a knife.

Hattie offered to write her words for her, but Mama shook her head. She needed to do this herself.

Hattie watched in silence while her mother labored over a letter to Papa telling him that their precious little boy was dead.

She imagined her father up there in Alaska hoping every day to get news of Patrick's operation. There was a pay phone at the Coal Town drugstore and probably other places in town, but most likely Mama didn't have a number to call. She could have asked Mr. Sedgwick's secretary to get word to him, but maybe Mama didn't think of that or maybe she thought that she should be the one to notify her husband about their son's death. She erased a lot and started over several times, but finally she folded a single piece of paper and put it in her purse. The next morning they went to the post office. Mama bought a stamped envelope. Hattie wrote the address on it and dropped it in the slot.

For years, Hattie would find herself imagining how happy her poor father would have been to get his first letter from home. He would have just gotten off his shift and be covered with whatever kind of dust came from chromium mines. He would have ripped the letter open and eagerly read Mama's printed words. He would probably have had to read it a second time to make sure he understood. Then he would have gone off by himself to cry. Even though he was a grown-up man, he would have cried and cried for his little dead boy. And there was no one to comfort him. Not his wife. Not his daughter. Not the preacher from the church.

As it was, Papa did not return from Alaska when his year was up. There was an accident at the mine, and he'd been trapped underground for almost a week. Papa and one other man were the only ones who survived. The mine was closed. Papa was sent to a hospital on Kodiak Island for many months before he finally came home. Hattie and Mama picked him up at the train station in Billings. Papa was so skinny that Hattie didn't even recognize him when he got off the train. He hugged them and sobbed like a baby, saying over and over how glad he was to be home. How much he had missed them. How he could hardly recognize Hattie, who had grown so tall.

Even with Papa back in the house, it seemed eerily quiet and empty. That first night Mama stewed a hen and made dumplings, and Papa told her it was the best food he'd eaten since he left home. And Mama bragged about Hattie's being the best student in the eighth grade. Then they just ate. Hattie had become accustomed to her and Mama eating their meals in silence, but she was surprised that first evening with her papa back home that no one seemed to have anything to say.

Mama and Papa never talked about Patrick, at least not in front of their daughter. But one day Hattie found her father out in the shed crying over the box with Patrick's toys that used to be in the corner of the kitchen. When he saw her, he opened his arms to her. His cheeks were wet with tears.

Sixty-five years had passed since that day, yet Myrna could almost feel the wetness of her father's tears. He had loved Patrick. And he had loved her.

TWELVE

ILY and Beth had not been sure that they wanted to leave their friends and softball and soccer teams behind and spend the entire summer in France with their grandmother, and Vanessa felt as though she would wither up and die without her daughters for so long a time. But Penelope insisted that they had to come for the summer or not at all. She enticed her granddaughters with promises of visits to Paris and London, and, yes, she would take them to see where Marie Antoinette had lost her head. And where Anne Boleyn lost hers. And Penelope explained how the town where she and Jean Claude lived offered a veritable smorgasbord of exceptionally handsome boys just about their age, and that of a summer's eve the residents of Château de Roc strolled about the town center visiting with friends and neighbors while the younger children ran about and the older boys and girls flirted with one another—all under the careful supervision of their parents and grandparents, of course. And their mother and aunts would be joining them at the end of the summer, and by then Lily and Beth would be knowledgeable enough about Château de Roc and the surrounding area to serve as their tour guides.

When Penelope sent Lily and Beth's plane tickets and flight information, Vanessa was surprised to see a generous and quite unexpected check from Penelope made out jointly to her three daughters with an accompanying letter explaining that the money was to be used for an early-summer getaway. For just the three of them. Out West, if they liked. Or a cruise. Or a beach house on Cape Cod. She wanted them to go someplace where they could put their day-to-day lives on hold and simply enjoy each other's company.

"I am so proud," Penelope had written, "of the way Georgiana and Ellie supported their sister and nieces in their time of need and proud of Vanessa for having the sense to lean on them."

After she read the letter, Vanessa called her mother.

"Is everyone all right?" Penelope asked.

Her mother's voice was full of concern, and Vanessa understood why. In the eight months Penelope had been a resident of France, she had been the one who placed the calls. Vanessa sent an occasional e-mail to her mother, but this was the first time Vanessa had called her.

"Everyone is fine, I suppose," Vanessa said.

"You don't sound fine. Please don't tell me that you've changed your mind about letting Lily and Beth visit me."

"No. The reason I called is to set the record straight."

"Which record would that be?"

"It is true," Vanessa began, "as you pointed out in your letter that accompanied the surprising and quite generous check, my sisters helped me through a very bad time, but I haven't seen them in months. They don't seem to understand that, as a single parent, I no longer have the money or the time to lunch with them in some charming bistro or to join them for a night at the theater seeing some wonderful new play or to go shopping with them in trendy boutiques. Ellie e-mailed me yesterday to tell me about a face cream that she swears has made her skin look five years younger in just three weeks, and it only cost two hundred dollars! Georgiana spends hundreds of dollars every week looking after her hands and feet, and I can't remember the last time I had a professional manicure or pedicure. I absolutely fell apart yesterday because Beth lost her lunch money."

"Does this mean you refuse to take a trip with your sisters this summer?"

Vanessa took a deep breath. Was that what she was trying to say? Looking back, she wasn't sure how she would have managed after Scott left without Ellie and Georgiana. But after she sold the house and moved into her new residence, her sisters seemed to think she no longer needed their support. "No, I suppose not," she allowed. "I'd planned to ask you to let me use my share of the trip money to pay down my credit cards and let Ellie and Georgiana go off on their own. But then maybe you figured out that we hadn't been seeing much of each other lately and this is your way of remedying the situation."

"Something like that." Her mother sounded so close. Vanessa could even hear a clock chiming in the background. But her mother was not close. She was half a world away. "Vanessa, if things are as bad as you say, why haven't you asked me for help?"

"Pride, I guess." Vanessa pulled a pillow out from under the bedspread that she had carefully smoothed over the bed this morning because she was the sort of person who made the bed every morning whether anyone else was ever going to see the bed or not and propped it against the headboard, kicked off her shoes, and leaned back. She'd had to purchase a new bed because the king-size bed she'd shared with Scott would have all but filled the so-called "master" bedroom of the cardboard town house where she now lived with her daughters except when they were with their father, which they were now, making her the lone occupant of the domicile. She grabbed the other pillow and clutched it against her middle. "Things are improving now that Scott's making child support payments," she told her distant mother as she studied her own image in the dresser mirror, an image of a lonely, worried, unhappy woman who wasn't as young as she used to be. "And now, in addition to my regular job, I'm moonlighting as a fund-raising consultant for a private school in Montclair. It doesn't pay a lot, but every little bit helps."

Vanessa hesitated, then asked, "Why a trip, Mother? If you want your daughters to spend more time together, why not just subsidize our having lunch together once a month and maybe an occasional theater night?"

"Because I want you girls to have some time together in a more meaningful way," Penelope explained. "You may not realize it, Vanessa, but your sisters need you. You are the oldest and the most sensible. When I'm gone, you'll be the matriarch of the family. How close my daughters are to one another in future years depends on you, my darling."

Vanessa wanted to say that in a very real sense, her mother was already "gone," but instead said, "I didn't ask to be the firstborn."

"That's true, but I'm so very glad that you were. Your father was, too."

Vanessa remembered her father's last visit to Central Park. He'd told her that she had taught him how to be a father. Tears sprang to her eyes now as they had then.

Vanessa had blown her nose and reluctantly agreed to take a vacation with her sisters and told her mother that she loved her, something she had not done since she'd learned that

Penelope was moving to France. Not that she had stopped loving her mother, but not saying the words was a way to punish her. It had been a relief to end the moratorium.

And maybe a trip with her sisters would be a good thing. Maybe Ellie and Georgiana did not fully appreciate how lonely and weary she was, but they had come through for her when she needed them the most.

She would never forget how grateful she was to see her sisters sitting on her front porch the night after Scott left—the night after she'd found the note from him that changed her life. Ellie and Georgiana had taken charge. When Lily and Beth arrived home after their trip to the mall, Ellie and Georgiana ordered everyone to the kitchen table. Lily and Beth regarded their mother's pale countenance and puffy eyes and exchanged fearful glances. Ellie nodded in Vanessa's direction, indicating that it was time for her to explain to her daughters what was going on, but before she could convince her mouth to speak, Beth blurted out, "You and Daddy are going to get a divorce, aren't you?"

Somehow Vanessa found her voice and told them that she and their daddy were having some problems that had nothing to do with them. "Your father and I both love you girls very much, and he will always be your father and I'll always be your mother even if we no longer live together, but I am hoping that will not be the case." She said she was sure that their father would be getting in touch with them soon and inform them about his plans. She explained about his note and how he needed some time away to think. She hoped that she and their father could work things out and their lives would get back to normal, but that might not happen.

Lily and Beth cried, of course. And they only picked at the meal that their aunts had prepared and served. Every time the phone rang, everyone jumped. Vanessa would feel four sets of eyes watching her each time she picked up the receiver.

None of the calls were from Scott. One of his golfing buddies called. A neighbor wanted them to be on the lookout for a missing dog. The other calls were for Lily or Beth, who would tell their friends they had loads of homework and didn't have time to talk.

Three long days passed before Scott called—three days of worry and fear and anger and disappointment. Vanessa was in her office at the college. "Where are you?" she asked, struggling to keep her voice even.

He ignored her question. "How are the girls taking this?"

"How would you expect them to take it? They're very upset. They miss you and want you to come home." Then she realized that he was sobbing.

"Oh, God," he said. "I don't know what to do."

Vanessa understood. He was debating whether he should come back home and be miserable or try to make a new life for himself.

"Who is she?" she asked.

"No one," he insisted. "I just needed to—"

"Yeah, I know," Vanessa interrupted, her tone as flat and unsympathetic as she could make it. "You needed time to think. In the meantime, you need to at least call your daughters."

"I don't know what to tell them."

"That makes two of us," she said, then carefully—as though it were made of eggshells—replaced the receiver on its cradle. She waited for the tears to start flowing once again. But for now at least, the reservoir was dry, and she turned back to her computer:

> We here at the college want to know how very
> grateful we are for your loyalty and support . . .

She had wanted to be mad at Scott. To hate him. To find some way to punish him. Of course, she had an obvious weapon with which to do that. She could make it difficult for him to have a satisfactory relationship with their daughters. She could limit the time he had with them. And poison their minds against him.

But she couldn't do that to him or their daughters.

The new woman in Scott's life turned out to be the younger sister of his high school girlfriend, Nellie, who'd died in a car crash their senior year. The sister's name was Dana. Eventually Vanessa learned the whole story. Dana had called Scott to tell him that her mother had died and how, in cleaning out her mother's house and getting it ready to sell, she had come across Scott's old high school letter jacket, his class ring, and the letters he'd written to Nellie from college. Dana offered to mail the items to him. They chatted for a time sharing fond memories of Nellie and exchanging information about themselves and their current lives. Dana lived in Brooklyn with her two young sons. Her husband was dead—a police officer killed in the line of duty. Scott decided he didn't want her to go to the trouble and expense of boxing the items and mailing them to him and offered to drop by and pick them up. She suggested they meet someplace in Lower Manhattan.

Vanessa could well imagine how things progressed. Dana reminded Scott of Nellie, his first love. No doubt he'd read the letters that he wrote to Nellie all those years ago, and they brought back wonderful memories of how it was to be young and completely in love and loved completely in return and to be filled with high hopes for the future. He probably convinced himself that he and Dana finding one another was meant to be. And maybe it was, Vanessa came to acknowledge. Maybe the end of their marriage was inevitable. If Dana hadn't come along, some other woman would have.

In the weeks after Scott left, Vanessa had spent a great deal of time with her sisters. The first two weeks they took turns staying with her. Then one or the other of them would come out on weekends to help with the shopping and cleaning and to do their best to convince Vanessa that life would get better and that she was not a bad person and her marriage to Scott had never been all that great. Of course, when Lily and Beth were around, they were careful what they said. Lily told her aunts that she wished they would stop reminding them at every opportunity that their father still loved them. "That's for him to say," she said in a very adult voice.

Lily, especially, gave Scott a hard time, refusing to talk to him on the phone or spend time with him. The missing hurt too much, however, and finally she agreed to have dinner with him, but only on the condition that he wouldn't talk about "that woman." Scott brought along Dana's two-year-old son, who apparently won over Lily with no trouble at all. Now her daughters were doting stepsisters to two young children. When Vanessa thought of the third baby she had never had because they could not afford it, the bile of bitterness rose in her throat. When she looked in a mirror, she hardly recognized herself. Bitterness was etched on her face.

Selling the house brought tears and recriminations from her daughters, but she really had no choice since she could manage neither the upkeep nor the mortgage. In spite of the realtor's insisting that location was everything, Vanessa was surprised and grateful that the house sold within a month of being listed. She'd leased a town house near enough to the girls' school that they could walk.

Scott saw the girls every Wednesday evening, and they spent every other weekend with him beginning after school on Friday and ending when he took them to school on Monday morning.

The weekends Lily and Beth were away were the most difficult. At first, Vanessa would go into town to be with her sisters, but Ellie often wasn't available in the evenings, and Georgiana would drop everything when Freddy came to town. Vanessa realized that her sisters considered her move into a new residence to be an indication that she was getting on with her life and no longer needed their constant support and concern. On one level Vanessa understood. Ellie and Georgiana had their own lives to lead. Now she seldom went into town. When her daughters were with their father, she used the time to get caught up on chores. And she would try to read or watch television, but she found it difficult to concentrate. It seemed as though she had a finite number of hours a week when her mind could function on a significant level, and she had to use those hours for her paying jobs. Not that she was doing those jobs well. Sometimes in the middle of a presentation, her mind would go blank and she would frantically sort through her notes.

More and more she dedicated several hours every weekend to walking or bike riding. Her walks and rides got longer and longer. When she was challenging her body, she wasn't thinking about how lonely and poor she was.

The most fulfilling and the most frustrating part of her life was motherhood. At times she had some of the best moments with her daughters that she'd had since they entered adolescence. Other times they acted like such selfish little bitches that she looked forward to summer and her time away from them. She never lost her temper, though, which was amazing. Divorce had made her sadder and lonelier and poorer and more afraid of the future than ever before, but it had also made her calmer and physically stronger.

The worst moments came in the night. Scott was not there beside her. It wasn't sex that she longed for—although moments of need in that department sometimes came rolling over her like an avalanche, need that was far deeper and greater than she had felt in years—it was his presence. Or maybe it was just *a* presence that she longed for. Whatever. Wakefulness brought forth soul-searching.

With all her focus on the present and getting through each hour and day and week and trying her damnedest to be a good mother to her daughters, Vanessa had long since lost interest in the mystery of Hattie.

But suddenly Hattie became an issue once again.

When she e-mailed her sisters that Penelope was bankrolling an early-summer vacation for them, Vanessa suggested they go someplace reasonably close to home. Charleston, South Carolina, perhaps, which she'd heard was a great place to visit. What she did not put in her e-mail was that a trip to Charleston would give her a chance to visit a potential donor who lived there, which meant she could charge her portion of the trip to her expense account and pocket part of her share of Penelope's money.

But Ellie and Georgiana both wanted to head for Montana and look for Hattie.

Ellie e-mailed that she wouldn't mind meeting "a nice, uncomplicated cowboy" while she was in Montana. And after a hectic spring, she was looking forward to leaving high fashion and the magazine behind for ten carefree days and hoped she would be inspired to write something other than over-the-top picture captions describing fashion-forward attire and accessories.

While Ellie was fantasizing about cowboys, Georgiana was dreaming of taking "exhibition-quality photographs." After a trip to the library to learn about Montana, she longed to photograph what early travelers to the region called the Land of the Shining Mountains. And she admitted that she got teary-eyed when she thought of the pictures she would take when they actually found their long-lost grandmother.

Overruled two to one, Vanessa searched for bargain tickets on various Web sites, but there were none. In fact, they could fly to California for considerably less than it would take to fly to Helena, Montana. Any hope she had of having money left over from their sisterly journey vanished.

Vanessa ran hot and cold when it came to the search for Hattie. It might be a joyous meeting they would remember all their lives. Or Hattie might be a hermit on a mountain who chased them off her property with a shotgun.

The night before their flight, Ellie and Georgiana spent the night with Vanessa in New Jersey, their first visit since they'd helped her move into the town house back in February.

The next morning, as the plane lifted off the runway at Newark Airport, Vanessa found it somewhat unbelievable that they were really on their way to Montana. With the last eight months of her life consumed with the dissolution of her marriage, selling her home, finding a new home for herself and her daughters, and trying to bring some semblance of normality to their lives, the trip to Montana had seemed like an abstraction. Something that might someday happen.

Vanessa read during the first segment of the flight out of Newark while her sisters dozed. They ate lunch during their two-hour layover in Salt Lake City.

Vanessa found herself nodding off before the flight out of Salt Lake City had even left the ground and was as soundly asleep as one could be on an airplane when Georgiana shook her arm. "Nessa," she said. "You've got to wake up and look out the window."

Vanessa dutifully leaned across Georgiana. "Oh, my God," she said as she stared down at the most incredible landscape she'd ever seen. She'd driven through the Alleghenies in

West Virginia and flown over the Appalachians on the way to Chicago, but those mountains didn't even begin to compare with the endless landscape of towering, snowcapped peaks she was looking at now. These mountains were beyond steep, beyond rugged. They were daunting beyond belief with a beauty so awesome and timeless that the incredible panorama they formed brought reverent tears to Vanessa's eyes.

The plane wasn't full, so she found a window of her own. For the first time since she'd reluctantly agreed to this trip, she actually felt glad. And there hadn't been much gladness in her life since Scott left. Mostly she'd experienced fear and sorrow and anger and a sense of loss that she suspected would be with her to some degree for the rest of her days— even if she fell in love with another man and created a new life for herself.

Maybe Montana's spectacular beauty would provide a bit of sustenance for her empty, tired spirit.

THIRTEEN

$\mathcal{A}$s she walked down the ramp at the Helena airport, Georgiana felt both excitement and apprehension. Apprehensive that Henrietta Polanski might not be *their* Hattie. And while the photographer in her had been thrilled by what she'd seen out of the airplane window, she worried that she wasn't skillful and talented enough to capture Montana's awesome beauty.

As they headed for baggage claim, Ellie tugged on Georgiana's sleeve. "Look," she whispered, and nodded in the direction of a lean, underforty guy wearing a cowboy hat, cowboy boots, faded jeans, and a worn leather vest. "Have you ever seen anything so gorgeous?"

By the time they had retrieved their luggage and rented a vehicle, Ellie was all but swooning. There were cowboys—or at least men dressed Western attire—all over the place. Old cowboys. Young cowboys. In-between cowboys. When a well-worn saddle came around the luggage carousel, a guy who could double for the Marlboro Man grabbed it and hoisted it onto his shoulder.

"I'll bet not one of them is gay," Ellie observed in a reverent voice.

"Probably not," Georgiana observed, "but that most likely means they probably already have a woman in their life."

As Vanessa drove their rented van through Helena's generic downtown, Georgiana was a bit disappointed. She had expected hitching posts, wooden sidewalks, and a saloon or two. But the mountains that encircled the city were impressive. "I hope we have enough time to find Hattie *and* take in all the scenery," she said.

After they checked into their hotel they drove around a bit, checking out the impressive state capitol with its copper-covered dome, and determining which of the buildings in the capitol complex housed the Montana Historical Society.

Like dutiful tourists, they ate barbecue in a restaurant made of fake logs. When they asked their waitress how to spend the rest of the evening, she directed them to the Lewis and Clark Casino.

As Georgiana looked around the garish casino, she wondered what the two explorers would have thought of having their legendary names affixed to such an establishment.

Ellie decided she would just "wander around a bit," which Georgiana interpreted as "check out the guys." She and Vanessa decided to head for the slot machines.

"Do you ever get lonely for a man's company," Georgiana asked her older sister as they wound their way through the crowded casino.

"Right now, I'm still licking my wounds," Vanessa admitted. "Besides, if someone as young and glamorous as Ellie can't find a man, I don't like my chances of finding a sweet, considerate, industrious man who isn't thirty years my senior."

"Yeah, but at least a guy's sperm count isn't a major issue for you like it is for Ellie."

Vanessa laughed and linked arms with Georgiana. "Well, I am still of childbearing age, but probably I'm never going to have another kid. I would be an excellent aunt, though, should either one of my sisters ever produce a child. What about you and Freddy? Think you two will ever get married and have a kid or two? Or not get married and have a kid or two?"

"Not anytime soon. Maybe never. I can't see myself getting frantic about having a baby like Ellie is, but maybe the alarm on my biological clock will start ringing one of the these days. Who knows?"

" 'To each according to his needs,' " Vanessa said. "Or in your case, *her* needs."

"Who said that?"

"Karl Marx."

"What did he know about having babies?"

"I have no idea."

Georgiana regarded Vanessa. She had changed since Scott left. Not only was she leaner and tanner, she was quieter and more introspective. "I'm glad we're taking this trip together," Georgiana said, and squeezed her sister's arm. "The three of us haven't seen much of each other lately."

"That's the whole point. Our mother is trying to manipulate us from afar."

"Well, I'm glad she is," Georgiana said as she pointed to two empty seats in front of quarter slot machines.

They hurried to the seats and agreed they would limit themselves to twenty dollars each. Georgiana immediately won a hundred-dollar jackpot. Vanessa used up her twenty dollars within minutes and watched Georgiana play until her winnings were gone. Then they went in search of Ellie.

Ellie was sitting at the bar with a nice-looking man in jeans and boots. When she saw them coming, she immediately slipped off the stool and headed in their direction.

"Are we interrupting something?" Vanessa asked.

Ellie rolled her eyes. "He thinks that gays go straight to hell and women should not work outside the home."

After a nightcap in the hotel bar, they turned in for the night. Georgiana couldn't sleep. On one hand, she found herself imagining a sweet, poignant scene in which the Wentworth sisters meet Hattie for the first time. But what if they came all this way only to discover that the woman named Henrietta Polanski hadn't had a baby sixty-two years ago and could not possibly be their father's mother?

Georgiana watched a group of schoolchildren petting and even talking to a huge stuffed buffalo that greeted those who climbed the steps to the second-floor reading room at the Montana Historical Society. She was growing increasingly nervous as she and her sisters waited to meet Janet Jordan, the archivist who'd told her that a woman named Henrietta Polanski had once been incarcerated at the state prison in Deer Lodge.

Georgiana stole a sideways glance at her sisters. Vanessa was watching the children. Ellie was listening to cell phone messages.

Ellie was wearing her notion of Western attire—a black-velvet, Western-cut jacket with a longish denim skirt and some New York designer's version of cowboy boots in cherry-red leather.

Shortly an attractive woman in a navy pants suit and carrying a manila folder started up the steps. She paused at the top of the staircase and smiled when she spotted the three women. "You must be the Wentworth sisters."

As she seated herself at the table, she asked, "Which of you is Georgiana?"

Georgiana nodded and, taking note of the *Ph.D.* following the woman's name on her name tag, introduced her sisters and thanked *Dr.* Jordan for agreeing to help them.

"Don't get your hopes too high," the archivist warned as she placed the folder on the table. "As I told Georgiana on the phone, most state prison records are destroyed. The ones we do receive are culled of material that has no historic significance. But we have hung on to the questionnaires that prisoners were asked to fill out when they arrived at the Deer Lodge prison because they offer an overview of the prison population through the years and have proven useful to numerous researchers."

Georgiana watched while Dr. Jordan opened the manila folder and carefully removed three sheets of fragile, yellowing paper. "This is the questionnaire that Henrietta Polanski filled out," the archivist said.

Vanessa moved from the other side of the table so the three of them could examine the pages together.

Georgiana saw that Henrietta had not given her middle or maiden name and had skipped more questions than she answered. She gave her age as sixteen and claimed to be in good health, and—in spite of her young age—to be a widow.

"She was awfully young to be in prison," Georgiana observed.

"Yes," Dr. Jordan acknowledged, "but not unheard of back then or now."

Henrietta's place of birth was Coal Town, which Dr. Jordan explained was a small mining community in the south-central part of the state. Henrietta Polanski also listed Coal Town as her place of residence prior to her arrest and incarceration.

As for her skills, Henrietta had checked sewing, cook-

ing, ironing, and gardening. She did not check typing, dicta-
tion, operating a switchboard, dairy farming, and operating
farm equipment.

Georgiana was disappointed to see that Henrietta had
left blank the line for the name and address of her next of
kin.

"Do you know why Henrietta was in prison," Georgiana asked, "and how long she was there?"

Dr. Jordan shook her head. "I was unable to discover
why she was incarcerated, but I did find some of the prison's
monthly censuses and know that Mrs. Polanski was incarcerated at the Deer Lodge prison for at least one year. Unfortunately, though, we're missing several years' worth of the
censuses, and she could have been there longer. What I would
suggest is that you visit Deer Lodge, which is only about an
hour's drive from Helena—a bit longer if you take the scenic
route—and see if you can track down anyone who worked in
the prison while Henrietta Polanski was there. They might
remember a prisoner who had a baby if indeed this woman is
the person you are looking for. I've been working with a resident of the town—a man named Franklin Webster—who is
writing a history of Deer Lodge. I told him about you ladies
and your search for your grandmother, and he said he'd be
glad to lend a hand. Also you might want to visit Henrietta
Polanski's hometown in John Coulter County. It's a longer
drive than to Deer Lodge but still doable as a day trip from
Helena.

"If the criminal act that led to her incarceration was
committed in John Coulter County," Dr. Jordan continued,
"she would have been tried in Hayes, which is the county
seat. You should be able to find the records of her trial at the
county courthouse along with her birth certificate—and her
marriage license, too, if she got married in the county. And

most likely you also can read about the trial in the archives of the local newspaper."

Dr. Jordan paused and folded her hands in front of her. "I realize that the three of you have undertaken this search for sentimental reasons. But if this woman does turn out to be the mother of your father, before you go any further in your investigation, you need to realize that the details of her life might be distressing to you. Whatever her crime was, it would not have been a minor one if she was incarcerated at a state penitentiary. Sometimes it's best just to let sleeping dogs lie."

FOURTEEN

*W*HILE Ellie inspected the large statue of a bison skull mounted in front of the historical society building, Georgiana used her cell phone to call Franklin Webster in Deer Lodge, and Vanessa used hers to call the high school librarian in Coal Town.

"Mr. Webster says that he's been looking for an excuse to play hooky this afternoon," Georgiana said. Then she sighed. "I hope you guys won't be mad at me if this turns out to be a wild-goose chase."

"Don't be silly," Vanessa said, linking arms with her baby sister. "Hattie is just an excuse to take a trip, and no one's going to be mad at you if we don't find her. Isn't that right, Ellie?"

"Sure," Ellie said with a shrug, "but it's going to be hard to write something publishable about a wild-goose chase."

In less than an hour they'd reached Interstate 90, which took them into Deer Lodge, a town of three thousand according to the directory on the back of the map. They stopped for lunch at a roadside restaurant on the outskirts of town and got directions to the old prison from their waitress.

The town had an Old West look to it with many vintage buildings still in use along its broad main street. The former prison looked like a medieval fortress complete with stone walls and turreted towers. A tall, thin man in his sixties wearing faded jeans and worn cowboy boots stepped forward as they approached the front gate.

"You must be the sisters from New York," he said with a glance at Ellie's outfit. "I'm Frank Webster."

Georgiana introduced herself and her sisters. "I can't tell you how much we appreciate your taking the time to help us."

"Well, anyone who's interested in the history of Deer Lodge is a friend of mine," Frank Webster told them.

He explained that he'd lived in Deer Lodge all his life. His day job was running an abstract company but his passion was local history.

He took them on a tour of the prison, which was now a museum, showing them the stark cellblock and the underground hole where prisoners were kept in solitary confinement. He explained that the facility had held both men and women prisoners until it was closed in 1977. Prior to 1963, the women were housed in a building that eventually became a maximum-security facility for male prisoners.

Ellie asked him to describe the life of a female prisoner.

"They worked," he said with a shrug. "They ran the prison laundry, scrubbed floors, washed windows, baked bread, cooked, sewed and mended, and maintained a vegetable garden."

Vanessa took in the twelve-foot-high walls that had once separated prisoners from the rest of the world. Had their father been born inside these walls? And even if he had been, what relevance did that information have to her life or those her sisters? It would be an interesting tidbit to drop into a conversation, she supposed. *My father was born in a Montana prison.* But as the archivist in Helena pointed out, Henrietta Polanski's crime must have been serious for her to have been incarcerated here. Probably her prison record and the nature of her crime were things she allowed to be buried and forgotten with the passing years.

"I've checked around to see if anyone knows of a former prison guard from that era who still lives around here," Frank told them, "but I had no luck. That was a good many years ago, and probably most of them moved on after the Deer Lodge prison closed. But there is someone here in town you need to talk to."

From the prison, they followed Frank to a nursing home on the outskirts of town to meet one of the community's oldest citizens. Mildred Fisher was the daughter of a family physician who had looked after the citizens of Deer Lodge from 1924 until his death in 1970, Frank explained as they walked down the wide hallway. Several residents in wheelchairs watched them walk by. An elderly man wearing a pair of overalls winked at Georgiana. She smiled and winked back.

They found Mildred Fisher in the parlor. Also in a wheelchair, she was sitting with several other residents in front of a large-screen TV tuned to a soap opera. Her face lit up when she saw Frank, and she reached for his hand.

Vanessa had never seen a person with so many wrinkles. Mildred had wrinkles on top of wrinkles. Even her sags had wrinkles. What little hair she had left hovered over her scalp like a white cloud, and she suffered from a palsy that caused a continuous bobbing of her head.

"Mildred is my best girlfriend," Frank told the sisters. "She has lived in Deer Lodge her entire life, has an amazing memory, and has been gracious enough to allow me to pick her brain."

Frank wheeled Mildred into a small sitting room with numerous overgrown philodendron vines that crawled across tabletops, over bookcases, and along window ledges, giving the room *A Little Shop of Horrors* look. The four visitors drew chairs in a semicircle around Mildred's wheelchair.

"These ladies have come all the way from New York City," Frank explained. When Mildred cupped a hand around an ear, he raised his voice. "*New York City*. These three ladies are from *New York City* and would like to ask you some questions."

Mildred scrutinized her visitors with a pair of faded blue eyes and began speaking in a quavering old-lady voice. "I used to have a postcard with a picture of the Empire State Building."

Georgiana scooted her chair closer to the woman. "The Empire State Building is my very favorite building in the whole world," she told the old woman, carefully enunciating each word in a voice that was just short of shouting. "I'll send you another postcard with its picture on it just as soon as I get back to New York City."

Mildred regarded Georgiana for a minute, then reached out and touched her hair. "Shirley Temple had hair like that."

"Yes, I believe that she did," Georgiana said. "Did you like Shirley Temple?"

"Oh, indeed I did. *Little Miss Marker* was my favorite of all her movies. She was left as an IOU at a gambling hall. Did you ever see it?"

"No, I didn't. But I've seen photographs of Shirley

Temple." Georgiana moved her chair closer to the old woman. "Mr. Webster tells us that your father was the town doctor."

Mildred nodded.

"I bet you were very proud of him," Georgiana said.

"Oh, yes, I surely was." Mildred clasped her knarred hands together. "My father was a kindly man and a fine physician. When he died, everyone in town came to his funeral. Dr. Wilburn Samuel Fisher was his name."

"Did he ever take care of prisoners incarcerated at the state prison?" Georgiana asked.

Mildred nodded. "Yes, Father would go to the prison. Mother didn't like for him to go there, but he had to obey that oath."

"The Hippocratic oath?"

Mildred nodded. "Yes, that's the one."

Georgiana took the old woman's hand. "Do you remember if he ever delivered a baby at the prison?"

Mildred looked beyond Georgiana, her faded eyes looking past the wall of this room, past this day and year, gazing down the tunnel of time.

Vanessa found herself holding her breath. Waiting. A part of her wanted the old woman to say that no inmate at the Deer Lodge prison ever gave birth to a child, and that would be the end of it. They had tried and failed to find a trail that would lead them to their birth grandmother, who had, after all, wanted to sever all ties with her newborn child and with the woman she called Aunt Vera, and who most likely meant for that severance also to include any progeny her cast-off child might produce. Vanessa and her sisters could spend the rest of their time in this breathtakingly beautiful corner of the world sightseeing. She and Ellie could help Georgiana haul about her photographic equipment and assist her in taking photographs of wildlife and soaring mountain peaks and the tiny wildflowers that grew above the timberline in high mountain meadows. And perhaps the experience would help the three of them become more accepting of one another's quirks and foibles and become better friends and deal more successfully with their mother's absence from their lives. But Vanessa also felt an intense curiosity about the woman named Hattie who had given birth to their father and hoped that the incarcerated Henrietta Polanski and Hattie were the same person. And that her crime had not been horrendous.

Vanessa watched Mildred's face as she searched back through her life. At one point, the elderly woman closed her eyes, and Vanessa was sure she had fallen asleep, but a small sigh escaped from her lips and she began to speak.

"My father delivered two babies at the prison. One of them was stillborn. That was back when my mother was still alive. Father brought the baby home, and Mother washed the poor little dead thing and swaddled it in strips torn from an old blanket until it looked like a tiny Egyptian mummy. My father made a wooden casket for it, and he and Mother took it to the cemetery for burial."

"What about the other baby?" Georgiana asked.

"Father brought that baby home, too. My mother was dead by then, and I kept house for Father and assisted him in his practice of medicine. I dressed the baby in clothes from my mother's cedar chest, then went to the store to buy baby bottles and evaporated milk and corn syrup so I could make infant formula for the child. When I returned from the store, Father was making a long-distance telephone call to a lady back East who was a relative of the baby's mother. As I recall, she lived in the state of West Virginia. And that fine lady rode the train all the way from West Virginia to Deer Lodge, Montana, to fetch the baby. A little boy it was. I cried to see him go."

Georgiana looked over her shoulder at her sisters, tears welling in her blue eyes.

Vanessa felt as though all the air had been sucked out of the small room. Overwhelmed with emotion, she put her hands to her mouth. This frail old woman had once held their newborn father in her arms.

Beside her, Ellie was whispering, "Oh my God! Oh my God!"

Vanessa knew this trip had been worthwhile if only for this one sweet moment that she and her sisters would remember for the rest of their lives.

They lingered for a time while Georgiana wheeled Mildred outside and photographed her in the shade of an ancient oak tree. After a time the old woman began to nod off, and they each hugged her and thanked her. "I won't forget about that postcard with the Empire State Building," Georgiana promised.

The scenic drive back to Helena was magnificent. They stopped along the way so that Georgiana could photograph the spectacular vistas.

It was dusk when Vanessa pulled off the road so that Georgiana could photograph a crumbling stone house beside a rushing stream with soaring mountains all around. Vanessa drove as far as she dared down a rutted lane. Ellie and Vanessa poked around the ruins speculating about the people who had once lived there, then sat on streamside boulders and dangled their feet in the rushing water while they watched Georgiana march around through the high grass in her flip-flops, checking the building from different angles. Finally she got her tripod out of the back of the SUV and set it up near some overhanging branches, explaining that the branches would frame the house in the picture. "Isn't it too dark to take pictures?" Ellie asked.

"Not for a timed exposure," Georgiana said.

After she attached the camera to the tripod, she looked through the viewfinder and adjusted the lens, then moved the tripod back a bit. Satisfied with what she saw, she used a pen-light in the waning light to adjust the settings.

Vanessa and Ellie watched while Georgiana took several pictures, changing the settings between each exposure to make sure she came away with one that would suit her.

"So much beauty," Ellie said in a reverent tone. "I can understand why so many movie stars want to buy land and build homes in Montana. They have enough money to live two lives—the glamorous one in New York or Los Angeles and a secluded one on an isolated piece of land where they build a palatial log cabin for themselves and another for their horses. When they get tired of solitude, they go back home and party with their buddies."

"If I had that kind of money," Vanessa said, "I would buy a penthouse in Manhattan for home base and travel the world. What about you, Georgiana?"

"If I were rich, I'd buy a bunch of land out here and establish a summer camp for poor kids and teach them how to take pictures," Georgiana said as she fussed with her camera.

"That's a lovely idea," Vanessa said. "Probably the most gratifying thing about having a lot of money is that one can afford to be generous."

"You know, the best part about coming to Montana is it gives you a different perspective," Georgiana said. "I'm going to buy some hiking boots even if they leave marks and make calluses."

"Your Chinese podiatrist might give you another sort of boot when you get back," Ellie warned.

"I'm getting tired of Dr. Lou."

Vanessa and Ellie exchanged glances. *Georgiana was getting tired of Dr. Lou?*

"What about you?" Vanessa asked Ellie. "If you found a wonderfully virile cowboy who was looking for just the right little honey to complete his life, would you move to Montana?"

Ellie frowned. "So, you are assuming that, as a woman, I would have to be the one to give up my career and lifestyle and the only home I've ever known to move to a completely alien environment."

"Seems to me that one of you would have to," Georgiana observed. "Either the guy stops being a cowboy, or you stop being a New York fashion editor."

Ellie was silent for a minute. "Actually, Boone and I kind of made up before I left."

When neither sister commented on her announcement, Ellie demanded, "So what do you two have against Boone?"

Vanessa recalled the day she met Boone at the picnic and how, on the way home, her daughters seemed surprised that she wasn't going to tell Ellie that Boone had been putting the make on Georgiana.

With her back to Ellie, Georgiana pressed her hands together prayerfully and gave Vanessa an imploring look.

"I know it was painful for you when he went back to his wife," Vanessa said, choosing her words carefully. "Are you sure he's sincere about you this time around?"

"Look, Boone and I enjoy being together. Maybe something will come of it, or maybe it won't." Then Ellie added with a shrug, *"Que sera, sera."*

Once they were back on the main highway, Vanessa stopped for gas and Ellie headed for the restroom.

As Vanessa dealt with the gas pump and washed the windows, Georgiana hovered. "Boone was waiting outside my building a couple of weeks ago," she said. "He pretended like he ran into me by accident and tried to get me to have a drink with him. I told him to go to hell. Then he calls later that evening, supposedly to apologize if he was out of line, but goes on to say all this other stuff about how he can't stop thinking about me. The man is a collector."

"What do mean?" Vanessa asked.

"He's the kind of guy who brags to his buddies in the bar how many chicks he's screwed."

FIFTEEN

 $\mathcal{M}$ YRNA poured her evening glass of wine, turned on the television set in the sitting room that adjoined her bedroom, and curled up in an easy chair to watch her son Randall being interviewed on the NBC Denver affiliate's evening news. The news anchor cut right to the chase, asking if Randall was planning to run for governor.

Randall admitted that he was considering the race but would be making an announcement one way or the other. He did, however, speak on issues he would want to tackle should be become governor—job creation, protection of pensions, affordable heath care, a balanced budget. When asked about the protection of the state's wilderness areas, he said that protecting the environment and making sure the mining and tourism industries continued to thrive were not only possible but essential to the continued prosperity of the state. Randall grinned when kidded about his score in a recent pro-am charity golf tournament sponsored by the station and said that his wife was the best golfer in the family. Next year the station should invite her.

Randall had always reminded Myrna of her father, but

this evening as she watched him on the television screen, that resemblance had never seemed more pronounced. Her father lacked the education and polish that Randall had achieved, but Randall's expressions, his grin, his sense of humor, all made her think of her father. Her beloved Papa.

Myrna had always regretted not being able to tell her children anything about her past. They had been curious, of course, but all she told them was that she'd grown up dirt-poor and been on her own since she was sixteen, and that she had put those difficult times behind her and never planned to discuss them with anyone.

Sometimes, though, Myrna wished she could at least tell her children how her father died and make them understand why mine owners had to do right by their miners. It was not only humane to make the mines as safe as possible and treat miners fairly, but over the long haul it enhanced the bottom line. People nowadays seemed to have forgotten that loyal employees were the most productive.

She watched the rest of the news program, then had dinner with Willy while they watched an old Debbie Reynolds movie. Willy absolutely adored Debbie Reynolds.

Myrna read in bed until she was nodding off, then turned out the light. But when she closed her eyes, memories of her father filled her mind. Her past had been much with her lately, which was puzzling. She hadn't revisited those years in any significant way for decades, but of late she found it difficult to keep thoughts of that time at bay.

When she closed her eyes, she could see the unpainted shack where she had been raised.

Her papa never got his health back after the mine accident in Alaska. The bad air he breathed while waiting to be rescued all but ruined his lungs. For the next two years, he somehow managed to get up at dawn and trudge down to Mr. Sedgwick's mine, each week and month worse than the one before as his health deteriorated. The days when he collapsed and Mama had to go fetch him in the old Ford became more and more frequent until finally the mine manager told him not to return. The company physician said it was tuberculosis that had destroyed Papa's lungs and not the mine accident in Alaska or working in the Coal Town mine, which meant that Papa wouldn't get any sort of settlement from Mr. Sedgwick. And when Papa died, Mama wouldn't receive any sort of widow's benefit from the mine owner.

After her father was let go at the mine, he lived for another long, agonizing year. He was constantly coughing up blood, and each breath was labored and painful. The sound of his gasping filled every corner of their small house throughout the day and night. He had no appetite, and his body was reduced to skin and bones. The black-clad preacher came often and would ask Hattie and her mother to kneel beside the bed and pray with him. The man prayed endlessly in a singsong voice that Hattie was sure God found annoying. The prayers were so long that she thought her thighbones were going to poke right out of her knees. The preacher kept asking God to forgive and to open the doors of heaven to "this craven sinner." Hattie wanted to tell him that her papa wasn't a sinner. He was a good man who had done the best he could, and God should have done a better job of looking after him.

When neighbors and church folk dropped by with food and cast-off clothing. Hattie could tell that her parents were grateful but also uncomfortable with being on the receiving end of charity. Her father especially. He would weep because he wasn't able to look after his own family.

Mama begged Papa to let her write to his father and

ask for money to help them through, but Papa made her swear on the Bible that she would never do such a thing. Not more than a month or two after that, Papa received a letter from an attorney in Pikesville, West Virginia. In addition to a one-page typed letter, the envelope contained a dollar bill. The letter informed Papa of the death of his father and that according to the terms of old Mr. Wentworth's last will and testament, his bequest to his only son was one dollar.

Papa tore up the letter and the dollar.

By then Hattie knew that the scars on Papa's back were from a razor strap. His father had beat him from the time he was a little boy until finally he announced that he'd had enough and was heading West. His father said that if he left, he was no longer a member of the Wentworth family.

Papa had walked out the door with only the clothes on his back, and to distance himself from his father, he dropped the *Went* from his name and went by *Worth*. William Thomas Worth. From time to time he would write his mother, but he never knew if she got the letters. He wouldn't put it past his father to keep them from her.

One snowy Saturday morning, Hattie and Papa were alone. It was too early for the preacher to make his rounds, or maybe he didn't want to venture out in the snow. But the snow had not deterred Mama in setting off for town on foot, pushing a wheelbarrow loaded with cartons full of fresh eggs. The Ford had a dead battery, and Mama needed to deliver her eggs to the grocer on schedule or else he might start buying eggs from someone who had a more reliable way to deliver them, and it was the egg money and the generosity of others that kept them from starving. When she returned, she would have a sack of cornmeal and one of beans and a tin of syrup to pour on the cornmeal mush Mama cooked for breakfast.

With Mama gone to town and the house surrounded

by silently falling snow, the only sound was her father's labored breathing. Hattie carried her library book into the bedroom and asked Papa if he wanted her to read to him. "This week I'm reading *Robinson Crusoe*," she told him.

Papa grabbed her arm. Gasping for breath between every word, he told Hattie that he needed to die and would she please help him.

Then he handed her a pillow.

Hattie understood. Her mama would not have had the courage to do such a thing, so he had waited until she was gone to ask. With a pounding heart, she shook her head and pulled her hand away. "I can't," she whispered.

"Please," he begged. "I need to die. It's time for me to die."

Hattie stood there for a long time, knowing that she had to do this thing for her father but would almost rather die herself. She was wearing a tattered flannel robe over her clothes to keep warm. Her belly was empty because there would be no food until Mama returned. And if she was going to do this thing, she had to do it before Mama came home.

She hugged him and kissed him and told him that he was the best papa in the whole world, then put the pillow over his face and lay across it using the weight of her body to keep it in place. He struggled a bit, but she knew it wasn't because he had changed his mind. His body was rebelling on its own. Finally the struggling stopped and his body was still. She didn't move for a long time just to make sure. Then she rolled away, removed the pillow from his face, and began to scream, a terrible uncontrollable sound that came from deep inside her. Her beloved Papa was lost to her.

Finally she was too exhausted to scream anymore. She wiped her nose with the sleeve of the flannel robe, then picked up the book and began reading to her father's dead body. She had gotten to the part when Robinson "was exceedingly surprised with the print of a man's naked foot on the shore" when she realized her mother was standing in the doorway.

"Is he . . . ?" Mama began, but could not say the word. She walked slowly to the bed and touched his face. Then she knelt beside the bed and kissed his face and his hands with tears running down her cheeks, but Hattie could tell she was relieved. That part of the nightmare was over.

And now, all these years later, as Myrna looked back on that time in her life, she realized how liberating her father's death had been. She would never have thought about leaving while he was still alive. With him gone, however, it was only a matter of time.

Sixteen

HE red cowboy boots were hurting Ellie's feet, and she considered changing footwear before heading downstairs for dinner with her sisters, but that would have required changing her outfit so she stayed with the boots.

Only two tables were occupied in the hotel dining room. The couple at one table was making moves to leave. At the other a lone male diner was eating a piece of pie. Ellie glanced at her watch. It was only nine thirty! But she could tell by the looks on the hostess's and wait staff's faces that they had been poised to close and were not pleased to see three diners walk in the door.

After they were seated, Vanessa beat Ellie to the wine list and ordered a California Chablis. Ellie started to protest but was feeling mellow after what had turned out to be a very successful day what with visiting the place where their father was born and meeting the woman who cared for him until Vera took over. When Vanessa lifted her glass and said, "Here's to Mildred," Ellie chimed in with "I'll drink to that."

"And to Hattie," Georgiana added.

Over coffee they put together a game plan for tomorrow's day trip to the county where Hattie had been born and raised.

Vanessa and Georgiana headed for the elevator, but Ellie decided she needed some time away from her sisters and announced she was going to have a nightcap and would be up shortly.

Or maybe she just wanted to see if any attractive, single heterosexual men were patronizing the bar. And with that thought, she headed for the ladies' room to freshen her makeup.

Except for the bartender, the bar was empty. And he was getting ready to close. "It's a weeknight," he explained.

She bought a beer and carried it out to the pool, where she settled herself on a chaise lounge, pulled off her boots, and dialed Boone's cell phone number. Which was insane. It was after midnight in New York, and he was probably either at home in bed with his wife or in bed someplace else with someone other than his wife.

She had lied to her sisters. She and Boone were not back together. He had not called her in months. But she was tired of being teased about cowboys and about always being on the lookout for an eligible man.

As much as she liked the fantasy of the perfect man or even a marginally acceptable man simply showing up at the next table in a restaurant or the next seat in a bar or asking for her help in selecting vegetables at the greengrocer's and they would both instantly know they were meant for each other, it simply wasn't going to happen. She had to make something happen.

As Boone's phone rang, she wondered if he was looking at the screen to see who was calling. Did he even have her number in his log after all these months? If he was back with his wife, he'd probably deleted her number—just in case his wife was the snoopy sort.

So why in the hell was she calling him in the first place?

Why? Because she was lonely. Lonely in a way that being with her sisters could not appease.

Boone answered, "Hi, babe."

His voice was surrounded by a sea of other voices. And laughter. He was in a bar that hadn't closed down for the night and not in bed with some woman. "Is that a generic *babe* or do you know who this is?" she asked.

"Mmmm, let me think. Your number is familiar, but you need to give me a clue." She hung up and continued to sip her beer. But shortly her cell phone played its musical summons.

She pressed the green button but didn't say anything.

"I've missed you, Ellie," he said in his sexiest voice.

She turned the phone off. She thought of the word Vanessa had used today. *Sincere.* Boone was not a sincere man. But if he were here, she would probably go to bed with him. And hate herself for it.

She was thinking about babies more than ever. Which was probably something hormonal. Something that happened to childless women once their hormones started to wane. The less fertile a woman becomes, the more she wants a baby. Nature's big fat nasty joke.

She wondered how old the bartender was and wished she'd looked to see if he was wearing a wedding ring.

He hadn't even tried to flirt with her.

Briefly she considered taking a cab to some other bar if for no other reason than she really wanted a second beer. Except she would have to put her boots back on. And she wanted more than another beer. A whole lot more.

She worried that she was on the verge of becoming a slut. And with that thought, she picked up her boots and headed for the elevator.

Lying in bed next to her sound-asleep younger sister with her sound-asleep older sister in the room's other bed, Ellie didn't like her chances of drifting off to sleep. Normally she would have turned on the television to take her mind off whatever thoughts were roaming inside her head. Being able to toss and turn herself into a comfortable sleeping position would be nice, too. But since she wasn't alone and neither option was in the cards, Ellie let her thoughts roam, and they took her straight past Boone to what had happened today at that nursing home in Deer Lodge. Ellie now had no doubt that the woman named Hattie who wrote the letter to Vera Wentworth that was mailed in Deer Lodge, Montana, had given birth to a baby boy who grew up and married a woman named Penelope and fathered three little girls named Vanessa, Ellie, and Georgiana. Their wonderful father. He called her his Elegant Ellie and said he loved walking with her and seeing how people took notice of her excellent posture and her impeccable style. Thoughts of her father took her back to those terrible days when he was in the last weeks of his life. He had tried to talk to her about it—about his dying—but she didn't have the courage to go there, couldn't bring herself to acknowledge that he was going to leave them, couldn't allow him to say whatever he wanted to say to her, and the very next day he lapsed into a coma.

The hospice people had come with their bed and equipment. Ellie and her sisters and mother took turns sitting with him. Round the clock, they did that, listening to his labored breathing, watching his chest rise and fall. Ellie was with him when he took that one final gasp.

Ellie had held her own breath waiting for him to take

another breath, but there was only a deathly silence in the room. He'd been living one instant and dead the next. She'd called out for her mother and sisters, who came in their nightclothes and wept with her. They kissed his lips and face and hands and stroked his hair and told him how much they loved him and that they would miss him for the rest of their lives.

Ellie got out of bed and tiptoed to the bathroom, where she could blow her nose and wipe her eyes. Then she carefully crawled back into bed and worked on taking her mind down another pathway that had nothing to do with death. Or with pregnancy, motherhood, and babies.

She tried to compose the first lines of the looking-for-Hattie piece she would write, but she had no idea how the search was going to turn out. Hattie might be dead or demented. She might be angry that they had tracked her down.

Okay, what now? Ellie asked herself. She had to figure out some way to make herself fall asleep.

In spite of her best intentions, her thoughts slid down a slippery slope straight to Boone. Maybe he knew who she was all along and was just teasing on the phone. He did say her name when he called her back.

She didn't trust him, but she had loved being with him. They were compatible in so many ways. On politics and religion and music and books. They liked the same wines and food. He'd even liked to shop and had good fashion sense. She admired the way he dressed and he felt the same about her. And they were good in bed.

Maybe it was out of desperation, but in spite of all her promises to herself about not getting overly involved with a man until she was sure about his intentions and his character, she had fallen a little bit in love with Boone. Maybe not just a little bit. If only he had just told her that he was going back to his wife, which was after all a laudable thing to do. She would still have been devastated, but she would have put her feelings on hold while he gave his marriage a second chance. Of course, she would have been praying that his wife was a frigid bitch who had let herself go and was chronically flatulent. But Boone tried to keep it a secret, and when she found out from the friend whose friend had gotten them together in the first place that Boone was back with his wife, she had been doubly devastated. Apparently he thought he could have home cooking *and* a little something on the side. On *Sex and the City*, a person whose sole purpose in one's life was to alleviate horniness was called a fuck buddy. That's what Boone wanted. Clandestine sex. No strings attached. He wanted a woman who would be grateful for a quick fuck every now and then and not expect more.

And she was almost of a mind to settle for that.

Ellie groaned when Vanessa shook her shoulder and announced it was time for her to get up. "We have another day ahead of us," Vanessa said in her most cheerful voice. Then she burst into song. "Open wide the windows, open wide the doors. Let a little sunshine in," which was the same stupid song their mother had used throughout their childhood to wake them up, but at least their mother could carry a tune.

"God, I feel sorry for poor Lily and Beth if they have to listen to that in the morning," Ellie moaned.

She was exhausted but managed to get herself out of bed and dressed. Then she downed enough coffee to make her human.

An hour and a half later, they were speeding across the middle of no place. Ellie couldn't believe the vast emptiness that they were now traversing. Traveling on Highway 287 out of Helena, they encountered only an occasional vehicle.

There were more trucks than cars, a number of them hauling coal. The long stretches of empty roadway in between the vehicle sightings gave her an otherworldly feeling. She and her sisters were a hell of a long way from New York City.

There were mountains in the distance, but they had left the breathtaking scenery behind. With no stops for Georgiana to take pictures, they reached Interstate 90 in less than an hour. The traffic increased but not by much. Midmorning, they left the interstate and headed south on a two-lane highway.

The landscape was hilly and wooded—pretty but not spectacular. Most of the traffic was now huge dump trucks piled high with coal, with no indication they might be approaching a town. "Are you sure this is the right road?" Ellie asked Vanessa.

"No."

"Maybe we should ask someone?" Georgiana said from the backseat.

"And just who would you suggest I ask?" Vanessa responded, glancing at her watch.

But soon there was an intersection and a sign indicating that Coal Town was twelve miles straight ahead.

The twelve-mile drive took them by vast blights on the landscape that even three city girls recognized as strip mines and the source of all that coal piled on all those trucks.

A billboard announced that Coal Town was home to Bitterroot Mines, a division of Aquila Industries.

The outskirts of town consisted of a large trailer park, salvage yard, numerous bars, a McDonald's and several other fast-food establishments, a Super Wal-Mart and a nonsuper Target, and a huge prefabricated Church of the Saved surrounded by a vast parking lot.

The prosperous-looking downtown was a bit of a surprise. The buildings along the tree-lined street had all undergone restoration or were new buildings with a Gay Nineties look. At the end of the street was Coal Town High School, a handsome brick building of recent vintage with a large marquee out front announcing that the building was the home of the Coal Town Eagles.

"I have a feeling that Coal Town has changed a great deal since Hattie lived here," Ellie observed.

Vanessa parked in front of the high school. The school was all but empty with only a few summer-school classes in progress.

The school librarian, a tall, angular woman with graying hair, led them to a collection of yearbooks from years past and left them to their browsing. The yearbooks featured high school students and their activities, but each edition also included group pictures of students in the first through eighth grades. Since they weren't sure of the exact years that Henrietta/Hattie had attended the school, they selected a range of years and carried the books to a nearby table.

After fifteen minutes or so, Georgina said, "Hey, guys, I found a Henrietta *Worth*."

Vanessa and Ellie came to look over her shoulder as she pointed to a knock-kneed little girl in pigtails standing in the front row of Miss Evelyn Teague's second-grade class.

"Maybe her family dropped the *Went* part of *Wentworth*," Vanessa suggested.

Ellie showed the librarian the picture of Henrietta Worth and asked, "Do you see any sort of familial resemblance between us and this little girl?"

The librarian studied the picture. "The quality of the picture is poor. All I can tell is that this little girl had scrawny legs and her dress is too small."

By the time Henrietta Worth was in high school, she

wore her hair in a ponytail. And while the other girls had smiled and tilted their heads coquettishly to one side—as the photographer had apparently instructed—Henrietta's head had no tilt and her face was without expression.

Her picture appeared only among the alphabetized class photos. She hadn't acted in any of the class plays. She hadn't sung in the choir or been a member of any organization. Her picture did not appear in the yearbook at all for what would have been her senior year.

"Okay, the form that Henrietta Polanski filled out said that she grew up in Coal Town," Vanessa pointed out. "Since this girl is the only Henrietta we've found, she has to be the right one—unless she lied on that questionnaire."

"But why would anyone bother to change their name from Wentworth to Worth?" Georgiana wondered.

"Maybe they didn't get along with the West Virginia branch of the family," Ellie speculated.

They looked in the librarian's copy of the current Coal Town telephone directory, a skinny little thing no thicker than a comic book. There were no Worths listed. Or Wentworths. Or Polanskis.

"That would have been too simple," Ellie observed.

"On to Plan B," Vanessa said.

They selected the picture taken Henrietta's junior year. The librarian directed them to the second-floor computer lab.

Even though class had been dismissed, several students were gathered around their instructor, a geeky young man with an engaging smile. He scanned the photograph of Hattie onto a CD and made several hard copies for them.

When they returned the yearbook, Ellie asked the librarian if she knew any Coal Town residents old enough to have known Henrietta Worth.

The woman shook her head. "I've only lived here for four years, but I know that Coal Town was all but a ghost town in the sixties and seventies. Mining operations had closed down, and folks couldn't earn a living here anymore. But Aquila Industries arrived in the late 1980s, and the town has thrived ever since. The high school was built with Aquila money and has state-of-the-art everything."

Hayes, the county seat of John Coulter County, wasn't much bigger than Coal Town, and obviously no benefactor had come along and rebuilt the town. Half the storefronts around the courthouse square were boarded up, and the courthouse was an ugly, square, two-story structure of more recent vintage than the town's other buildings. "I guess they couldn't afford an architect," Georgiana observed.

They found their way to the court clerk's office on the second floor, only to learn that the original courthouse had burned down more than fifty years ago, destroying all court records along with birth and death certificates, marriage licenses, and property abstracts. And all these years later, the clerk lamented, they were still trying to sort things out.

Next they tried the newspaper office. The young woman at the front desk showed them to a dingy back room with long-ago issues of the newspaper bound by month in large folders arranged chronologically. "The newspaper has been bought and sold several times over the years, and our morgue is far from complete," she explained.

The sisters pulled out the binders that covered the year leading up to the date that Hattie was first incarcerated at Deer Lodge. Some of the issues were missing. Articles had been torn or cut out of others. They found nothing about the trial of a young woman named Henrietta Worth or Henrietta

Polanski. If anything had been printed about the trial, it had been removed or lost.

Ellie asked if they could see the editor, who seemed quite willing to turn away from her computer and visit with them. Her name was Joan Harris.

Ellie pitched their story to her.

"And you came all the way from New York City to find this woman?" Editor Harris asked as she studied the yearbook picture through a pair of reading glasses parked on the end of her nose.

"Yes, ma'am," Georgiana said. "Or at least we're pretty sure she's the one we're looking for." Then she explained about the letter from Hattie.

Even while Georgiana was speaking, the editor turned to her computer and began tapping away on the keyboard. "How's this for a lead?" she asked. "'Three sisters raised in New York City have come to Montana in search of a woman they believe to be their long-lost grandmother.'"

"I'm feeling a bit uncomfortable about this," Vanessa interrupted. "If our Hattie is still alive, there are some parts of her story that she probably wouldn't want published in a newspaper article."

"No problem," Joan Harris said. "I'll identify the person in the photograph as a long-lost *relative* who grew up in Coal Town and focus the piece on you ladies." Then she turned to Ellie. "Tell me about your boots."

SEVENTEEN

*A*FTER making her trek down to the mailbox and back, Myrna went through her usual morning ritual, arranging the mail on her desk in the order it would be opened, seating herself, and pouring her first cup of coffee.

She tackled the stack of newspapers first, scanning headlines, then checking to see what topics were being addressed by editorial writers and what was being reported in the business sections. She paused to e-mail her children, telling them to read an article in the *Wall Street Journal* concerning the future of coal.

She saved the *Denver Post* until last and gave it more careful perusal since it did the best job covering state news and issues pertaining to the mining industry. She refilled her mug, then looked through the front section. Some articles deserved only a glance, others she read with care.

A picture on the back page of the front section of the Denver paper caught Myrna's eye—a head-and-shoulders shot of a somber-faced teenage girl with stringy blond hair. The face looked vaguely familiar.

The headline of the accompanying story read, "New York Women Seeking Long-Lost Relative." The dateline was Hayes, Montana, which made Myrna take a second look at the picture.

Then she closed her eyes, placed a hand on her chest, and took a deep breath in an attempt to slow her racing heart.

After all these years, how can this be?

She took off her glasses, rubbed her eyes, cleaned the lenses, replaced the glasses on her nose, and looked again at the picture. Then she opened a drawer and pulled out a magnifying glass and examined the picture more closely.

Only then did she allow herself to read the story. Myrna quickly scanned it, then went back and reread it with great care.

Three sisters with the family name of Wentworth had grown up in New York City believing their father had been orphaned at birth and only recently found a letter that led them to believe that his mother might still be alive.

They had traveled to Coal Town, a mining community, in Montana's John Coulter County and then to Hayes, the county seat, searching for information about a woman they believe might be related to them and might have information about the circumstances of their father's birth. Henrietta Worth Polanski, who was also known as Hattie, had grown up in the county. The article stopped short of saying that Polanski was their father's birth mother, but anyone reading the article would wonder if that wasn't why these women were looking for her.

The rest of the article was a lot of nonsense about the sisters and their careers. The oldest sister had two children and was a fund-raiser for a private college. The middle one was an editor at a fashion magazine and was described as wearing "couturier Western." The youngest sister was a hand and foot model but was interested in pursuing a career in photography.

The article ended by saying that anyone who had information about Henrietta Worth Polanski was asked to contact the editor of the *John Coulter County News.*

Myrna carried the newspaper and the magnifying glass to a window where she examined the grainy picture in the bright morning sunlight.

So long ago it had been taken. For the yearbook.

For the goddamned yearbook!

Myrna closed her eyes, the pain of that time folding back upon her.

It was her junior year. She hadn't wanted to have her picture taken. Not for that yearbook or for the ones that had come before it. But none of the other students declined to have their picture taken, so when her turn came, she sat on the stool and stared at the camera. Most of her classmates would order copies of the yearbook and for days after they arrived would eagerly sign each other's book. The signing ritual took place in front of the building before school, in the halls between classes, in the lunchroom, in classrooms when the teacher wasn't looking, even in the restrooms. But the girl named Hattie couldn't afford a yearbook and had no friends to sign it even if she could. Once the other miners' children had been her friends, but she had become their worst nightmare. Mining had killed her father, and the owner of the mine denied her mother a widow's benefit, leaving them poor as dirt. She became a misfit who wore her mother's made-over dresses to school and her mother's shoes, which were too narrow and made her feet hurt. Not a day went by that Hattie didn't promise herself that someday she would wear shoes made of such soft leather that they felt as if she were wearing velvet bed-room slippers.

Just thinking about that time and her mother's narrow shoes made Myrna's feet hurt. She wiggled her toes inside the supple leather of her handmade shoes. Then she touched the unsmiling face of the girl whose shoes would have been pinching her toes when the picture was taken and who—after the yearbook was published—would not be asked by a single classmate to sign her name below that picture or to write some clever remembrance on the flyleaf.

Myrna had remade herself since that picture was taken, and she had systematically set out to destroy all evidence that Henrietta Polanski had ever existed. Once that task was completed, she had mentally let go of her. Months and even years could go by without her giving more than a passing thought to that time in her life and the person she had once been. She had erased the person she used to be and created a new being—a confident, clever woman who had made a tremendous success of herself.

But now she felt that confidence slipping away.

Myrna went into the bathroom and studied her face in the mirror. After all these years, would anyone see a resemblance between the face in the mirror and the one in the newspaper? Her company officers would be having their breakfast now in their expensive suites in Steamboat Springs' finest resort before being brought to Eagles Nest in limousines for the afternoon meeting. They would have their newspapers spread out in front of them. Were they staring at the picture of Hattie at this very moment? Would they see something of the woman she now was in that long-ago photograph and wonder why she had changed her name? Why she was living a lie?

Panic rose in her chest and pushed against its walls,

causing her breath to come in short gasps. What if after all these years her true identity became known?

She took a deep, calming breath. That was not going to happen, she told herself. She would do whatever needed to be done to make sure that it didn't.

She wondered if the appearance of the picture and article in the *Denver Post* on the day that the company officers of Aquila Industries were scheduled to be in the state was not coincidental.

Maybe she should postpone the meeting and give the company officers time to forget about a picture in the newspaper that might have looked vaguely familiar.

But she had never once postponed a meeting. They would think she was ailing or unprepared.

She returned to her desk, opened a drawer, and pulled out a pair of scissors. Carefully she cut out the picture and placed it in the exact middle of her desk. She had been born Henrietta Rose Worth, but her parents had always called her Hattie. But that person no longer existed, she reminded herself. Hattie had been pushed out of existence by the person she had become.

The person she had become. When she needed a new name, she had pulled one out of thin air and become Myrna Miles. With no middle name. Not even her children or Willy knew her real name.

She had changed her last name three different times as three different men came into her life. For the last five decades she had been Myrna Miles Cunningham.

She looked down at the picture of Hattie. "Stupid girl," she said. "Why did you let them take your picture? Why did you even go to school that day in your mother's tacky old dress and her skinny shoes? You already knew you were going to run away and leave that awful town behind. What were you waiting for anyway? If you'd already left, you would have saved yourself a whole lot of trouble. And I wouldn't be looking at this picture of you."

What else was waiting out there for the three sisters from New York to discover? Myrna wondered.

She closed her eyes and rubbed her temples. *Think,* she told herself.

After a time, Myrna's breathing began to slow. And her pounding heart. She opened her eyes, picked up the phone, and punched a button.

"Good morning," the familiar voice responded.

"Would you please come to my office?" Myrna said.

EIGHTEEN

*S*TILL in bed, Ellie mumbled that she hadn't slept well and had no intention of going downstairs for breakfast. She requested that her sisters bring her coffee and juice, then burrowed back under her pillow.

Vanessa and Georgiana were discussing their plans for a return trip to Coal Town as they headed toward the elevator. "Maybe we could visit the old folks home like we did in Deer Creek," Georgiana suggested. "Surely there's someone in the town who remembers Hattie Worth."

They were crossing the lobby when Georgiana's cell phone began playing its tune. Vanessa waited while Georgiana dug the phone from her canvas backpack. She glanced at the number on the screen, then with a puzzled look put the phone to her ear and said, "Hello. . . ."

"Yes, this is she," she responded, and listened for a few seconds more, then grabbed Vanessa's arm and gave her a wide-eyed look. "But you just interviewed us yesterday!" she told the caller. "You mean the article has already been published and you've heard from someone?"

As Georgiana listened, she kept glancing at Vanessa, her head bobbing. "Wire service! You mean it's running in other newspapers, too? That's amazing." Georgiana indicated to Vanessa that she needed a writing implement.

Vanessa dug a pen and a scrap of paper from her purse and watched while Georgiana wrote down a phone number, then repeated it to make sure she had it right. "And this person said that she recognized the picture and had information on Hattie?" Georgiana asked the caller.

"Oh my gosh! That's so cool!" she responded with a little hop and jump. " . . . Yes, I'll let you know what happens."

Georgiana ended the call and yelped, "Bingo!" Then she took a deep breath. "The newspaper editor in Hayes filed the article she wrote with a wire service, and someone in Colorado has already contacted her about it."

"That really is amazing," Vanessa acknowledged, "but don't get your hopes up too high. It could be just a crank call. Or it could be someone who knew Hattie back in high school and hasn't seen her since and hasn't a clue as to where she might live or if she's even still alive."

"But it could be her next-door neighbor who called," Georgiana said, not trying to contain the excitement in her voice, "or it could have been Hattie herself."

Georgiana glanced at the phone number on the scrap of paper, then thrust it into Vanessa's hand. "You're better on the phone than I am. You call."

Vanessa used her own cell phone to call the number. Almost immediately a voice said, "Hello."

"Is this the person who called the John Coulter County newspaper about the story on Hattie Worth?" Vanessa asked.

"Yes, are you one of the Wentworth sisters?" asked a pleasant but nervous voice that could have been male or female.

"Yes, this is Vanessa, the oldest sister."

"This is so exciting," the androgynous voice said. "You came all the way from New York looking for information about your grandmother!"

"Do you know something about Hattie?" Vanessa asked.

"I sure do. She's not named Hattie anymore, but she's the same person. I didn't know about her other name until this morning. I work for her and live in her house, and she's my best friend in the whole world. She would like to meet you and asked that I call you and invite you to come here. She recognized the picture in the Denver newspaper right away. It was taken for the school yearbook back when she was a junior at Coal Town High School. She didn't like the picture or the high school, but she wants to meet you three ladies as soon as possible. Are you still up there in Montana?"

"Yes, we're in Helena."

"That's good. What's the name of your hotel?"

"The Big Sky Inn. Is Hattie coming to see us?"

"No, but she would like you to visit her."

"Where does Hattie live?" Vanessa asked.

"In Colorado. We'll send a plane for you."

"I need to talk this over with my sisters. Where in Colorado do you live, and how can I get back to you?"

"Why don't you girls just stay with us for the rest of your visit?" the voice continued. "It will give us all a chance to get to know each other. The newspaper article said that your sister Georgiana is interested in nature photography, and we live right in the middle of a whole lot of nature. There are lots of birds and animals and snakes and trees and rocks. Lots of rocks. I guess we got more rocks than anything else. Except maybe trees. Trees are all over the place. One of our planes will fly up there to Helena and bring you back here. I'll arrange for someone to pick you up at the Big Sky Inn at one o'clock and take you to the airport. This is really exciting, don't you think?"

"Yes, I suppose I do," Vanessa acknowledged.

"Well, I guess that's everything I'm supposed to tell you. Now don't forget. Be ready at one o'clock. I'll be waiting when the airplane lands."

"I need to call you back after I make sure this is okay with my sisters," Vanessa said. But she was greeted with silence. The line was dead. And she didn't even know the name of the person to whom she had been speaking.

"So, what's the story?" Georgiana asked, her eyes wide with curiosity and excitement.

"According to this individual, we have found Hattie, and it would seem that she has come a long way from her days as an inmate in the Deer Lodge prison."

Georgiana hugged Vanessa, then performed an impromptu dance around the lobby to the amusement of the desk clerk and bellhop. "Just wait until Ellie hears!" she said as she dispensed another hug.

Georgiana's lovely face was positively glowing with joy. "Aren't you just thrilled, Nessa?"

"I'm not sure. I don't know Hattie's current last name or the name of the person I just talked to. But she expects us to fly off to some unknown location in Colorado in 'one of their planes' to meet Hattie. It would seem that Hattie has overcome her modest beginnings. *And* her prison record."

"Well, good for her!" Georgiana said enthusiastically. "Come on, let's go tell Ellie."

"What about breakfast?"

"We'll call room service." Georgiana headed for the elevator.

When Vanessa unlocked the door to their room, Georgiana rushed inside and pounced on Ellie's sleeping form.

Vanessa closed the door and watched while Georgiana straddled Ellie's body. "Wake up, kiddo! We've got news. Big news."

"I don't smell coffee," Ellie said with her eyes still closed.

"We found Hattie!" Georgiana said, shaking Ellie's shoulders.

Ellie's eyes popped open. "You're kidding!"

"No, I'm not." Georgiana rolled off Ellie. Then, sitting cross-legged in the middle of the bed, she explained about the phone call from the newspaper editor in Hayes and Vanessa's conversation with some nice person who worked for Hattie. "Was the nice person a man or a woman?" Georgiana asked Vanessa.

Vanessa shrugged and sat across from her sisters on the other bed. "I never said this person was 'nice,'" she pointed out. Although he or she probably was, Vanessa decided. And somewhat unsophisticated. Childlike almost.

"Well, anyway," Georgiana continued, "this person said that Hattie is anxious to meet us and wants us to visit her in Colorado and is sending a private plane to fetch us, so we've got to get packed and I need to wash my hair and buy batteries and I am so excited I can hardly think."

"Oh my gosh!" Ellie said, giving Georgiana a high five. "The old gal must be loaded. A real American success story. From rags to riches. And through the years she's always wondered about the baby she gave away and if he had children and if he wondered about her from time to time. And now in her twilight years, she meets the grand-daughters she never knew she had. It is a story begging to be told."

"A story by Ellie Wentworth," Georgiana said with a grin.

"With pictures by Georgiana Wentworth," Ellie said, giving her sister a high five.

Then Ellie turned to Vanessa. "How come you're not excited?" she demanded.

"I guess I'm more amazed than excited," Vanessa explained. "And I don't think you should count on Hattie wanting you to tell her personal history to the world."

"You're just miffed," Georgiana said in a teasing tone, "because the person that you talked to hung up before you found out his or her name and its exact spelling or Hattie's current last name and its exact spelling or told him or her where to fax Hattie's current curriculum vitae or to specify the exact geographical positioning coordinates from where the person was calling."

Vanessa ignored the teasing as she flipped open her cell phone and called the last number on her calls-received list.

A recorded voice informed her that no one was available to take the call. She was not given an opportunity to leave a message.

Georgiana ordered three continental breakfasts while Ellie hurried into the bathroom to take a shower. Vanessa sat immobile sifting through her thoughts. Why was she being such a spoilsport? Wasn't finding Hattie the reason why they came on this trip? She and her sisters were being presented with the opportunity to share an incredible adventure.

Unless the seemingly ingenuous person on the phone was a con artist.

She went downstairs to the gift shop. The *Denver Post* was sold-out, the clerk informed her, but she could probably buy it at the drugstore just up the street.

Vanessa walked up the block and purchased a copy. Before she left the drugstore, she began leafing through the newspaper. The article and picture were on the back of the front section.

The three sisters were presented as "bright, attractive New York career women searching for their late father's birth mother." The article mentioned that Vanessa was a single mother of two and explained what each of them did for a living. Nothing in the article would make an embezzler or con artist think the sisters were worthy of attention.

But perhaps it was someone other than Hattie herself who'd recognized the picture. A someone who knew that Hattie was rich and planned to kidnap her long-lost granddaughters and hold them for ransom.

Which seemed too far-fetched even to consider, Vanessa decided. And the voice on the phone had said that Hattie recognized the picture as being from her high school yearbook and that it was taken her junior year, information that was not mentioned in the newspaper article.

Vanessa reread the article. This time she felt a bit of adrenaline flowing into her veins. The Wentworth sisters had pulled off a minor miracle. Looking through the high school yearbooks had been Vanessa's idea. And now they were going to fly to Colorado and meet the woman who gave birth to their father.

Their own mother would be pleased when she learned the success of her little scheme. Penelope's daughters had renewed their sisterly bonds and accomplished their mission.

Vanessa imagined the three of them relaying their adventure to Penelope and Lily and Beth as they all sat on the terrace enjoying the view of the French countryside. Georgiana's photographs would be spread out on the table. Vanessa could almost feel the wineglass in her hand.

For the first time since learning that her mother had a French lover and planned to live with him in the south of France, Vanessa felt her heart beginning to thaw. Life did go on. And she did want her mother to be happy. Happiness was so much better than unhappiness.

Before heading up to the room, she arranged to have the rented SUV picked up at the hotel garage and checked out.

Ellie and Georgiana were rushing around the room pulling clothes out of drawers and the closet and packing their bags, Georgiana with her cell phone tucked between her ear and shoulder as she told Freddy her "amazing news." Their girlish exuberance reminded Vanessa of Lily and Beth packing for their trip to Europe, a thought that caused a pang of missing to dart through her breast. She wished they were going with her and their aunts to meet Hattie. Maybe she would bring her daughters out West someday soon so that they could meet their great-grandmother and experience yet another corner of the world.

NINETEEN

$\mathcal{S}$o they had agreed to come, these children of the child she gave away.

Myrna needed to prepare her remarks for today's meeting. And she should call the kitchen to tell Mrs. Sanchez that her coffee had gotten cold.

But she just sat there. Stunned. Angry. When only hours before she had felt such an incredible sense of well-being. The weather was perfect. Her morning descent down the mountain to get the mail and the climb back up had been especially invigorating. She had been looking forward to today's meeting of her company officers. And to next week's meeting in Denver of Randall's gubernatorial campaign committee. They had already rented the ballroom at Denver's historic Brown Palace Hotel for the announcement event. Already the pundits were speculating that Randall would be a presidential candidate four years from now. She was approaching the pinnacle of her life. Everything she had planned for these last six decades was beginning to come to fruition. Her health was excellent. Her power and wealth vast. Her resolve unyielding. She had no doubt that she would live to see her son elected president of the United States.

Of course, it had occurred to her over the years that the Deer Lodge baby would have grown up and probably married and had children. But when she'd escaped from the prison, she had drawn a line across her life. From that day forward, she had been a new person with a new name and new goals. And as the years went by, she had taken great pains to make sure her past would never come back to haunt her. But obviously she had failed in that endeavor.

Ironic how things had turned out in her life. If her brother hadn't been born with a clubfoot and her father hadn't gone to Alaska to earn money for an operation to fix Patrick's foot, maybe her life would have taken a different course. Maybe she would have stayed in Coal Town and married a miner. Maybe she'd be living there still—a dried-up old woman living on her Social Security checks.

Their driver arrived at the hotel at precisely 1 p.m., and the sisters were delivered by limousine to a hangar on the back side of the Helena airport where a small, sleek jet with an eagle in flight and the words AQUILA INDUSTRIES painted on the side was waiting for them.

A man came out of the small office, loaded the luggage onto the plane, and told them the pilots would return shortly. "Make yourself at home," he said, indicating a bench beside a vending machine.

Ellie pulled out her cell phone and, with it pressed to her ear, walked to the other side of the aircraft.

Vanessa glanced at Georgiana. "Boone?"

Georgiana shrugged.

They sat on the bench. "Are you nervous about this trip?" Vanessa asked.

"Why would I be nervous?"

"We don't even know where we're going."

"That just makes it more exciting," Georgiana said, running a hand through her unruly curls. "Just think how incredible it is that we actually are going to meet the woman who gave birth to our father. I wonder if she's excited over the prospect of meeting three granddaughters that she never even knew she had until today. And how sad she must be to learn that the long-ago baby she was forced to give away is dead. Surely a part of her wished that he would come looking for her someday. But at least she can learn about him through us. I brought pictures of him and a copy of his obituary from the *New York Times* and some samples of his reporting—just in case we really did find her."

Vanessa leaned over and kissed Georgiana's cheek. "That's so thoughtful of you."

"I want Hattie to know what a special person he was," Georgiana said, then paused before adding, "I miss him a lot."

"Me, too." Vanessa stared at the plane that would soon be taking them to meet the mother their father never knew. "Back on Mother's birthday, when we first saw the note from Hattie to Daddy's Miss Vera, you said that looking for Hattie is what Daddy would expect us to do. I wasn't so sure about that at first, but I am now. I think Daddy would be proud of us for taking this trip, don't you?"

When Georgiana did not respond, Vanessa realized she was watching Ellie emerge from behind the plane and march toward them, cell phone in hand.

"Something's wrong," Georgiana whispered.

Yes, judging from the scowl on Ellie's face, Vanessa could see that something was definitely wrong.

Ellie was staring at Georgiana as she approached. "You bitch!" she said, spitting out the words. "You little bitch!"

The mechanic stuck his head out of the office to see what was going on, then quickly pulled it in and shut the door.

Vanessa stood. "Hey, that's our sister you're talking to. What the hell is going on?"

"Why don't you ask her?" Ellie said, pointing an accusing finger at Georgiana. "She knew that I'd fallen for Boone and that something really special was happening between us. And then she goes and ruins it. She ruined *everything*."

For an instant, Vanessa thought that Ellie was going to attack Georgiana and stepped in between them. "All right, Ellie, you need to calm down and explain why you think she has 'ruined everything.' But before you go any further, I'm going to tell you something that I should have told you the day of the picnic in the park. Boone was coming on to Georgiana. You were too busy passing out food to see what was going on, but even Lily and Beth noticed it and asked me about it on the way home. And recently, he has been calling her and not the other way around."

"Why do you always take her side?" Ellie demanded. "Boone wouldn't lie about something like that. He said that she called him after the picnic last fall, but he thought he'd made it clear that he wasn't interested in seeing her. Then after he went back to his wife, she would call him at home. He and his wife weren't getting along very well anyway, but with Georgiana calling it just made matters worse. Long story short, the reason he's been avoiding me was because he didn't want to come between me and my sister."

Vanessa glanced at Georgiana, who was shaking her head, a look of disbelief on her face.

"Have you considered the possibility that he was involved with someone else and she dumped him?" Vanessa asked in her most conciliatory, reasonable-sounding voice.

"And now he's made up some cock-and-bull story to get back in your good graces and to get back at Georgiana because she wouldn't have anything to do with him, which means the man is not only sleazy but malicious."

Vanessa realized that two men in matching blue uniforms had entered the hangar and were heading their way. "The pilots are here. We will settle this later," she said, changing her tone from conciliatory to adamant.

"I'm not going," Ellie said, tears pouring down her face.

"Come on, Ellie," Vanessa said, putting an arm around Ellie's trembling shoulders and guiding her away from the bench and Georgiana. "We've come this far. Let's see this Hattie thing through."

"No," Ellie said, shaking her head.

"Ladies," one of the uniformed men called to them. "We are ready to board."

"Please, Ellie honey," Vanessa implored, "don't do something you'll be sorry for the rest of your life."

"*I am not going.*"

"This is all my fault," Vanessa said. "Georgiana called the morning after the picnic to tell me that Boone had called her the night before and tried to invite himself over. She was worried about telling you herself and thought it would go down better coming from me, but I convinced her that it would be best just to let it go. I realize now that I shouldn't have done that. I should have let you know what sort of person he was before you got any more involved with him."

"You're just lying to protect her," Ellie said, ducking from under Vanessa's arm. "You've always taken her side in everything. Sweet little Georgiana who never does anything wrong."

"I am not lying, and neither is Georgiana," Vanessa

said, working to keep her voice even and calm. "I'm sorry if the truth hurts, but Boone is not worthy of you, Ellie. The man is a jerk, and I'll tell him so to his face if given the chance. But if you're hell-bent to take up with him again, I can't stop you, but you are going with us to meet Hattie."

Vanessa grabbed Ellie's hand and pulled her along as she would a balky child.

"Is there a problem?" the pilot asked.

Vanessa shook her head.

"There's no restroom on board," he said. "I suggest you ladies use the facility here before we take off."

Ellie jerked her hand away from Vanessa's grasp and marched to the restroom. She was there for a long time. The two pilots kept looking at their watches. When she finally came out, she looked pale and her eyes were swollen. But she said nothing and headed for the plane.

The plane had only six passenger seats, three on each side with a narrow aisle down the middle. The copilot stuck his head through the curtain as the plane taxied out of the hangar onto the runway. "Fasten your seat belts," he ordered.

Shortly they were in the air. The noise from the engines in the small craft was so loud normal conversation was impossible, which was just as well, Vanessa decided. The altercation in the hangar had left her upset and tense. Maybe the flight would give them a chance to calm down.

Vanessa leaned her head back and closed her eyes. She would gladly have wrung Boone's neck. The man was scum. Thank God he showed his true colors before Ellie married him and/or had gotten pregnant by him.

With nothing to read and too upset to doze, Vanessa was left to her thoughts, which were bothersome. She had no idea how long the flight was but found herself checking her watch every few minutes. After a time even the fabulous pan-orama provided by the Rocky Mountains became too much of a good thing.

After an hour, the plane began its descent. Vanessa watched out the windows as they flew over a small city that occupied a mountain valley. Soon they were landing on a small one-runway airport.

The pilot made a perfect landing then taxied to a stop near a modest terminal building. A sign welcomed them to Steamboat Springs. A very large person clad in jeans, a plaid shirt, and red, high-topped athletic shoes was waiting beside a shiny black Hummer.

As they descended from the aircraft, the person ap-proached. At first Vanessa thought this oversize individual was a man, but a substantial bosom was evident under the plaid shirt. The woman's short brown hair was standing on end in the swift breeze. Her broad face was wearing an ex-cited smile.

"Welcome, ladies. Now let me guess which is which," she said, putting a finger alongside her mouth.

Vanessa recognized her voice. The person on the phone this morning. The woman who'd said that Hattie was her employer and best friend.

Fascinated, Vanessa watched as the woman pointed at Ellie and said, "This must be Ellie," which was a rather obvi-ous guess since the newspaper article mentioned that Ellie worked for a fashion magazine and she was wearing a khaki safari outfit and carrying a zebra-print handbag.

"And you must be Vanessa, the oldest sister," the woman said as she pointed at Vanessa. "And that leaves Georgiana, the photographer." She nodded in Georgiana's direction. "And you all are really pretty," she added with a shy smile.

"Thank you," Vanessa said. "And you are . . . ?"

"I'm Willy." The woman touched a hand to her chest. "My real name is Wilhelmina, but everyone calls me Willy."

Willy helped the pilots unload the luggage and put it in the Hummer.

Ellie climbed into the front passenger seat of the Hummer even before Willy boarded the oversize vehicle. Ellie looked straight ahead while Vanessa and Georgiana got in the backseat. "I've never ridden in one of these things," Vanessa said in an attempt to take the tension down a notch or two.

Neither of her sisters responded.

Willy had soon left the airport far behind as she headed north on Highway 40, passing other vehicles at what seemed to Vanessa an excessive rate of speed. After a half hour or so, Willy left the highway behind and continued on a blacktop road.

Vanessa leaned forward and asked Willy in a voice loud enough to be heard over the road noise. "Where are we exactly?"

"In Colorado."

"Yes, but in what part of Colorado?"

"The western part. The eastern part doesn't have any mountains."

"What town is Hattie's house near?" Vanessa asked, trying a different tack.

"Closest town is a wide spot in the road named Folly for all the folks who came to these parts thinking they were going to get rich mining gold," Willy said over her shoulder. "Not much left there now. You can buy gas and a hamburger, but that's about all."

They passed an occasional mailbox beside a lane that disappeared into the pine and spruce trees. But after a time, the only sign of civilization was the road itself.

The grade was steeper now, the road winding. Willy whipped the Hummer around the curves like a race car driver. Vanessa and Georgiana held on for dear life and exchanged apprehensive glances.

Finally Willy turned onto a gravel road and stopped in front of a massive iron gate on which was mounted a large sign that read:

Private Property
Keep Out
Trespassers Will Be Prosecuted

Willy pointed a remote opener at the gate, and slowly it swung outward in a graceful arc. She drove the Hummer through, then slowly rounded switchback after switchback as the road wound its way higher and higher up the mountain until a second iron gate, this one higher than the first, loomed in front of them. Once the gate had opened itself, they entered a spacious parking area that had either been carved into the mountain or utilized space provided by a naturally formed cavern. Willy came to a stop beside a late-model Lincoln sedan.

One corner of the parking area was occupied by a small concrete-block building. "That's for the security officer," Willy said with a nod in its direction. "Myrna fired him this morning. I'm not sure why."

They helped Willy unload their luggage onto a cart, which she pushed toward what looked like an elevator door. Which it was. They entered its spacious interior and headed upward.

When the elevator came to a stop, the door slid open to reveal a huge split-level living room with floor-to-ceiling windows that showcased a spectacular view of the mountainous landscape. "This is Hattie's house?" Georgiana asked in awe.

"Yes, this is her house," the large woman said with pride. "She planned the house in her head for years, then finally had it built. Her and me, we used to live in Denver, and this house was where we came on weekends. But we live here all the time now. The people who run her mines and her trucking company and all the other stuff she owns come here when they need to see her."

"Is Hattie here now?" Georgiana asked reverently.

Willy nodded. "You'll see her at dinner. Her company officers were here for lunch and a meeting, and she still has some business things to take care of."

"You said on the phone this morning that Hattie has a different name now," Vanessa said.

"Yes. I was surprised when I saw that other name in the newspaper story. But I wasn't supposed to say that on the phone," Willy added, looking contrite. "She wants to explain everything to you herself."

Willy herded them back onto the elevator and took them up another level to their suite of rooms—a sitting area and two bedrooms. Willy said that they would have an early dinner so they could have a nice long evening with Hattie, after which a late-evening snack would be served. Once Willy had departed, Ellie said that she was going to lie down before dinner, then headed for the smaller of the two bedrooms and closed the door. "She'll come around," Vanessa told Georgiana. "At some level she realizes that awful man has been playing her for a fool."

"I'm not so sure about that," Georgina said, kicking off her shoes and stretching out on the bed. "It really takes the fun out of finding Hattie, doesn't it?"

"Yeah, but I am curious to see what she's like. Can

you believe this . . ." Vanessa paused, searching her mind for something to call Hattie's home. The word *house* seemed too conventional. "This dwelling!" she said with a wave of her hand, indicating the structure around them. "It is certainly not what comes to mind when one thinks of 'over the river and through the woods, to grandmother's house we go.'"

Suddenly the door to Ellie's room swung open, and she appeared, cell phone in hand. "My cell phone doesn't work," she announced.

"You need to borrow my charger?" Georgiana asked.

"It has a charge."

Georgiana pulled her phone from her purse and switched it on. "It says 'no service.' I wonder why."

"Because we're in the middle of no place," Vanessa said, checking her own phone, "and there probably aren't enough people for the cellular companies to bother with." She looked around the room for a regular telephone. There was none. "Is there a phone in your room?" she asked Ellie.

"There's a jack but no phone."

"We'll ask Willy at dinner to bring us phones," Vanessa suggested.

Vanessa stretched out for a time, then took a long shower and put on slacks and a silk blouse.

Georgiana wore jeans with a glittery sweater and jeweled flip-flops and was carrying a large manila envelope.

Looking as though she had just stepped out of her magazine, Ellie was wearing a long skirt of swishy taffeta, a slinky jersey tank top, a fabulous multistrand necklace of turquoise and garnets, and high-heeled sandals. She carried a tapestry purse.

"I'm nervous," Georgiana admitted.

"Me, too," Vanessa said, then put a hand on Ellie's arm. "Can we please declare a truce for this very special evening?"

Ellie marched past Vanessa without responding and punched the elevator call button.

Willy, with a long face replacing her earlier smile, was waiting in the living room to take them down a circular metal staircase in a stairwell carved out of solid rock.

"My cell phone doesn't work," Ellie said in an accusatory tone as she fell in behind Willy. "And there's no phone in our rooms."

"Cell phones aren't much good around here," Willy said.

"I need for you to bring me a regular phone," Ellie asked.

"I'll see what I can do." Willy stood to one side and allowed them to precede her into the dining room.

One wall of the room was formed by the mountain, and the wall of windows at the other end of the room framed the beginnings of what promised to be a spectacular sunset, coloring the horizon.

The table was set for three. Willy explained that Hattie was resting and that they were to join her in her office after dinner.

Vanessa felt a stab of disappointment. Obviously Hattie wasn't pumped up about seeing them if she hadn't managed to greet them when they arrived and was resting rather than having dinner with them.

"Aren't you going to join us?" Vanessa asked Willy.

"I've already eaten," she said, looking down at her feet.

An array of food was laid out on a massive slice of polished wood that was mounted directly onto the stone wall. Willy explained that the household help had the weekend off, but the cook had prepared a meal before leaving. Then she uncorked a bottle of wine and filled their glasses while Vanessa and Georgiana helped themselves to the food. Ellie stood with her back to them staring out at the view.

Vanessa filled a small bowl with clam chowder and put it on a plate along with some grapes and a slice of French bread, then seated herself at the head of the table, hoping to act as a buffer between her sisters. Georgiana put an assortment of fresh fruit on a salad plate and carried it to the table. Ignoring the food, Ellie sat down and picked up her wineglass.

Once they were seated, Willy told Vanessa, "If you need anything, just press the button on the underside of the table. I'll come get you when you're finished and take you to"—she paused, obviously having to remind herself to use the name by which the three guests knew her employer—"to meet *Hattie.*"

Willy left and the room grew quiet. Vanessa took a sip of her wine, which was superb. Even Ellie would have to approve of it. Vanessa wondered what it was, but the bottle was closest to Ellie, and she didn't care enough to ask her what the label said. She needed to say something though. Needed to start a conversation. Ellie certainly wasn't going to. And poor Georgiana was miserable.

This was not the way it was supposed to be.

TWENTY

*W*ITH silence hanging like a cloud over the table, Vanessa felt it was her responsibility as the oldest sister to negotiate a truce. But the events of the day had left her exhausted. Anyone watching them would think they were strangers.

Except strangers would at least make polite small talk.

The notion of watching eyes stayed in her head. But why would anyone bother? And, if Willy was to be believed, there were only two other people in the house—Willy herself and Hattie, who had not yet bothered to greet them.

So much for making an old woman happy!

Obviously Hattie had not been waiting all her life to find out what had happened to the son to whom she'd given birth inside the walls of the Deer Lodge prison or to meet any children he might have fathered.

When Ellie spoke, Vanessa jumped.

"I'm leaving in the morning," Ellie announced. "Willy will have to drive me to an airport where I can catch a flight to New York."

"I wish you would wait until after we meet Hattie to

decide that," Georgiana suggested, her voice timid as though speaking to her own sister were terrifying.

"You think I give a damn about what you wish for?" Ellie said, her voice dripping with venom.

"Come on, Ellie," Vanessa said sharply. "You know very good and well that Georgiana isn't the sort of person who would try to steal her own sister's boyfriend, and besides, the man is a piece of scum."

Immediately Vanessa wished she could recall her last words. She was only making matters worse.

And what if the room was bugged and Hattie and Willy were listening in? The Wentworth sisters should not be airing their dirty linen.

Ellie didn't bother with a retort. She finished her glass of wine, then reached for the bottle and poured herself another.

Vanessa glanced around at the dining room trying to decide where a microphone might be hidden. Or a camera. The room was furnished with only the table and chairs and the massive ledge on which their meal was laid out. Above the ledge was an abstract sculpture made of twisted metal. Vanessa wondered what the sculptor had in mind. Anguish, perhaps. Or confusion.

The sculpture could hide a microphone. Or one could be stashed under the buffet perhaps. Or the table. In the chandelier.

But why in the hell was she feeling so paranoid? Why would anyone want to watch or listen to them? This business with Ellie had gotten to her—along with the absent Hattie and her strange house. She found the mountain abode cold and stark, which probably was a reflection of its owner.

Vanessa nibbled on grapes as she took in the view through the floor-to-ceiling windows.

She fervently hoped that Hattie was a warm, kindly woman who would put them at ease. Maybe she really did need to rest after her business meeting this afternoon. After all, she was getting on in years.

Georgiana had only picked at the fruit and sat staring at her plate. Ellie was polishing off her third glass of wine. Vanessa pushed the button on the underside of the table, and shortly a still somber Willy appeared and led them back up the circular staircase and put them on the elevator.

They rode up two levels. The elevator door opened to a large room surrounded by windows on three sides. French doors opened onto a deck shaped like the bow of a ship. The sun, now a glowing red ball, was just beginning to slip below the peak of the nearest mountain.

Vanessa looked around the large room and took a tentative few steps. "Hattie?"

"I'm here," a voice to her right said.

Vanessa prickled with apprehension as she turned to face the woman who'd given birth to their father. She was seated in a large armchair at the head of a massive conference table, her back to the windows, and her face in shadows.

"Come sit here with me." Hattie's voice was neither welcoming nor unwelcoming. Not a quivery, old-lady voice. An authoritative one. The voice of a woman who expected to be obeyed.

Georgiana took the first step. Vanessa and Ellie followed.

Ellie went around the table and took a seat Hattie's right. Georgiana and Vanessa sat across from Ellie.

Hattie sat erect in her chair, shoulders square, chin high, clasped hands resting in front of her on the glossy surface of the table. At her elbow were a folder and three pens. Her thick head of hair was so white it seemed to glow. With her handsome face, strong voice, and commanding posture, Vanessa would never have taken her for a woman who must be approaching eighty. Not just any woman, though. This was the woman who had given birth to their father. Vanessa had thought she would be filled with emotion when this moment came. She was nervous and apprehensive but not emotional.

"Which one of you is Georgiana?" the woman asked.

Georgiana leaned forward. "I am."

"The newspaper article gave you credit for launching the search for me. Tell me how you did that."

Georgiana cleared her throat and explained how they came to have the letter with a Deer Lodge postmark that someone named Hattie had written to Vera Wentworth. And how, with a computer search and some phone calls, she learned that a woman named Henrietta Polanski had been incarcerated at the Deer Lodge prison during the time their father had been born. But they weren't sure that Henrietta was Hattie until they talked to the daughter of the doctor who'd delivered a baby boy at the prison and helped place him with a relative of his mother's who lived in West Virginia.

"Yes," Hattie said. "I told the doctor the name of an aunt I'd never met but heard my parents talking about over the years, and the name of the town in West Virginia where my father's people were from. How fortunate for you that the doctor's daughter was still alive after all these years."

"Yes, ma'am," Georgiana agreed. "It was a very special moment when we realized she had cared for our newborn father. And now, it's quite overwhelming to actually meet the woman who gave birth to him."

Georgiana paused before adding, "Before you continue, I've been wondering what we should call you. You said that you hadn't been Hattie since you left Deer Lodge."

"'Hattie' is fine. I do go by another name now, but you girls are a remnant of my other life. So tell me, what led you girls to Coal Town and the yearbook picture?"

"That was Vanessa's idea," Georgiana said, touching Vanessa's arm. "A questionnaire that you filled out when you arrived at the prison said that you'd attended Coal Town High School. Vanessa called the high school and found out that the school library had a complete collection of yearbooks dating back to the early 1900s."

"You own Coal Town now, don't you?" Vanessa asked, thinking of the sign announcing that the town was home to an Aquila mine.

"At one time in my life I regretted not burning the town down," Hattie said with a defiant lift of her chin. "That town and the man who owned the mine there brought a great deal of grief to my family, but the state closed him down after an anonymous whistle-blower began sending the state depart-ment of mines and various influential newspapers informa-tion on mine operations and detailing the various accidents and illnesses suffered by miners over the years. The mine had been closed for a number of years when my company acquired it. We closed down much of the underground opera-tion, especially the older shafts, and established strip-mining, which has been most profitable."

Hattie turned to Ellie. "And you must be Ellie. What did you contribute to this endeavor?"

"Not much," Ellie admitted with a shrug, "except that I'm planning to write a magazine piece about the trip to find Hattie. Of course, your reaction is hardly what I had expected. Obviously you're not exactly thrilled to meet three granddaughters you never knew you had."

"It is a shock," Hattie allowed, her chin lifting a bit, "something I'd never thought would happen, and it does bring back a time in my life that was very difficult—a time that I've spent a lot of years trying to forget."

"I'm sorry if we've brought back bad memories," Georgiana chimed in, "but out of those difficult times came our father, who was a wonderful man and a fine journalist. I've brought you pictures of him and some of the pieces he wrote over the years." She put the manila envelope on the table.

Hattie shook her head. "I never knew him, and he represents a very painful time in my life. You must understand that I willingly signed the papers giving up my parental rights to him. I had just turned seventeen and already knew exactly how I was going to escape from that prison and exactly how I was going to change my identity and my life. There was no place in my plans for a newborn baby. It's nice to know that he turned out well, but I never called or wrote Vera Wentworth to ask about him. I had my own life to live, and I put him and those grim times out of mind."

So much for great expectations, Vanessa thought. Poor Georgiana's body sagged like a deflated balloon. And Ellie, who wanted a baby more than anything, so much so she was willing to alienate herself from her own sister in an effort to hang on to a contemptible man she hoped would get her pregnant, was staring at Hattie in much the same manner that one would stare at an alien creature.

Vanessa regarded their father's birth mother anew, taking in her upright posture, her hands resting on the table—ungnarled hands, her nails unpolished but well tended. Her clothing was simple but appeared to be finely tailored. She wore no jewelry except for a watch. But it was not so much the way she looked that made her formidable, Vanessa decided. It was her voice and her body language announcing that she was a woman accustomed to having her own way.

"Then why did you contact us if you had no feelings for the baby who grew up to be our father?" Vanessa asked.

"Let's just call it curiosity." Hattie paused a few seconds before adding, "Oddly enough, after all those years, the past has been much with me over the last few months. Maybe the Fates put us on a collision course, and we were destined to meet. And since the three of you have come all this way, I've decided to tell you how it was that your father came to be born. But there is a stipulation."

Vanessa almost didn't want to hear what the woman had to say. Obviously it was not going to be a heartwarming tale. Vanessa had had no preconceived notion as to what sort of a person Hattie would be, but she had expected the woman to find some satisfaction or closure or maybe even pride to learn that the son she'd given away grew up to be a decent, worthy man. Apparently she had no feelings at all for the baby she'd birthed all those years ago in the prison at Deer Lodge.

Vanessa wished they'd never seen Hattie's note to Miss Vera. Wished they'd never come in search of her.

But they had come, so they would hear her tale and politely take their leave, the sooner the better as far as Vanessa was concerned. No way were they going to remain in her home for the rest of their vacation as Willy had suggested. Vanessa now realized that Willy must have assumed too much in that regard. Probably she was lonely living in such an isolated place and looked forward to visitors.

"I haven't been Hattie since I escaped from prison," the woman who gave birth to their father said. "I became someone else altogether, and no one knew about the early part of my life—not the men I married or my children, and I am speaking of the children I raised. When I think of my children, I have never included that long-ago baby in my maternal musings."

"But you wrote that sweet little letter to your aunt Vera thanking her for taking in your baby," Georgiana reminded Hattie.

"I'd forgotten about that until I read that newspaper article," Hattie admitted as she gazed past them into lengthening shadows taking over the large room. "The doctor told me that my aunt had come to fetch the baby. He asked if I wanted to visit with Vera before she headed back to West Virginia. Since I'd never seen the woman before in my life, I didn't see any need to meet her. But she had done a laudable thing, so I expressed my thanks with that note. I find it beyond amazing that the note survived for all these years.

"When I saw that picture this morning in the Denver newspaper, the past came rolling back," Hattie continued. "And oddly enough, after all these years of never speaking about what happened back then, I had pretty much convinced myself that the past was no longer relevant, yet I find that I am willing to tell you girls my story mostly because I want to hear it myself and perhaps in doing so figure out some things that have always puzzled me."

Ellie reached into her handbag and pulled out a small tape recorder.

"No recorders," Hattie snapped. "What I tell you is never to be revealed. There will be no magazine article. After tonight, we will never see each other again. Now, before we begin, I expect you girls to sign a confidentiality agreement in which you agree never to tell anyone what you learned here tonight. And if you violate the terms of that agreement, you do so at great financial risk."

"What will you do if we refuse to sign it?" Vanessa challenged.

"Then you will never know the story of how your father came to be born." Hattie focused on Vanessa's face, her tone almost wistful. "My dear, the only reason I thought of the agreement was to make you and your sisters feel entirely comfortable hearing things that I have never told anyone—and to let you know that I am quite serious about confidentiality. You came here wanting to know about your father's birth and why I gave him away, and I have decided that you have a right to know these things. But I need to know that what I divulge is secure and that you girls will never reveal it to anyone. *Never.* You also need to know that I am a woman with immense resources and can make life very difficult for you should you not honor this agreement, which I assure you is entirely legal. Willy is a notary public and will certify your signatures."

Hattie rose and placed a copy of the document and a pen in front of each of them just as the elevator door slid open, revealing Willy's enormous form. Hattie went to the head of the table and reached under it, and panels slid open in front of each place at the conference table, and brass lamps, each with a green-glass shade, magically rose into place.

Vanessa turned on her lamp and read the agreement. The wording seemed pretty straightforward. If she or one of her sisters violated the privacy of the woman they knew as Hattie Worth Polanski, they would open themselves up to a lawsuit that would probably leave them penniless.

Amazing, Vanessa thought. It must be some story Hattie was planning to tell them. She thought of her fantasy about her and her sisters sharing the Hattie story with her mother and Lily and Beth during their late-summer visit to France. Apparently that was not to be. The agreement spelled out everything. They couldn't even tell anyone that they had made this trip to Colorado.

Vanessa read the document again to make sure she hadn't misunderstood. "Is this okay with you?" she asked her sisters. "Or should we just pack up and leave?"

"We've come all this way . . . ," Georgiana said, her voice trailing off.

Ellie shrugged. "It better be a damned good story. And come morning, I'm out of here even if I have to walk."

With Willy watching, they each picked up a pen and signed their name.

Willy was all thumbs as she signed each document and affixed the seal, almost dropping the device used for making it when she got to the agreement Vanessa had signed. Once Willy was finished, she handed the agreements to Hattie and headed for the elevator, and the green-shaded lamps magically disappeared from view. Once again the only light in the room was provided by the night sky outside the expanse of glass.

So many stars. More than Vanessa had ever before seen. Scattered about like fairy dust. And the moon was in its slightly deformed, more-than-half, less-than-full configuration that Vanessa now knew was its "gibbous phase," a factoid that she had picked up from Lily, who had actually liked her science class last year and claimed to have found the unit on astronomy "fascinating." But maybe that was because the teacher was a young, attractive male, whom both Lily and Beth agreed was "drop-dead gorgeous."

Vanessa looked at the glowing dial of her watch. The time difference between Colorado and France was seven hours, and her daughters would still be in bed. They awakened to crowing roosters and church bells in the morning and always had their *petit déjeuner sur la terrasse*. Every conversation with them was peppered with more and more French. She wished she were there with them, even if her mother was sleeping with a Frenchman under the same roof. She missed her daughters. Missed her mother. Missed her dear departed father.

She was glad that her father never knew his mother. What a disappointment she would have been.

TWENTY-ONE

*M*YRNA felt the gaze of the three women who genetically were her granddaughters but for whom she had no feeling whatsoever. Of course, it was no surprise that the baby she'd had in prison probably grew up to have children of his own. She'd always had a codicil in her will that excluded any progeny who were not mentioned by name. But that was just a precaution. She never really expected to meet these hypothetical grandchildren.

Myrna thought she had erased Hattie decades ago, long before she began her rise to prominence. When the John Coulter County Courthouse burned down, the record of Hattie's birth and the court records of her trial were destroyed. Doing away with newspaper articles that detailed her crime, trial, and the trial's outcome had been easier to accomplish: all it took was a visit to the newspaper morgue of the *John Coulter County News* with a pair of scissors in her purse. And all it took to purge the state archives of her prison records was to slip them in a briefcase and walk out the door.

But she had forgotten about the yearbooks.

And she had forgotten about the stupid questionnaire she had filled out the first day of her incarceration. Not an official record. Just a piece of trivia. Who would think that such an insignificant artifact would survive all these years? Maybe other incriminating information was stashed away in other files. Maybe no one could ever completely escape his or her past.

The three sisters were watching her expectantly. Myrna realized that the middle sister—Ellie—looked a bit like her favorite granddaughter but immediately pushed the thought aside.

Their meddling into her life was beyond annoying. It threatened all her hopes and dreams for the future.

So why was she willing to share with them the story of how she came to bear the child that had become their father? It certainly wasn't because she thought they had a right to know. But she might as well give them what they came for before she dealt out their punishment.

So strange that they should come looking for her at this particular time. For more than six decades she had lived in the present and for the future, but over the last few months thoughts of the time when she was still Hattie had been much with her. In fact, the past had been so much with her of late that it was as though she had been mentally preparing for her part in this evening's proceedings.

She would begin with her memories of her parents and her little brother, Patrick.

Patrick. Myrna closed her eyes and searched her mind for an image of him. A little red-haired, blue-eyed boy with a clubfoot riding on his father's shoulders. Those were hard times for her family. But even though Patrick was crippled and her parents had to work hard from dawn to dusk, those had been the sweetest years of her life. And so she began telling them about the shanty house and the poverty and the love. And how that period of her life ended with her father leaving for Alaska and her brother's death.

"I had just finished the eighth grade when my father returned from Alaska, already a broken man, his health compromised and his grief over losing Patrick profound," she told her listeners. Then she described her father's illness and how the only thing between them and starvation was charity and the eggs her mother sold. She described her papa's suffering in excruciating detail and explained the role she had played in his death.

"You really ended your own father's life?" Vanessa, the oldest of the sisters, asked, incredulous. She glanced at her sisters, who obviously shared her shock.

"One does not lie about something like that," Myrna snapped. "Wouldn't you have done the same thing if your terminally ill father was suffering mightily and had asked it of you?"

Vanessa drew in her breath. "I . . . I don't know," she stammered.

"Were you with your father when he died?" Myrna asked.

Vanessa shook her head.

"Well then, how would you feel if your mother or one of your sisters had committed a mercy killing?"

Vanessa felt her cheeks grow warm with frustration or anger, but before she could respond, Ellie said, "I was with him. Daddy was in a coma at the time of his death. And if he hadn't been, there would have been drugs to alleviate pain, so there would have been no need to do something like that."

"I suppose," Myrna said. "And you are city girls.

You've never put a suffering animal out of its misery. Never wrung a chicken's neck. Never seen a screaming pig hanging by its hind feet from the rafters and bleeding to death out of a slit in its throat so its flesh will be edible. Never prepared a human body for burial."

"Why are you even bringing up such things?" Vanessa demanded. "I am deeply sorry that your father suffered so much, and I realize it took a tremendous amount of courage for you to do what you did. But what happened that night is between you and your conscience. I was expressing surprise, not condemnation."

"Maybe we should continue this in the morning," Georgiana piped in with a worried frown on her face.

Hattie shook her head. "I have other plans for tomorrow. If you want to hear the rest of the story, you will hear it tonight or not at all."

"Willy said that you wanted us to spend the rest of our vacation here with you," Vanessa pointed out. "Obviously she was mistaken."

"I never should have involved her," Hattie said. "I wasn't thinking straight when I asked her to track you down. Apparently the poor dear got all caught up in the idea that three granddaughters I didn't know existed had come looking for me. Probably she thought I would want to get to know you and for you to meet my family, but she now realizes that is not the case."

Hattie paused. "So do you want to hear the rest, or not?"

Vanessa glanced at her sisters.

Ellie and Georgiana both responded with a nod. They'd come all this way to hear Hattie's story. If tonight was to be their only opportunity, then they wanted to let her finish.

"Very well," the woman they knew as Hattie said. "But first I need to take a break."

Myrna used the restroom then went out on the deck for a few minutes to breathe in some of the crisp night air and calm the anger seething within her at how those three women had disrupted her life and peace of mind.

The stupid little newspaper story about their search for a woman named Hattie would appear in other newspapers. It was just the sort of mindless human-interest story with which newspapers like to pad their pages and could eventually be in dozens of newspapers. Maybe hundreds. The story *and* the yearbook picture. With these three being from New York City, she wouldn't be surprised if they ended up in the *New York Times*.

Why, just as decades of dreaming and meticulous planning were falling into place, was this happening to her?

She would see to it that any yearbooks from her years at Coal Town High School were removed from the school library, but that was like closing the barn door after the horse had already departed. Of course, there would be numerous copies from those years stashed away in attics or on closet shelves. How many students from that time were still alive? she wondered. The majority were probably dead, but not all. There would be others who, like her, were still active, still with all their mental faculties. Probably just a glance at that picture in a newspaper would not ring a bell, but if they read the article and discovered that the girl in the picture had gone to Coal Town High School, they would take a second look and then pull a yearbook down from the shelf or from a box in the attic. But even if they recognized the girl from back then, there was no way they could connect the girl named Hattie Worth to Myrna Cunningham.

Myrna touched her face, wondering how much had she'd changed? Would people in her present life see a resemblance between her and the girl in that old yearbook picture?

That was highly unlikely, she decided. Not after all these years.

The only people who could connect Hattie Worth to the woman she was now were the three women sitting here in this room.

And Willy. Her dear Willy.

Damn those three women! Damn them to hell.

TWENTY-TWO

*M*YRNA would have loved to have a glass of wine to calm herself, but she needed to keep her head clear and poured herself a glass of water from the pitcher on the credenza. Wine would come later when Willy served their late-evening repast.

And after the business of the evening had ended, she would never have to deal with these women again.

She downed the glass of water, then returned to her place at the head of the conference table and allowed her mind to return to Hattie and the drab little shack of a house just outside Coal Town.

"I helped my mother wash my father's dead body," she said.

All that was left of her papa was skin and bones. Her mother had covered his private parts with a towel, and Hattie looked away when she washed him down there. They dressed him in his best clothes, and Hattie sat with him while poor Mama walked back to town to get the undertaker. By then the snow had buried the road and was drifting against the house. Hattie waited all through the day wondering if her mother was lost in the snow and had maybe frozen to death. Then she would be both fatherless and motherless. An orphan like she read about in books.

So quiet it was without Papa's breathing. Just the sound of the house creaking under the weight of the snow on the roof.

To push back the quiet and pass the time, Hattie picked up her book and kept on reading to her dead father, stopping every so often to put some coal in the potbellied stove. When she finished *Robinson Crusoe*, she read from the Bible, understanding little and questioning such passages as "But if any provide not for his own and specially for those of his own house, he hath denied the faith, and is worse than an infidel." Her papa had done his best. What sort of God would judge him badly?

It was evening before Mama and the undertaker arrived in the hearse.

The funeral was two days later. It was bitterly cold, but the snow had stopped, and the sun was shining. Along with neighbors and church people, many of the men Papa had worked with in the mine attended, even though they would have their pay docked for the hours they were away from work.

Like Patrick, Papa was buried in a wooden casket. Hattie wondered how Mama had paid for even that. Perhaps the undertaker was letting her pay for it a little bit at a time.

The preacher droned on, but the hymns sounded especially beautiful in the crisp, cold, snow-covered stillness. The hymns made her papa's funeral beautiful. Hattie wasn't sure there was any such place as heaven, but if there was, her father should be there. With Patrick.

Hattie began to realize the very next day just how much her father's passing would change her life. Each of her teachers called her to their desk and told her in a soft voice how sorry they were for her loss. When she walked back to her desk, her classmates averted their eyes.

Hattie had never had a best friend, but she had always been accepted by the other miners' daughters and congregated with them in the halls between classes. But after her father died, when she walked down the hall even the daughters of miners acted as though they didn't see her. Hattie now represented their worst nightmare. The miner's life had killed her father, and Mr. Sedgwick had not done right by him and his family. Hattie and her mother were facing even harder times than they had just endured.

The landlord had told Mama that he wouldn't put a dying man out in the cold, but after Papa was gone he expected them to pay up or leave. After the funeral, when the landlord came on the first of the month to collect the rent, Mama would hand Hattie a blanket and send her to the shed.

Mama began taking in ironing, with the ironing board becoming a permanent fixture in their tiny front room. The old Ford still needed a battery so Mama still put her eggs in the wheelbarrow and pushed it into town every Saturday morning, but at least the worst of winter seemed to be over.

That spring she and Mama planted their garden as always, and Hattie did most the tending. Then one night a man who wasn't the landlord came knocking at the door, a man Hattie didn't know. Mama stepped out on the porch to talk to him, closing the door behind her. Shortly, she came back in the house and told Hattie to go to the shed. As Hattie was going out the back door, she heard Mama opening the front door to let the man in.

Other men began to come. Sometimes, while Hattie was alone out in the shed, she would revive an old fantasy. Her little brother, Patrick, was still alive. The doctor in Billings thought he was such a pretty little boy with his red curls and blue eyes and rosy cheeks, and he and his wife had never been able to have children so he told Mama that Patrick had died and took him home to be raised as his own. The wooden casket that Mama buried had contained a bag of sand. Hattie imagined the day that she would be strolling along a street in a place that wasn't Coal Town and she would see this handsome boy and know at once that he was her little brother. They would come fetch Mama and the three of them would live together someplace nice with no winter and no coal mines.

When winter rolled around again, Hattie refused to go to the shed when men came and went to her room instead. Her "room" was a lean-to that Papa had built on the house after Patrick was born. It was furnished with a narrow bed and a table and chair. Her clothes hung from hooks on the wall, and her other possessions were kept under the bed. The only light came from a lamp plugged into the same extension cord they used for the iron. Instead of a door, there was a curtain made from an old blanket. In the evening, whenever there was a knock on the door, Hattie went to her little room. Sometimes she peaked around the blanket to see who it was that night. Sometimes she didn't want to know. Because of those men, they had a roof over their heads, a car that ran, and money for food and coal. When men didn't come, she and her mother ate eggs and whatever their garden had provided, and Hattie would pick up the coal along the railroad tracks to fuel the potbellied stove and the cookstove. They managed. But there was no money for clothes and shoes. By then Hattie was a beanpole of a girl and taller than her mother. Mama would let down the hem and take in the waist of her own well-worn skirts and dresses so that Hattie would have something to wear to school.

Hattie hated going to school in her made-over clothes and shoes that hurt her feet. She hated Coal Town, hated the mining company that had caused her father's death, hated the man who owned that company, hated the men who came in the night and kept her and her mother from starving, hated the schoolmates who snubbed her, hated the people who looked the other way when she and her mother walked down the street, hated the preacher who told Mama she was a fallen woman and that she and her daughter could no longer attend his church. Except for a few of the teachers who loaned her books and encouraged her, Hattie hated the entire population of Coal Town, Montana.

Her goal was to leave as soon as she graduated from high school and never come back, not even to see her mother. Maybe Mama had done the best she could, but what she had done made Hattie not love her anymore. Hattie had lost her little brother and her father, and she no longer respected her mother.

Hattie started thinking about West Virginia, a state that she knew nothing about except that the aunt she'd never met lived there. Papa had asked Mama to let his sister in Pikesville, West Virginia, know when he died and tell her that he always remembered her kindly and was sorry things had been the way they were. Pikesville was not a pretty name, and maybe it wasn't any nicer than Coal Town, but it would be a place to start over. When Mama never got around to writing to Vera about Papa's passing, Hattie decided to do it herself. And not just because Papa had requested that Vera be informed. Hattie figured since Vera had inherited a farm that should by all rights have been bequeathed, at least in part, to Hattie's father, Vera couldn't very well turn away his only living child. And since Vera was a spinster lady with no children of her own, she would have to bequeath the farm to Hattie, who was her closest living relative.

Hattie was a late bloomer but finally began to fill out. And some of the men who visited her mother began asking about her. She could hear such conversations just the other side of the curtain. Mama would laugh as if they were making a joke. "Why, she's just a child," she would say.

Then one evening while they ate the last of a pot of watery stew in the shabby kitchen with the linoleum worn clear though and soot on the wall behind the cookstove, Mama took only a few bites, then put down her spoon and stared past Hattie's shoulder at the corner of the room and told her that a man had offered a lot of money to be the very first to have "sexual intercourse" with her.

Hattie had never heard the term before, but she realized what it meant. "How much is 'a lot of money'?" she asked.

At first Mama looked shocked by her question, then her eyes filled with tears. "I shouldn't have told you about him."

"How much is 'a lot of money'?" Hattie repeated.

"He said he would pay fifty dollars if he really was the first," Mama said, looking down at her lap.

"How would he know?"

"The first time a woman bleeds."

"Why?"

"Because the man uses his thing to poke open a hole in her."

"And men like that?"

"Yes, I guess they do," Mama said with a sigh. "The first time a girl doesn't know anything about pleasing a man, but I guess it gives him something to brag about."

"Does it hurt?"

"Yes."

"Is there a lot of blood?"

"Can be."

"Did Papa do it to you the first time or did some other man?"

"He was the first," Mama said, toying with her spoon. "It was our wedding night, and I never had sexual intercourse with another man until after your father passed away. But even before that, men had been asking, and sometimes they would slip me money and say they would settle with me later, meaning after your poor father was dead. The undertaker was one of those men. He knew I wouldn't have any money to bury your father when the time came."

Mama put her hand on Hattie's. "We are dirt-poor, Hattie. You might not like what I do, but we still have a roof over our heads and a car that gets us where we're going and so far we haven't starved."

Hattie pulled her hand away. "Why didn't you go to work in a store or clean houses?"

"I tried to find work," Mama said, rubbing her forehead the why she did when she was getting a headache, "but I was tired after taking care of a sick husband and peddling eggs and vegetables and keeping his poor dying body clean and washing all that soiled bedding. My hands have been raw for years from all that washing and wringing and hanging laundry no matter what the weather. I just didn't have the energy for cleaning up after other people or standing on my feet all day in a store. After I paid my 'debt' to the undertaker with coffins all around and his wife upstairs in the apartment cooking his dinner, the only man I did it with was Mr. Hadley, so he wouldn't kick us out of the house. He said his wife was real sick and couldn't do it anymore and he sure missed it and he thought I was a pretty lady and the money he gave me seemed more like a gift than a payment. I was sort of hoping that when his wife died, he would marry me, and our troubles would be over. But she didn't die, and other men started coming. I tried to be discreet and not let the word get around town. I tried to make each man think he was the only one. But before I knew it, I was the town whore and no man is ever going to marry me."

"This man who wants to be the first, how was he dressed?" Hattie asked. "Was he a farmer or a miner?"

"Neither. He works at the front office at the mine and was wearing a suit and tie."

"What about his shoes?"

"What about them?"

"Were they shiny and new or ratty and old?"

"He was wearing shiny black shoes that looked brand-new."

"Has he been in your bed?"

"No. He came here to ask about you."

"How does he know about me?"

"He said that he's seen you waiting for the school bus."

"How did he know that I'm your daughter?"

Mama's shoulders sagged. "I don't know, Hattie. I just opened the door and he asked if I had a daughter named Hattie. Then he wanted to know if you were a virgin." Hattie frowned. "What's that?"

"Oh, God," Mama moaned and began shaking her head. "Just forget the whole thing."

"What is a virgin?" Hattie demanded.

"It's a girl who has never had sex with a man."

"Tell this man I'll do it if he gives me two hundred dollars up front, and I want the money the day before so I have time to hide it away someplace where he won't find it and take it back."

Mama shook her head. "No man is ever going to pay that much for sex—not in a hundred years. And besides, that's not how it's done."

"I know how it's done. After they pull on their pants, they're supposed to leave money on the bureau before they leave. But sometimes they don't leave as much as they promised, do they? And sometimes they just walk out the door without leaving a dime."

Wordlessly Mama picked up the two soup bowls and carried them to the sink. Her shoulders were hunched over. Hattie realized that her mother wasn't pretty anymore. The skin under her chin was starting to sag, and dark circles were under her eyes. She looked gaunt and haggard and just plain worn-out.

"I want the money first," Hattie repeated.

For the next two days, Hattie felt as though she were holding her breath. With two hundred dollars she could ride the train to West Virginia and maybe even have some left over in case Aunt Vera wouldn't take her in. On the third afternoon, when she got home from school, her mother had been crying and her lip was split open. "I shouldn't have told you about him," she said. "You don't have to do this, Hattie. I don't want you to do this. I forbid you to."

"Is he going to pay two hundred dollars?"

Mama sank into a chair. "He'll bring it by this evening and then leave for thirty minutes so you can hide the money away."

Hattie was too nervous to eat dinner. She put on the only halfway decent dress she owned and put her hair up.

When the knock on the door came, she remained in the front room.

Mama opened the door.

He was a tall, well-built man in his midtwenties and looked vaguely familiar. He was wearing a brown suit, and his fingernails were clean. He looked Hattie up and down. She could see the desire in his face, and it made her feel powerful.

She held out her hand for the money that he was supposed to put there.

"You little bitch!" he said. "For two hundred dollars I could buy this shack and burn it to the ground."

Then suddenly Hattie knew exactly who this man was. She'd seen him years ago standing beside his father in front of the bank. He was Mr. Sedgwick's son, who had gone to a fancy college back East and was now back in Coal Town with his new wife to learn how to run the family business.

Her mother had been watching this exchange with a look that was half fear, half bewilderment. Hattie understood. She had always been such a meek, quiet girl. Her mother didn't know the girl who had stood up to someone as high-and-mighty as Mr. Sedgwick's son.

Mr. Sedgwick's son threw a wad of bills on the floor. "I'll be back in thirty minutes, and I want you alone in this house and buck naked."

He slammed the door so hard the entire house shook.

Hattie realized that she had overplayed her hand. Mama was crying and waving her hands around like a crazy woman. "He's real mad, Hattie. He's going to hurt you."

Hattie stared at the bills scattered on the floor. Tens and twenties. She had planned to the take the money and run. Under her bed was a freshly laundered feed sack filled with her clothes. But if she wasn't here when he returned, Mr. Sedgwick's son would take his anger out on her mother. She didn't love her mother anymore, but she didn't want anything bad to happen to her.

Using her mother's gesture, Hattie rubbed her forehead. Harder and harder she rubbed it. She had to plan. Had to think.

First the money.

She picked it up and put it in the feed sack with her clothes. Then she went to the kitchen and grabbed a butcher knife.

When her mother saw the knife, she started to scream, "No, Hattie. No!"

"Shut up!" Hattie yelled. "Just *shut up*. I want you to go out to the shed and stay there until I come get you."

When the car pulled up into the yard, Hattie stood by the door, her back pressed against the wall, the butcher knife in her hand.

The door burst open:

Mr. Sedgwick's son took one step, then stopped, looking around the seemingly empty room.

Hattie plunged the knife into the side of his neck. Then she pulled out the knife and slid it across his throat.

Mr. Sedgwick's son fell to his knees, blood gushing from both wounds.

Hattie stabbed him in the back, the blade scraping against bone.

He fell on his side. His eyes were wide and bulging, his mouth opened as though to scream, but no sound came. Only blood.

She pushed him onto his back and began stabbing his belly again and again. Stabbing the son of the man who had killed her father. The son of the man who denied her mother money that was rightfully hers and turned her into a whore. It was hard work, all that stabbing. And so bloody. So much blood. The man's eyes were still open, but she could tell that he was dead.

She sat back on her haunches, put down the knife, and regarded the mutilated body.

Then she went to fetch her mother.

Mama took one look at her bloody dress and began to scream. Hattie put a hand over her mouth. They had no close neighbors, but she didn't know how far a scream could travel.

Hattie told her mother to drive the man's car around back. Then they rolled his body onto a blanket and dragged it out to the car and somehow wrestled it into the trunk of the man's shiny black Oldsmobile sedan. Hattie siphoned some of the gas from the Oldsmobile to put in the Ford's almost empty tank.

Then they went inside to change out of their blood-stained clothing, and Mama filled a jar with water and made two sandwiches with stale bread and sliced tomatoes. "What do we do now?" she asked her daughter.

"Remember the quarry lake we went to one Sunday afternoon?" Hattie asked. "You and Papa and Patrick and me."

"I remember the lake but I don't remember where it was, Hattie. That was a long time ago."

"Think, Mama. Close your eyes and think. You fixed a picnic lunch. We stopped for gas at a service station that had an old Model T Ford sitting on the roof. Papa gave me a nickel to buy a Coke from a machine. I shared it with Patrick. We went through a town where the signs on the storefronts were written in German."

Hattie's only experience driving a car consisted of driving into town with Mama at her side. But it was night and there was little traffic. She focused on the taillights of the Oldsmobile. Mama drove slowly heading east. Hattie never saw the service station with the Model T on the roof, but she followed the Oldsmobile's taillights through the town with signs on the storefronts written in German. It was almost dawn when the headlights of the Oldsmobile illuminated a wooden sign that said QUARRY LAKE with an arrow pointing down a rutted country lane that disappeared into a thick growth of pine trees. The lane sloped downward, and when they emerged from the trees, it continued to the edge of the quarry, then began a gentle circling descent down the steep walls to the water's edge. Mama went in the other direction heading for the far side of the huge man-made crater where there was a sheer drop to the water below. Hattie followed.

Mama pulled the Oldsmobile close to the edge and got out.

Side by side, mother and daughter stood looking down at the water. Calm, black water reflecting the moonlight. "Let's get this over with," Hattie said.

Mama released the brake, and together they pushed the car over the edge. It hit the water front-first, then slowly and gracefully slipped from view.

Mama drove the Ford on the way home. It was daylight when they arrived.

They worked throughout the day cleaning the house. There was only one scrub brush so they took turns scrubbing the blood-soaked wooden floor, with the other emptying the bucket then refilling it. Again and again. Hattie burned their blood-soaked clothing in the potbellied stove. When they were finally finished, Hattie washed herself, put on clean clothes, and pulled the feed sack from under her bed.

Her mama had fallen asleep in the rocking chair, her head lolling to one side. Hattie wished it was Mr. Sedgwick

himself that she had killed. Because of him, her parents became paupers, and her mother had lost herself.

Hattie opened the sack and pulled out the roll of bills.
She peeled off a twenty and placed the rest in her mother's
lap.

She would get more money, Hattie vowed. And not
by spreading her legs for men. She would rob a bank if she
needed to and ride the train to Pikesville, West Virginia.

TWENTY-THREE

*G*EORGIANA realized she had been holding her breath and slowly exhaled while she watched the white-haired woman lean back in her chair, focusing once again on the present and her three visitors. "I never made it to West Virginia and I never met Vera Wentworth," Hattie said.

Georgiana glanced at her sisters to see how they were dealing with the woman's grisly story, which seemed too far-fetched to be true.

Could Hattie have made it all up?

But why would anyone lie about something like that? And why would she tell three people she'd only just met that she had once killed a man? Not a dying man like Hattie's father. Not an accidental killing either. She had deliberately killed the son of the man who owned the Coal Town mine. The man probably meant her harm, but Hattie and her mother should have left the house after he dropped off the two hundred dollars. They could have driven to town and sworn out a complaint against the man. After all, the man had been soliciting sex with a minor.

Of course, the man Hattie killed was the son of the most powerful man in the community, and maybe the sheriff took his orders from his father—from Mr. Sedgwick, who would have hired detectives to look for his son and the black Oldsmobile sedan. His son probably was as terrible a man as Hattie indicated. But his father would have loved him. Mr. Sedgwick probably spent the rest of his life trying to find his son. He would have grieved greatly. And his wife, too. Georgiana wondered if they had other children. If the bride that their son had brought from back East was pregnant and provided them with a grandchild who helped assuage their grief.

"Was that man's body ever found?" Ellie asked from across the table.

"No," Hattie said, rising. "As far as I know, he and that car are still down there on the bottom of that quarry."

"So that wasn't why you were sent to prison?" Vanessa asked.

"No, it was not."

"Then why did you tell us about it?" Georgiana asked, puzzled. "I'd think something like that would be the sort of secret one carried to the grave."

"Yes, that would be the most prudent thing to do, wouldn't it?" Hattie locked her fingers at the back of her neck and stretched a bit.

"It sounded like you planned all along to take his money," Vanessa commented. "Which given your situation, I can understand. But did you also plan to kill him?"

"I don't know that I planned anything," Hattie said, irritation in her voice. "I was just improvising. Killing him seemed like the best way out of a bad situation. Can you girls honestly tell me that you would have done otherwise?"

"When you put it like that, I suppose not," Ellie said from her side of the table.

Georgiana was tired. Exhausted really. And disturbed by the story she had just heard. She wondered how long Hattie's tale would continue. Hopefully they had already heard the worst, and the rest would be clear sailing. "I'm going to take a break," she announced, and rose from her chair.

She used the bathroom, then stepped out on the moonlit deck. It was cold, and her arms were bare, but Georgiana stood next to the railing for a time feeling as if she were on a ship at sea. Such a house. Like something out of a movie. Not real life.

Georgiana wished she had never left her real life. Wished she were back home in her cluttered apartment with Freddy on his way over. *Her darling Freddy.* She needed to hear the voice of that sweet, uncomplicated boy. She would remind Willy about bringing them a phone and call him tonight when their session with Hattie concluded.

What a disappointment the woman had been. Their long-lost grandmother was not likable. And maybe she was a liar. The more Georgiana thought about it, the more she found Hattie's story about stabbing that man and dumping him in a lake hard to believe. It was like something out of a movie and not from real life.

Georgiana inhaled deeply in an attempt to invigorate herself with the crisp, cold, clean air, then went back into the room. A lamp on the credenza had been turned on and cast long shadows across the room.

Hattie and her sisters were seated at the table, waiting in silence. Georgiana slipped into her place.

"Why were you sent to prison?" Vanessa demanded of Hattie.

Hattie held up her hand. "We'll get that in due time." Then she became very still.

For a long time she said nothing. When finally she began to speak, her gaze had once again grown distant.

Myrna recalled how, with no sleep the night before, she had been exhausted as she left her mother sleeping in the rocking chair and walked away from the only home she'd ever known.

She wanted to put some distance between herself and Coal Town as quickly as possible but didn't dare hitchhike for fear someone she knew might offer her a ride. Whenever a vehicle approached, she would duck into the tall grass that grew alongside the road. She walked all night to get to the highway, where she got plenty of offers for rides but always from men. She ignored them and kept walking. East. Finally she was so exhausted she curled up behind a tree and used the feed sack that held her possessions for a pillow and slept for a time.

When she started walking again, an elderly couple in a pickup truck stopped.

"If you don't mind sharing, you can get in back," the woman told her.

Hattie went around back. The bed of the truck had wooden-slat sides. A boy in overalls was sitting in the front leaning against the cab, a boy with red curls showing beneath his billed cap and blue eyes and rosy cheeks and a mouth so pretty she had to look twice to make sure he was a boy. Her breath caught in her chest. That's how her brother would have looked if he were still alive. And for an instant she wondered if her daydream had come true. If Patrick were still alive. But this boy was older than she was. Not younger.

He nodded at her.

She tossed the feed sack into the truck and climbed

over the rusty tailgate. Once again using the sack for a pillow, she tried to make herself comfortable, but the road was rough, and the truck's springs were shot. And besides, she was aware of the boy watching her.

She scooted to the front of the truck to get out of the wind and to inspect the beautiful boy. He smiled at her. "Where are you headed?" he asked, raising his voice to make himself heard.

"As far as they'll take me," she said, nodding toward the couple in the cab of the truck.

"You running away from home?"

Hattie pretended that she didn't hear him.

The boy dozed off and Hattie tried to do the same, but the bumps were too jarring.

The truck slowed as it entered a town that Hattie recognized as Hayes, which seemed like a metropolis compared to dinky little Coal Town. The truck stopped in front of the county courthouse, and the elderly couple got out. "We got business in town, then we're heading back home," the old man told them.

Hattie didn't want to be in Hayes. It was too close to home. When the pretty boy jumped out of the truck and headed east, she followed. On the outskirts of town, he reached in his duffel bag and handed her an apple. "Name's Josh."

"I'm Mary," she lied.

The apple was crunchy and tasted wonderful. When she finished, he handed her a canteen.

"Where are you going?" she asked.

"Eventually I hope to end up someplace where I can get paid to play baseball. A town with a farm club. But first I've got to make some money."

"Me, too," Hattie said. "What's a farm club?"

Josh explained about baseball farm clubs as they trudged along and how a fellow had to play for peanuts in hopes of getting himself noticed. He was good though—damned good—and had no doubt his big break would come. He had played high school baseball over in Big Timber, but major league teams didn't send scouts to little, no-account towns in Montana. So he was heading East. To Indiana maybe. Or Kentucky. States that had farm clubs. But in the meantime, he needed to find work. It was too early to get on with a combine crew, but he could do any kind of farmwork. He'd grown up on a hog farm. Nasty work. He never wanted to see another hog for as long as he lived.

Then Josh wanted to know where she was from and why a girl was out hitchhiking. Didn't she know that could be dangerous, especially for a pretty girl like her? She didn't tell him much—just that her father died and she left home. She was flattered that he thought she was pretty and worried that she was blushing.

A couple of miles out from Hayes, Josh stopped to study a large, white farmhouse in the middle of a field of sugar beets. "The beets need hoeing," he pointed out.

Hattie followed him down a rutted lane. Trash was blowing about the yard, and a rusting Chevy truck and a dust-covered Chrysler sedan stood in front of the barn. One of the barn doors was hanging on one hinge.

They walked around the house and Josh knocked on the back door. A tall, angular woman with graying hair appeared at the screen door, drying her hands on an apron.

"Good afternoon, ma'am," Josh said as he took off his cap. "My sister and I are looking for work."

Hattie coughed a bit to cover up her surprise at his words. The boy who reminded her of her brother had just called her his sister!

"I'll have to talk to my husband," the woman said.

"We'll work for food and a place to sleep and whatever you think we're worth in pay," Josh offered.

Hattie felt the woman taking a second look at them. "How old are you?" she asked Josh.

"Eighteen next month. My sister just turned fifteen. Our parents have both passed, and the sheriff sold our place up by Reed Point for back taxes. We've been on the road for two days now. We saw this fine-looking house and thought whoever lived here might need some help looking after things."

Just then there was a pounding sound overhead.

The woman closed her eyes and drew in her breath. "I need to see to my husband."

"Yes, ma'am," Josh said. "You go 'bout your business. We'll just sit here in the shade for a time, if that's all right with you."

They sat on the stoop saying nothing. They could hear the woman bustling about the kitchen. Shortly the pounding began again. Through the screen door, they could see her carrying a tray down the hallway and starting up the stairs.

"For the record, I'm sixteen," Hattie informed Josh.

He nodded.

"You'll full of blarney," Hattie said.

"Think so?"

"Know so."

"Yeah, but does the lady of the house know I'm full of it?" He nudged Hattie in the ribs with his elbow.

Hattie moved away from him. "I really am hungry."

"Tell the lady. Open those big blue eyes and get a pitiful look on your face."

When the lady came back to the screen door, they scrambled to their feet. Hattie took a step forward, then let her legs go limp under her. Josh kneeled beside her. "Please, ma'am," he said. "We could sure use a bit of grub. Then we'll quit bothering you and be on our way."

She brought them four fried-egg sandwiches stacked on a plate and a pitcher of water. She said if they would weed her garden, rake the chicken yard, and fix the barn door, she would feed them again that evening and they could sleep in the barn. The cow had died. They'd have the place to themselves.

At dusk she brought out two bowls of stew and another pitcher of water, then went to inspect the garden, chicken yard, and barn door.

When she returned, she said, "You can stay through the week. My husband is down on his back, and chores have gone undone."

Hattie was to work in the house, and for starters the woman wanted Josh to hoe the beets, clean out the barn, and whitewash the fences. If they did their work well, she would give Hattie four dollars and Josh seven at the end of the week.

That night Hattie carried a bucket of water to the barn, leaving Josh to wash up at the pump. She went into a stall for privacy and washed herself as best she could. She had a nightgown in the feed sack but thought it would be improper to wear it when she and Josh would be sleeping in such proximity and pulled a clean dress over her damp body.

She rinsed out her sweat-soaked dress and put it over the top fence rail to dry. With the blanket the woman had provided for her tucked under her arm, she climbed the ladder to the hayloft. Josh was already there, shirtless and stretched out on his blanket.

"I've never been so tired in my life," Hattie said as she spread out her own blanket on the hay some distance from his. "That woman expected me to do a week's worth of cleaning in just one day."

Josh told her good night and turned his back to her.

When Hattie closed her eyes, she still saw him—the young man who looked like her brother, Patrick. That was why she felt so kindly toward Josh, she decided. He reminded her of her brother.

Myrna paused, trying to decide just how much more of her story she wanted to share with these women.

She hadn't thought of that time in any significant way for years, yet it represented a turning point in her life. If she had submitted to Mr. Sedgwick's virgin-seeking son, would her life have taken a different course? Would the experience have been so dreadful that she would have been frigid for the rest of her life and hated everyone with a penis? Maybe she would have entered a convent and become a nun so she would never have to be around men again.

Perhaps she'd had sexual yearnings before that night in the hayloft of a barn east of Hayes, Montana, but she could not recall them. Unless her memory was playing tricks on her, she had never touched herself down there, never thought about sex. Her father had been the center of her life, the person she loved above all others, and in the last years of his life as she was changing from a child to a young woman, that relationship had taken on a somewhat sanctified meaning to her. Papa was the finest, dearest, gentlest, best person she had ever known. To this day she felt that way. No other man had ever even come close to his revered status in her life. And perhaps she had backed away from sexual thoughts because they would have somehow desanctified her relationship with her father. But whatever the reason, she was unprepared for her attraction to Josh, which had perhaps been tinged with incestuous overtones since he reminded her so much of the little brother she had loved and mothered.

Josh's breathing was peaceful and deep, not quite a snore but definitely the sound of sleep. Thanks to her mother's warnings over the years, she was knowledgeable enough about male behavior to know that most males, no matter how exhausted they were from their day's labors, would have forced themselves on a young, innocent, powerless runaway girl. Josh had chosen to do the honorable thing. She decided that he was the sort of young man Patrick would have grown up to be. And the urge to touch him was actually painful. In spite of her exhaustion, she desperately wanted to touch the skin on his chest. His hair. His lips. His chest. Her fingertips were on fire. Her heart was pounding.

She moved her blanket closer to him. With just the tip of a finger she touched his hair, still damp from washing. Touched his ear. Then his shoulder.

She wanted him to wake up.

But maybe he had been awake all along. When he finally rolled over to face her, he asked, "Are you a virgin?"

That word. *Virgin.* How strange to be hearing it again in such a short time. She'd heard the word before. The Virgin Mary. The Virgin Queen Elizabeth of England. The Virgin Islands, where Christopher Columbus landed on his second voyage. But she hadn't known what the word meant until her mother told her.

"Yes," she answered.

"You're supposed to save yourself for your wedding night. Every man wants his wife to be a virgin."

Hattie remembered her mother saying that the first time she had sex was on her wedding night and that she had been a virgin. Hattie wondered if it had been the first time for her father, too. "Are you a virgin?" she asked Josh.

"I don't think that's a word you're supposed to use for fellows, but I've never had sex before."

"Is it all right for a fellow who's never had sex before to kiss a virgin?"

"I guess so."

"Then I want you to kiss me," Hattie said.

He leaned over her and planted a soft kiss on her lips. She hadn't remembered putting her arms around his neck, but she must have because that's where they were. And she was pulling him back for a second kiss. Which lasted longer than the first. And was very pleasant.

But it ended too soon.

He whispered, "Mary." Again and again he said the word. At first Hattie wondered if he thought she was someone else. Then she remembered telling him that was her name.

Hattie rolled onto her side and pulled his face to hers. "My name is Hattie."

"Not Mary?"

"No, not Mary. Hattie."

"Hattie. Beautiful Hattie. Nice to meet you."

"Kiss me again."

This kiss was quite long with neither of them willing to end it.

Then suddenly his hand was touching her breast through the fabric of her dress, which made her gasp. And her back arched. Did she want him to do that?

His hand became motionless while he awaited her verdict.

For an answer, she placed her hand over his.

He groaned.

Hattie couldn't believe how wonderful it was to have him touch her breasts. A small mewing sound came from the back of her throat. Like a cat made when it was being stroked.

He was kissing her again, and his leg came across her body and he pushed his crotch against her leg. She experienced a momentary shock when the tip of his tongue began to make its presence known, tentatively as though he wasn't sure it was the proper thing to do. Hattie touched the tip of his tongue with the tip of hers, and her entire body responded as though it had been struck by lightning.

Hattie wanted the kissing and touching to go on forever. It was the most delightful thing she had ever experienced in her life. She opened her mouth for him and his tongue darted farther. She felt possessed by his tongue. It was magic. Josh of the magic tongue. And the magic lips. And hands.

And what about the rest of him?

By then their bodies had plastered themselves against one another, and he was rubbing his pelvis against her stomach. And of its own accord, her body reciprocated. They both were making animal sounds. Sounds of pleasure and desire and need.

He reached for her hand and placed it over the bulge in the front of his overalls. "I don't understand," Hattie whispered.

"It's because I want you," he whispered back. "It's what happens to a man when he wants a woman."

"Can I see it?"

She made him turn over on his back so that the square of moonlight streaming through the open hay door illuminated this most amazing sight. She had seen Patrick's little peepee many times when she changed his britches. And occasionally caught glimpses of her father's privates when he washed up out by the pump in the backyard. But neither her father's nor Patrick's privates looked anything like what was now poking out of the fly in Josh's overalls.

She was even more amazed when she touched it. It was as hard as a post. No wonder a man could poke a hole in a virgin.

But a man like Mr. Sedgwick's son, a man who didn't really like women, wanted to poke it in a virgin to hurt her. To make him feel big and strong and powerful and better than she was. Josh wasn't like that. Josh was nice. As her father had been. She unfastened the clasp on Josh's overalls. And he began inching her dress up her thigh.

"I like you," she told Josh, startled by the husky sound of her voice. "I want you to make me not be a virgin anymore."

Myrna closed her eyes and leaned her head against the high back of her chair. So long ago that had been, yet the memory of that night brought forth those same responses in her body.

What she wouldn't give to be young again. To have a man want her again.

She realized that she was clutching the arms of her chair and forced herself to relax. To push sexual thoughts aside.

"That young man in the barn was the father of your father," Myrna told her listeners.

"I'm glad he was someone nice," Ellie said.

"Did Josh ever get to play big-time baseball?" Georgiana asked. "Our father played baseball in high school. He had a framed certificate on his office wall that said he'd been named to the West Virginia All-State Baseball Team."

Myrna ignored Georgiana's question. She was thinking about the creek that Josh had discovered at the bottom of the back pasture that had a lovely swimming hole surrounded by willows and the spreading branches of a box elder. At the end of their second day, after the woman had brought them their meal, they raced each other the length of the pasture, kicked off their shoes, and jumped in. Splashing and laughing and ducking, they managed to rid themselves of clothing and made love in the water and again on the moss-covered bank. Then they put on their wet clothes and walked back to the barn and made love in the loft.

Making love was the most wonderful thing in the world. And Josh was the most beautiful boy in the world. Hattie found herself laughing and crying at the same time so great was her delight. They had little knowledge of their own bodies and the mechanics of lovemaking. For all they knew they were the first people ever to discover the secrets and delights of sex. And when they were satiated and poor Josh's penis could no longer be teased to erection, they fell asleep in each other's arms but awoke after a time and made their plans.

Deep into the night, they discussed and planned. They needed money. With enough money they could go anyplace they wanted and do whatever they wanted.

And the place where one went to get a significant amount of money was a bank.

Twenty-four

*E*ACH morning, the woman told Hattie what she wanted done and scrutinized her carefully throughout the day. Hattie tried just once to engage her in conversation, asking how long her husband had been bedridden.

"That is none of your concern," the woman said, her lips drawn in a tight line.

Even so, Hattie was able to learn a great deal about the occupants of the white farmhouse from their possessions. The framed photographs and certificates hanging on the walls revealed that the man was a Mason, a certified livestock auctioneer, and had fought in the war and was awarded a Purple Heart. The woman was past president of the John Coulter County Home Demonstration Club and a member of Eastern Star. They apparently had only one child—a son who had belonged to the Future Farmers of American and recently graduated from Eastern Montana College in Billings.

The man must also have been an avid hunter, judging from the gun case in the hallway.

And the woman liked to listen to radio programs in

the afternoon: *Young Widder Brown. Backstage Wife. The Guiding Light. The Romance of Helen Trent.*

The man glared at Hattie when she dusted his room. He kept a stick by the bed and pounded the floor with it when he wanted his wife to come tend to him—often during one of her programs—and spoke to her in a gruff voice that sounded as if he blamed her for his failing health. Hattie thought how her father had been sweet and kind through all his suffering.

She reported what she had learned about the man and the woman to Josh. He took a great interest in the gun case in the downstairs hallway.

The third morning when the woman was upstairs tending to her husband, Hattie motioned to Josh that it was all right for him to come inside. He stood in front of the gun cabinet, studying its contents and fiddling with the lock. Then he pulled open the drawer at the bottom of the cabinet, revealing boxes of ammunition, but quickly closed it and headed for the back door when he heard the woman's footsteps in the upstairs hallway.

The morning of their fourth day at the farm, the woman asked Josh if he knew how to drive. He assured her that he did. Then she asked if he knew anything about motors. Josh told her that his uncle owned a service station, and he had worked there weekends and summers since he was ten years old.

"I'd appreciate it if you'd take a look at the truck," she told him. "I haven't been able to get it started, and I'd hate to have to haul chicken feed in the Chrysler. If you get it started, I'll give you an extra two dollars."

An hour later he came to the back door and informed the woman that the truck needed a new battery and spark plugs. And she should really replace two of the tires. She put newspapers on the backseat of the Chrysler for Josh to sit on and drove him into Hayes so they could make the required purchases.

While they were gone, Hattie roamed about the downstairs opening drawers and examining what few books were on the shelves—almanacs, a history of the United States, *Robert's Rules of Order*, a Bible, and a book on etiquette called *The Perfect Woman* that said a woman should never raise her voice or say ungracious things to others. When the man pounded on the floor, she went upstairs. "Isn't she back yet?" he demanded.

Hattie shook her head and gave him a sip of water. While she was bending over, he pinched her breast.

The next time he pounded with his stick, she ignored the summons and continued her perusal of the downstairs.

When she heard the car pull up out back, she hurried back to the kitchen and busied herself scrubbing the floor.

By evening, the pickup was drivable, and the woman gave Josh the promised two dollars.

After dinner, as Hattie and Josh made their way down to the creek, he told her the truck would be their get-away vehicle.

"But the Chrysler would be faster and less likely to break down," she said.

"Yeah, but a big, shiny car like that would stand out like a sore thumb, especially with you and me inside. That old truck looks like every other old truck. And it will take us places that Chrysler can't go."

"Like where?"

"Like across fields and creeks and down rutted dirt roads. And besides, likely as not, I can fix it if it breaks down. I've already stashed a jack and some tools behind the seat."

Once again, after they made love, they talked long into the night. Josh had gone into the bank while the woman was at the feedstore. He explained how it was laid out. He wanted

Hattie to stand by the door with a rifle pointed at the bank president, whose desk was in the corner behind a railing, and Josh would deal with the two tellers. Much as he would like to empty the safe, it would take too long.

"We'll grab whatever cash the tellers have in their drawers and take off," he told her. "There's a deserted farmhouse just this side of town. You can hardly see it from the road for all the trees and weeds. I figure we'll go there and hide out for a few days. No one is going to look for us so close to town. The sheriff will think that we're heading south for the state line or north into Canada."

The next day, after the woman carried a breakfast tray upstairs, Josh came in the house and pulled the telephone cord from the wall, then pried open the lock on the gun cabinet. He loaded a rifle and carried it upstairs. Hattie followed.

She held the rifle while Josh tied the screaming man spread-eagled to his bed. The woman looked at them with accusing eyes but said nothing as Josh tied her to a chair.

Josh searched the house for money while Hattie carried food and blankets to the truck. She felt excited like when she was a little girl getting ready to go on a picnic. But she was worried, too. Worried that Josh wasn't smart enough to plan a bank robbery.

Josh stashed two rifles and boxes of ammunition behind the seat of the pickup and soon they were on their way into Hayes. Josh talked constantly, telling her over and over exactly where she was to stand and that she should keep the gun pointed right at the bank president's face. "If he tries to make a phone call, shoot him," Josh said.

Myrna's three listeners were looking at her wide-eyed and had obviously not been expecting guns and a bank robbery—maybe something less brazen such as taking money from a grocery-store cash register when the clerk's back was turned.

"I knew even then the scheme was a bad one," Myrna told them. "Josh and I were just two dumb kids. How could we expect to rob a bank and then drive off into the sunset and live happily ever after?

"But I never questioned his leadership in the endeavor," she admitted. "That was a mistake I never repeated. Since that time, I have run my own show.

"We parked directly in front of the bank and waited for two women to stroll past on the sidewalk." Myrna's heart grew heavy as she remembered that horrible day. The worst in her life. Worse even than when her father died. Her father's death had been inevitable. She had just hurried it along. But she could have prevented what happened that day in the First National Bank of Hayes, Montana.

"Josh gave me a kiss," she told her listeners, "and then he said, 'Let's go.' And there we were, two teenage kids carrying hunting rifles into a bank. There were two customers—a man in a straw hat and a woman with a little boy at her side. And just one teller—a middle-aged man with his thinning hair plastered to his skull. The president's desk was empty. It turned out that we arrived just after the bank president and the other teller had gone across the street to the café for their morning cup of coffee.

"Josh yelled, 'This is a stickup,' or something like that. The woman screamed and pushed her little boy behind her. The male customer put his hands in the air. And the teller ducked behind the counter. Josh leapt over the counter, and a shot rang out. And then another shot and Josh screamed. I found out later that the bank had been robbed before. Several times apparently. Each teller kept a loaded revolver in his cash drawer.

"The teller stood up and aimed his revolver at me and

told me to put the rifle on the counter. But I pointed the rifle at him and pulled the trigger. The look on his face was one of surprise. I don't think he thought a young girl like me would do such a thing. I dropped the rifle and crawled over the counter. Josh was on his back. The teller had shot him in the chest, but he was still alive. Not for long, though."

Myrna heard a gasp from one of her listeners. The young one—Georgiana—had her hands over her mouth and tears in her eyes for a man she'd never met. For Josh. The father of her father. The other two looked horrified that this was where her teenage love story had taken them.

"Fear was in Josh's eyes," Myrna continued, her voice a monotone. "He knew he was dying. I kissed him and told him that I loved him. Which I guess I really did. He was the only man I've cared for in such a sweet, trusting way. The teller was moaning beside us, blood spurting out of his chest. There was no point in trying to help him. He was dead before the sheriff arrived. Josh, too, but I stayed with him until the sheriff dragged me kicking and screaming off to jail. It wasn't going to jail I was protesting. I just didn't want to leave Josh.

"They put me in a cell with a concrete bench and a chamber pot, and a long time passed with no one coming to question me or turn me over to a lynch mob. Finally I called out that I was thirsty. When a deputy brought me a glass of water, I told him about the man and woman tied up in the two-story farmhouse. Finally the sheriff came. When he asked me my name, I told him Hattie Polanski. I don't really know why I did that. Polanski was Josh's last name. I'd asked him what his last name was only the day before. A Polish name. In the five days we had known each other, nothing had ever been said about marriage, but I guess I married him posthumously. Maybe I was trying to protect my mama or keep the Worth name untainted. But it didn't work. When a picture of Hattie

Polanski appeared in the county newspaper, people in Coal Town knew who it was. The daughter of the town whore. I was arraigned and tried as Hattie Polanski, though, and that's what I continued to be called in newspaper coverage of the crime and the trial. No one ever asked how I managed to get myself married while I was on the run. Not even Mama.

"Mama came to see me in the jail and brought me food and clean clothes. She never mentioned what happened to Mr. Sedgwick's son or the money I'd left for her. She never asked how come I tried to rob a bank or who the boy was that I was with and how I got hooked up with him. All she said was that she was sorry—like it was all her fault. But it wasn't. I'd been stupid to let an empty-headed boy tell me what to do. If Josh had been mean and ugly, I never would have gotten involved with him. But he was beautiful and tender and reminded me of my dead brother. And oddly enough, maybe the rest of my life wouldn't have turned out nearly as well if the two of us hadn't met in the back of that old truck with the wooden-slat sides. I would have just let one thing follow another and not set out a plan for myself.

"But after that dreadful fiasco, I have planned well and succeeded in every endeavor I have undertaken. I have exceeded even my own greatest expectations. After I escaped from Deer Lodge and established my new identity, I enrolled at the Western Colorado School of Mines, one of the first women ever admitted to what had been an all-male stronghold. They had no lodging for women students. Most of the buildings didn't even have restroom facilities for women. I managed, however, and worked harder and studied more than any of those male students and graduated at the top of my class. Instead of burning down Coal Town as I'd always intended, I bought—thanks to a wealthy husband—the mine from Mr. Sedgwick's heirs. It had been closed for years, and they probably thought they were unloading an albatross. But I'm getting ahead of myself," Myrna said, getting up to refill her water glass.

"Mama came back to Hayes for the trial," she told them as she reseated herself, "which took place less than a month after the crime. Nowadays cases like that can take months or longer to come to trial, but not back then. Not in John Coulter County, Montana, especially when the sheriff and the judge and the prosecuting attorney and the attorney assigned to defend me and every other person in the county already knew what the verdict would be. My attorney was a fat, old man with whiskey on his breath. In both his opening remarks and his summation, he claimed that I was an innocent young girl led astray by a man with a 'devious criminal mind.' I didn't know what *devious* meant, and I doubt anyone on the jury knew either. The trial lasted only a couple hours, and the jury deliberated about fifteen minutes.

"People in the courtroom were angry because the jury gave me life in prison when they wanted a hanging. The jury spared my life because the teller had two bullets in him. I hadn't realized it at the time, but Josh managed to shoot him at the same time I pulled the trigger of my rifle. The doctor who testified couldn't say for sure which gun killed the man. Or maybe the jury spared me and sentenced me to life in prison instead of hanging me because I was only sixteen and had long blond hair and blue eyes. No one knew I was pregnant yet. I'm not sure I even knew myself. Such irony. Josh never planned to kill anyone, but in his dying breath he shot the teller who was about to shoot me and in doing so not only saved me but saved what would be his only child.

"Mama waved as they took me back to my cell. That was the last time I ever saw her. They took me to the prison in Deer Lodge the next day.

"One of the other inmates had performed abortions and offered to help me get rid of the baby I carried. I'm not sure if I turned her down because of fear or because of Josh's memory.

"When the doctor in Deer Lodge came to the prison to deliver the baby, he asked if I had a relative who could take it in. Otherwise, it would be sent to an orphanage. My mother was out of the question. The doctor was nice enough to call Aunt Vera on his own dollar. Can you imagine how stunned Vera Wentworth must have been! But the doctor said she didn't hesitate. She just said yes, that she would get there as soon as she could. It amazed me that my father's sister came all that way to get that baby."

"Did you ever think about trying to get him back from Vera?" Vanessa asked. "Or maybe getting to know him or helping him financially? I know that Vera had to sell part of her farm to educate him."

Myrna felt a wave of anger at the oldest sister's question. "I went to great lengths to change my identity, and until you three came along, *no one* knew that I was a convicted murderer and gave away a baby and escaped from the prison by hiding in the trunk of the warden's car."

Hattie was a murderer, bank robber, and an escaped convict.

And if Hattie or whatever name she now used was telling the truth, Vanessa and her sisters were the only people to whom she'd ever told her story. Which made Vanessa nervous. *Very* nervous as she pondered why Hattie had responded to that newspaper story in the Denver newspaper. And why she had told them her secrets. None of it made any sense.

No sense at all.

If Hattie's story became known, she could be sent back

to prison and might very well spend the rest of her life behind bars. If she was as wealthy and important as she appeared to be, her arrest would be a major news story. Her hard-earned reputation would be ruined. Whatever family name she now used would be tainted. Her entire family would suffer.

Vanessa watched fascinated while Hattie stretched and yawned and marveled at how supple the woman's body was. And her mind was as adept as her body.

But her conscience was flawed.

Hattie had gone to great lengths to keep the secrets she had just divulged to them. Vanessa didn't approve of her killing the son of the man who owned the mine in Coal Town but could understand why she might have done that. But she had not spoken one word of remorse over the killing of the teller at the Hayes bank.

She and her sisters were virtual prisoners in the isolated mountain home of a sociopath.

Vanessa looked around the room and wondered where the telephone was.

She glanced at her sisters wondering if they were suffering from the same disquiet she now felt. Ellie was staring out at the nighttime sky, her mind obviously elsewhere.

Georgiana met Vanessa's gaze and reached for her hand. "I'm scared," she whispered.

TWENTY-FIVE

I'VE kept you girls much too long," Hattie said, glancing at her watch, "but I promised that we would have some wine and cheese before we bid farewell."

Vanessa glanced at her own watch. Hattie's seemingly endless story had taken less than three hours.

She wondered how they should bid farewell to a hostess who hadn't wanted them to visit her in the first place and made it very apparent that she never wanted to see them again.

Vanessa watched as Hattie reached under the edge of the table to press the button that would make Willy magically appear once again. Then Hattie rose from her chair and headed for the bathroom.

As soon as Hattie's back was to them, Vanessa put a finger to her lips warning Ellie and Georgiana to wait until Hattie was out of earshot before they said anything.

Once the bathroom door had closed behind her, Ellie spoke first. "Well, that was quite a story, but I don't believe a word of it. I think she was just having fun with us. Her tale is too far-fetched even for a novel."

"I believe her," Georgiana said softly.

"Me, too," Vanessa whispered. They now knew things that could ruin Hattie's reputation and the family name she had apparently worked hard to establish, Vanessa realized. The confidentiality agreements she and her sisters had signed were supposed to protect Hattie's secrets. As long as the Wentworth sisters kept their mouths shut, they should be safe from Hattie's wrath.

Vanessa wondered how legally binding the agreements were. Could they have been a ruse to put them at their ease?

"We should leave here," Georgiana whispered. "Now. Tonight."

"But how?" Vanessa wanted to know. "We can't just call a cab. And Willy is not going to take us anyplace unless Hattie tells her to."

Willy arrived just as Hattie emerged from the bathroom and opened folding doors that revealed a kitchenette. Vanessa and her sisters watched Hattie's silent helper remove a tray from the refrigerator and carry it to the conference table. The tray held cheese, fruit, and foil-wrapped chocolates. Willy brought a second tray with crackers and French bread. Then she placed a waiting bottle of wine on an ornate, freestanding opener and removed the cork. Once the cork was removed, she poured the wine into heavy silver goblets that looked like something out of King Arthur's court and carried them to the table. Then she opened a second bottle and left it on the credenza.

"Thank you, my dear," Hattie told Willy. "That will be all."

When the elevator door had slid closed behind Willy, Hattie said, "I selected a very special Beaujolais from the year your father was born, which was a vintage year in Burgundy and the most dreadful one of my life. Out of the events of that time, however, a baby was born who—judging from what I have learned from you ladies—grew up to be a good-hearted man who cared deeply for his family. But let us suppose that before he met your mother, he impregnated a woman and had a child out of wedlock that he never acknowledged. If that child showed up decades later, your father would probably have wished him or her well but could not possibly have the same feelings for the child as he had for the children he had cared for and loved from the day they were born. I know you find me harsh in my rejection, but you represent a very difficult time in my life.

I always believed that I was destined for a better life than my parents had—a far better life. And I spent years creating a new identity for myself and distancing myself from the person named Hattie with her crimes and prison record. I erased—or so I thought—all evidence that I was the young woman at the center of the unfortunate events that occurred that ill-fated year in a dismal little corner of Montana. Then all these years later when I am close to achieving a goal for which I have been striving for decades, you three track me down. Surely you can understand why I did not greet you with open arms and why I wish that we had never met or had any knowledge of one another. But here we are. So in the interest of making the best of things, I propose a toast to your father, who raised three bright, interesting daughters." And with that, Hattie lifted her goblet to her lips.

Vanessa took a sip from the surprisingly heavy goblet. The wine also was heavy and not all that pleasing. She didn't particularly like red wines, vintage or otherwise. And red wine didn't like her and usually gave her a headache. But a few sips probably wouldn't hurt. And after the stress of the evening, she longed for that mellow feeling a bit of wine would bring.

She looked over at Ellie to see what she thought of the wine. Ellie was regarding the contents of her goblet with a puzzled look. She tried another tentative taste, after which she shrugged and downed the entire glass. Then she rose and poured herself another glass.

Georgiana took sips of wine in between nibbles of cheese. When she realized Vanessa was watching her, she held up her goblet and nodded first at Vanessa, then somewhat fearfully at Ellie. "Here's to Vera Wentworth, the woman who raised our father," Georgiana said.

"Here, here," Vanessa said, lifting her glass. The wine tasted better now. Maybe it just took a little getting used to.

Ellie also raised her glass and said, "To Vera, who loved our daddy."

Vanessa tried to show her agreement with Ellie's statement with another sip of wine, but she could not lift the goblet. It seemed stuck to the table.

She looked at Ellie to see if she was able to lift her goblet.

Ellie was still sitting across the table, but the tabletop had expanded into a vast, glossy plane, and Ellie was far away. She was looking at Vanessa and her lips were moving, but her voice was just as distant as she was.

Something was wrong, Vanessa realized. *Very, very wrong.*

TWENTY-SIX

*M*YRNA followed the flashlight's beam to the metal stairs then climbed upward through the bowels of her mountain until she reached the garage. From there she entered the elevator, relieved to have the distasteful and exhausting task completed and to be returning to the fabulous home that she had designed and built and loved.

She wondered, however, if she was going to feel the same about Eagles Nest after the events of this night.

Damn those three women! How dare they come snooping into her life!

She punched the button for the office level.

The elevator door slid open, revealing the remains of the midnight repast still on the conference table, and the chairs her "guests" had occupied were still askew.

She made herself a cup of tea, then took her accustomed place at the head of the table and closed her eyes.

Living once again in Hattie's skin and telling her tale had exhausted her.

Of course, the memory of that time in her life had always been with her, but over the years only transitory recollections would flit through her brain when a bit of conversation, a line in a book, a familiar melody, or even the sight of an ancient pickup truck or a well-tended vegetable garden would set them free for a time. And even though thoughts of that time had haunted her of late, she had deliberately avoided living through that time in its entirety as she had tonight.

For she did have regrets.

She'd realized from the beginning that Josh's plan was clumsy and flawed, but she had allowed him to lead. And she had paid the price.

But those nights in the loft with moonlight streaming through the open hay doors as they explored the joys and mysteries of their own bodies had never been equaled for her in all the years since. Never. She remembered how the local newspaper vilified Josh as a cold-blooded killer. She didn't mind so much what they said about her, but Josh was just a sweet, ignorant boy with dreams that went amiss. He thought he could walk in that bank poor and leave rich. What happened was her fault because she went along with his stupid plan and hoped for the best.

She also regretted setting her mother adrift. Even though she'd never wanted to see her mother again, she should have provided for her needs. She should not have allowed her mother to die a pauper if for no other reason than her father would have expected better of her.

But she had no regrets over killing Mr. Sedgwick's son. None at all. The man was vermin and deserved to die. She wished she could have killed Mr. Sedgwick himself, but she managed to have his mine investigated and then closed, which ruined him financially and was a sort of death.

And she was sorry that beautiful Josh Polanski had died. But even though she had adored him and maybe even loved him, theirs would not have been an enduring relationship. She needed to figure out who she was and what she wanted out of life before she was ready to make that sort of commitment. Not that any of the men in her life had had a permanent place. They either died or disappointed her. The closest thing to fulfillment came from her children and grandchildren, who had disappointed her at times, but she made sure they learned from their mistakes as she herself had done. Of course, no one in her family knew about her mistakes. They thought of her as infallible.

Myrna wondered what time it was but was too weary even to look at her watch. She deliberately avoided thinking about Willy. She would come to terms with that later. Right now, in spite of her aching muscles and her brain crying out for sleep, there were things she needed to tend to.

Feeling unaccustomedly stiff and tired, Myrna finished her tea, then rose and carried the silver wine goblets to the sink, where she carefully washed and dried them and put them away. She poured the remaining wine down the drain and washed and rinsed the wine bottles before putting them in the trash can. Next she washed the dishes and utensils and dumped the leftover food down the garbage disposal. She took a clean dish towel and polished the fingerprints from the glossy top of the conference table and the arms of the chairs. In the adjoining bathroom, she carefully wiped down any surfaces her guests might have touched. Then she wiped off the French doors and the railing around the deck. She bagged the trash and carried it with her to the elevator. She wiped off the front of the elevator door and the controls inside.

In the dining room, she polished the table and chairs. Next she wiped down the banister for the circular staircase.

After inspecting the bedroom suite to make sure Willy had left none of the three sisters' possessions behind, she rubbed down any surface they might have touched and scrubbed down the bathroom, making sure no stray hairs remained in the corners or caught in the drains.

Then with the trash bag in hand she took the elevator back down to the garage area. So strange to have no security officer emerge from the security office.

She put the trash in the trunk of the Lincoln and drove into the nearby community of Folly, where she put the bags in a bin behind the service station.

Once she was back at Eagles Nest, she turned her attention to the Hummer, wiping every surface—both inside and outside the vehicle—that the women might have touched when Willy drove them from the airstrip.

So weary she could hardly walk, Myrna took the elevator up to the service level and placed all the cleaning cloths she had used in the washing machine and turned it on. Then she rode to the main level where the living room and her bedroom suite were located. When the door slid open, she made her way toward her bedroom with a lagging step.

She didn't even bother to undress or pull back the covers on the bed. She sank onto the chaise, pulled a throw over her exhausted body, and stared out at the predawn sky.

The moon had long since set, and the stars were beginning to fade, but Venus was still brilliant in the western sky. One of her granddaughters often brought a small telescope with her when she visited Eagles Nest and would try to get Myrna to look through the lens and admire worlds so distant that it took eons for their light to reach earth. But Myrna had no desire to ponder the universe. As far as she was concerned, the nighttime sky was no more than a theatrical backdrop for the nighttime activity and musings of human beings.

Her labors at last concluded, she allowed her mind to turn to Willy. In so many ways, this was Willy's home as much as it was hers. Eagles Nest was going to be impossibly lonely without her.

Willy had come into Myrna's life as a hulking fourteen-year-old at Myrna's Denver estate. Willy and her parents lived in quarters above the garage. Three years later Willy's parents slipped away in the night, leaving their daughter asleep in her bed. Willy ran errands for her reclusive employer and did things the gardener and housekeeper left undone. Willy's entire life revolved around pleasing Myrna, and her devotion to Myrna was absolute. The two women often had their lunch together while watching a noontime soap opera. And even in the evening they would often dine together while watching the news and the game show that followed. When Myrna decided to give up her Denver home and live full-time at Eagles Nest, she invited Willy to join her, and the large, awkward woman had knelt in front of Myrna and kissed her hands. Remembering made tears come to Myrna's eyes.

And now Willy was lost to her. Already loneliness was seeping into Myrna's bones as she realized how adrift she was going to be without her Willy. Willy had cared more about her than anyone else in the entire world. More than her own children.

I have always done what needs to be done, Myrna reminded herself. She had set a course for herself decades ago. Willy was not elemental to that course. An impeccable reputation was.

"I'm so sorry, Willy," she whispered. "Please, please forgive me."

TWENTY-SEVEN

*V*ANESSA opened her eyes to darkness.

She was lying on her back. *But where?*

She held her hand in front of her face but saw nothing. No hand. Just complete and total blackness.

She blinked several times, then waved her hand in front of her face. She could feel the movement of air the waving caused but still saw nothing. Absolutely nothing.

Had she gone blind?

The thought filled her with panic. She took a deep breath in an effort to calm herself and realized she had a headache. A terrible, throbbing headache. And she was thirsty. Her mouth was dry. Her tongue felt swollen.

She rubbed her forehead in a futile attempt to ease the painful throbbing. Maybe she couldn't see because she'd had a cerebral hemorrhage.

Then she remembered the wine that Willy had served.

She'd gotten headaches from red wine before, but it had never made her pass out. And she'd taken only a few polite sips. But it must have been the wine that rendered her unconscious because she had absolutely no memory of anything after drinking it. No memory of being brought to this place of total darkness.

Yes, that had to have been what happened. She wasn't waking from a deep sleep. She'd been unconscious, otherwise she would remember being carried or dragged from Hattie's office to wherever she was now. The last thing she remembered was looking across the table and seeing Ellie becoming farther and farther away from her and not being able to hear what she was saying.

"Ellie?" she said out into darkness, her throat so dry it hurt to speak the word and using her voice caused yet another pain to shoot through her head. Mentally she pushed the pain aside. "Georgiana?" she called out. "Are you guys here?"

She listened. Then called her sisters' names again. She could sense from the reverberations of her voice that she was not in a small space.

Whatever this place was, it smelled bad. Like vomit. Which meant that other living creatures were here with her.

And the silence was not total. She became aware of the soft sound of breathing.

"Who's there?" she said, her heart pounding. Images flitted across her mind's eye. A man with an ax. Hattie pointing a gun at her. A wild animal.

"Please answer me," Vanessa sobbed. "Whoever you are, please, please answer me."

She strained her ears trying desperately to hear a response. When there was none, she took a deep breath and reached out into the blackness. She waved her hands back and forth, up and down.

Then she touched the surface she was lying on. Solid rock covered with a sprinkling of dirt. But she was not outside. There was no sky above her. Even the darkest sky could be seen.

She rolled over. The movement brought the pain back to her head. Think around it, she told herself, and began inching her way toward the sound of breathing. Even if it was a wild animal, she needed to know with whom or what she was sharing this darkness.

Her hand touched something and instantly recoiled.

Then she forced herself to reach out again. She was touching warm, bare skin.

She allowed her fingertips to explore. It was a foot. A human foot. A warm, living human foot that was so soft and unbelievably smooth that it could only belong to one person. Her sister Georgiana.

Vanessa kissed her baby sister's extraordinary foot, then scooted up to Georgiana's face and kissed her cheek. Then her lips. Georgiana's breathing was shallow. Vanessa patted her face. "Honey, I need for you to wake up."

When Georgiana didn't respond, Vanessa pinched her cheek. Then she shook her, gently at first, then with vigor. "Please, Georgiana, I need for you to wake up."

But still there was no response.

Something definitely had been in the wine. They'd been drugged. Vanessa was sure of it now. She had taken only a few sips, but Georgiana had drunk more. Ellie, too. Ellie had poured herself a second glass.

"Ellie," Vanessa called out. "Ellie! God damn it, Ellie, answer me!"

Again there was only silence.

Vanessa felt all around Georgiana's body as she continued to call out. "Ellie, answer me, please. Where are you, honey? Just moan a little bit so I can find you."

She moved out into a wider circle until she bumped

into something. But it wasn't Ellie. Not a person. She explored the something with her fingertips.

It was a suitcase.

Next to it was another suitcase. And another. Then carry-on bags. And the cases that held Georgiana's photographic equipment. All lined up in a row as though some hotel bellhop had carefully placed them in this place of total darkness.

All that was missing was their purses. Vanessa knew she didn't have a flashlight or a water bottle in her purse, but maybe Ellie or Georgiana did.

On her knees, Vanessa felt her way back down the line of luggage. The purses were on top—Ellie's expensive leather tote, Georgiana's backpack, her own well-worn department-store purse. Blindly Vanessa searched through them for a flashlight or water bottle. There were none.

She pulled her cell phone out of its designated pocket and pressed a key. The familiar tiny screen lit up, but its light barely penetrated the darkness.

Hoping and praying for a miracle, she pressed 911 and the send key, but nothing happened.

She tried Ellie's cell phone. Its light was just as insignificant, and her phone also refused to connect with the outside world. Georgiana's phone was useless, too.

Frantic for any meaningful source of light, she started searching through Georgiana's photographic gear. Vanessa knew that Georgiana preferred to augment natural light with reflectors and probably hadn't brought along any sort of flash equipment, but maybe some sort of light source was among all this stuff.

Then Vanessa remembered how on the way back from Deer Lodge they'd stopped so Georgiana could make a low-light, timed exposure of a crumbling stone house with a stream in the foreground and mountains behind. She had used a penlight to check her settings in the fading light.

Somewhere in all this stuff was that penlight.

Vanessa frantically searched through the various cases. *Light*, she thought. *Please let there be light.*

Desperately trying to remain calm, she went through each case, checking each compartment and side pocket, until finally there it was—in a cloth bag along with spare batteries.

Vanessa took a deep breath and turned on the tiny flashlight. Never had a beam of light seemed so wondrous.

Slowly she moved the beam back and forth in an ever wider swath until finally she located Ellie.

Vanessa scrambled to her side and caressed her face. Ellie's skin was warm, and she was breathing. Dried vomit was on her face and neck, which Vanessa hoped meant that Ellie hadn't metabolized as much of the wine as Georgiana had.

"Open your eyes, honey. I need for you to open your eyes and talk to me. Georgiana is here. We're all together. Please, please, Ellie, please wake up. I know you're mad at me, but the three of us have got to stick together. We haven't been doing a very good job of that lately, and now we're being held prisoner in . . ."

Vanessa paused to scan their surroundings with the narrow beam of the tiny flashlight.

"We're underground in a cave of some sort. Willy must have brought us here."

Yes, one by one, Vanessa realized as she stroked Ellie's smooth, silky hair. The enormous woman would have carried or dragged their unconscious bodies to this place. And then she would have brought their possessions.

Willy had brought them and their possessions to a

place where they would never be found. A place that was supposed to become their tomb.

The privacy agreements had been a ruse so those two horrible women could get them to drink drugged wine. Rather than kill them in the house and risk leaving any incriminating evidence behind, they brought them here to die. It was tidier that way.

They must have been sure there was no way out of this place, Vanessa realized with a sinking heart.

But if there was a way in, there had to be a way out. Unless they'd locked or barricaded the only entrance. But maybe there was an air duct they could crawl through. Or they could dig their way out. There had to be a way. If there wasn't, she was never going to see her daughters again. Never see her mother.

"Come on, Ellie, I need for you to wake up," she said, rolling her sister's shoulders back and forth, then gently slapping her face. "Together we can figure a way out of this mess."

A small mewing sound came from deep in Ellie's throat.

"I'm here, sweetie," Vanessa said, stroking Ellie's forehead. "Your big sis is here."

The mewing turned to a moan. "My leg," Ellie gasped.

"What about your leg?"

"It hurts," Ellie groaned, gesturing toward her right leg. "It hurts like hell."

Vanessa carefully pulled up Ellie's elegant taffeta skirt, which had gone swish, swish when she walked, and shone the tiny beam on her right leg.

At first Vanessa couldn't believe her eyes.

A bone was jutting through the skin on Ellie's right

shin. Suddenly the hopelessness of their predicament came down upon Vanessa like an avalanche. Georgiana was barely breathing, and Ellie's leg was badly broken. Vanessa realized it was up to her to get help, and they would all die if she failed.

Fear gripped her like a vise. Bile rose in her throat.

"I can't stand the pain!" Ellie cried out. "Help me, Nessa. Please help me!"

"I will, honey. I will." But Vanessa hadn't a clue as to how she was going to do that.

"Is my leg broken?" Ellie asked, her jaw clenched.

"Yes. Don't try to move it. I'm going to find help."

"I need water."

"Yes, I'll get water and bring help."

Vanessa rose shakily to her feet and used the tiny beam of light to explore their place of confinement. A narrow set of iron rails ran through the middle of a long, narrow tunnel that must be part of an old mine. The rails disappeared into darkness at both ends of the space. Primitive wooden benches lined one wall.

She ran her tiny beam of light around the outside perimeter of the area. Then she followed the rails toward the opening at the far end. The tunnel curved out of sight, and Vanessa rounded the curve only to be greeted by a pile of boulders and rocks and loose dirt from a long-ago cave-in that had sealed off the tunnel.

Then she made her way back through the tunnel and explored the other end. But once she rounded the curve, the penlight revealed heavy iron doors covered with rust. She pushed on them and kicked them, but they didn't budge.

There was no keyhole. Probably the doors were secured by a sliding bar on the other side. She pounded on them and called out but could tell that such efforts were futile.

She walked back to the pile of boulders and dirt at the other end, put the penlight in her mouth to free her hands, and climbed. She could feel air coming through spaces at the top of the pile. She turned off the penlight long enough to see if any light was squeezing through the spaces.

There wasn't.

What she wouldn't give for a stick of dynamite and a match.

Ellie was calling out to her. Vanessa climbed down. "I'm coming," she called.

She knelt beside her sister. "I can't stand the pain," Ellie sobbed as she grabbed Vanessa's hand.

Vanessa kissed Ellie's forehead. "Remember what Daddy used to say about pain?"

"That it will feel better when it stops hurting," Ellie managed to say. "But I need a painkiller. And a doctor to set my leg. Where are we, Nessa? Can't you just go for help? Please," she sobbed. "The pain is unbearable."

"I'm working on it, honey," Vanessa said, tears rolling down her cheeks.

"And there isn't any water?"

"No."

"Are we going to die?"

"Not if I can help it. Close your eyes and try to think of something beautiful. Think of going to see Mother. Think of us all sitting on her terrace with Lily and Beth and watching the sun go down over French countryside, and Mother's Frenchman is serving us wine and cheese."

"I don't want any wine," Ellie said. "I'm never going to drink wine again."

"Never say never. Now close your eyes, honey. I need to work on things."

Vanessa closed her own eyes. *Please, please, please help me save my sisters.*

She felt Ellie's hand on her arm. "Is Georgiana here, too?"

"Yes, Georgiana is here. We're here together."

TWENTY-EIGHT

*A*FTER pulling clothing from the suitcases and improvising pillows to cradle her sisters' heads, Vanessa put some spare batteries in her pocket and began a more methodical search of their prison. She walked up and down the chamber using her narrow beam of light to search every inch.

At first she thought the object at the far end of the row benches was a boulder, until she saw the high-topped sneakers. Large high-topped sneakers belonging to a large person curled on his or her side and facing the wall. A person so large it had to be Willy.

But why would Willy be locked up with them? That made no sense. No sense at all.

Maybe Willy had locked herself in here by accident and soon Hattie would come let her out, a thought that made Vanessa's heart soar with hope.

When she was within a few steps of Willy, Vanessa said her name.

When she got no response, she knelt and touched the woman's massive shoulder. "Willy, can you hear me?"

"Go away."

"What's going on?" Vanessa demanded. "Why are we here in this place?"

"We are here to die," Willy said in a flat, emotionless voice.

"You brought us here, didn't you?"

"Myrna told me to."

"Myrna? Is that the name Hattie uses now?"

"Yes. Myrna Cunningham. I never knew she had another name until she showed me that story in the newspaper."

"Okay, I understand that Myrna told you to bring me and my sisters down here. But why are *you* here?" Vanessa demanded.

"I loved her," Willy said in the deflated voice of a person who had decided to give up. "She's the only friend I've ever had in my entire life."

Vanessa took a seat on the closest bench. "Willy, I want you to sit here on this bench with me and help me figure a way out of here."

Willy didn't budge. "There's no way out. Besides, I might as well die. Myrna doesn't want me anymore."

"How do you know that?"

Willy didn't answer. Vanessa knelt beside her again and shook Willy's shoulder. "I want you to tell me why Myrna doesn't want you anymore."

"When Myrna said that you and your sisters had to die, I didn't think that was fair. I told her you were nice ladies and really pretty and her own flesh and blood and that all she had to do was ask you not to tell whatever it was she didn't want you to tell."

Vanessa recalled the conversation she'd had with Willy on Georgiana's cell phone. Willy had said that Hattie was her dearest friend.

Willy had been chatty and friendly on the phone and when she picked them up at the airstrip. But when she took them to the dining room and later in Hattie's office—or rather *Myrna's* office—notarizing the confidentiality agreements and serving them wine and cheese, she had seemed nervous and dejected. Probably the drug was already in the goblets when Willy filled them with wine. And she knew it. She had been willing to commit murder for Myrna.

Had Myrna prepared for their arrival by obtaining some powerful sedative? Vanessa wondered. Or maybe she had simply doubled up on whatever she had on hand. Or tried to kill them with some sort of household poison and hadn't used enough to get the job done.

Vanessa wanted to scream and yell at Willy and tell her that she was just as evil as Myrna. She wanted to tell her that she deserved to die along with them for doing such a thing.

But maybe Willy could help her find a way out of this place.

Willy turned over onto her back and looked up at Vanessa. "Myrna heard me talking to Miss Rachel on the phone. Miss Rachel said that her mother hadn't quite been herself at the board meeting and wanted to know if something had happened to upset her. That was after I talked to you on the phone. Myrna told me that your visit to Eagles Nest had to be a deep dark secret, so I told Miss Rachel that I couldn't talk about it. Myrna was standing in the doorway and heard what I said. She grabbed the phone from me and told Miss Rachel that sometimes I said really stupid things. I know I'm not a smart person, but Myrna has never called me *stupid* before."

"You're not stupid, Willy," Vanessa said. "Myrna said that because she was angry that we knew a secret about her that she never wanted anyone to know."

"What was the secret?" Willy asked as she struggled to a sitting position.

"We discovered that when our father was born, Myrna was in prison. And we found out what her name was back then. Both her names. She was born Henrietta Worth, but she was Henrietta Polanski by the time she was sent to prison. I guess Myrna thought it wouldn't take much more sleuthing on our part to learn that her crime was trying to rob a bank and killing a man who worked there. As it was, she told us herself. The whole god-awful story. I guess she'd planned all along to bring us down here and leave us to die and took some sort of sadistic pleasure in telling it."

"She had to get rid of you girls because she knew that when she was on television, you would recognize her," Willy said, her eyes filling with tears.

"Why was she going to be on television?"

"After her son is governor of Colorado, he's going to be president of the United States. Myrna will be standing with Mr. Randall and his wife and children when they are up on the big stage with all the balloons coming down from the ceiling and the band playing happy music and everybody clapping and cheering and waving signs that say 'Cunningham for President.'"

Willy paused and took a deep breath before continuing. "Myrna told me that if I carried you and your sisters and all your things down here so she could lock you up and make sure that no one would ever know that you'd ever been to Eagles Nest, she would take me to Washington, D.C., after Mr. Randall is elected president and I can stay with her in the White House. Myrna never lets anyone take her picture and has never been on television and keeps to herself except when her family or the people that help her run her company come to Eagles Nest. Even when Mr. Randall was going all over the state campaigning for Congress, she wouldn't let anyone take her picture or put her on television. But when he runs for president, everyone will expect his whole family, including his mother, who is one of the richest women in the whole country, to be up there on the big stage, and Myrna wants to share in the glory because, after all, none of her children would have amounted to a hill of beans if it hadn't been for her.

"And if you and your sisters were still alive, you would look at the television and say, 'Oh my God, that's our grandmother, and our uncle is going to be president of the United States!' And you would tell all your friends, and then the newspaper reporters would find you, and you would tell them that your father is Myrna Cunningham's son and that he was born in prison because his mother had done bad things. And then maybe people wouldn't vote for Mr. Randall and he would never be president and Myrna has been working to make him president since the day he was born. Even though she has all that money, it might not be enough to make him be president if the American people learn her secrets."

"That's quite a story," Vanessa said, "but you're just as wicked as Myrna because you brought us down here and left us to die."

Willy sighed. "I know, and now I am going to die and go to hell and burn forever and forever."

Vanessa leaned over and pulled on one of Willy's meaty arms. "Maybe there's a way to keep that from happening, but we can talk better if you sit up here with me."

With a groan, Willy hoisted herself onto her hands and knees, then pulled herself onto the bench.

"Have you been in this place before?" Vanessa asked.

"Hattie used to have a wine cellar on the other side of the big doors. I've been in there lots of times. And I knew that on the other side of the doors was an old gold mine where a long time ago there was an explosion and a lot of miners died. That was before Myrna bought the mountain and built her house on it. I'd never had been inside this place until I carried Georgiana down here. Then I brought you, and last was Ellie. But I tripped and dropped Ellie, and now her bone is sticking out of her leg. I felt real bad about that, but Myrna said it didn't matter since Ellie was going to die anyway. Myrna helped carry down all your things. When I carried the last of your stuff in here, I heard the door close behind me. And I knew that she had left me here to die because she was afraid I might tell someone that you ladies had been to Eagles Nest and were left to die down in the old mine. And because I told her that I thought what she was doing was wrong. Myrna doesn't like people to disagree with her."

Vanessa took a deep breath and sat up straight. "You have done a very bad thing, Willy, but you can make up for that by helping me find a way out of here."

Vanessa realized the penlight was about to go out and changed the batteries. And thought to look at her watch. It was one twenty-seven. But she didn't know if it was night or day.

"How long have we been down here?" she asked Willie, shining the narrow beam on her face.

"I don't know."

"More than an hour?"

"It took more than an hour to get you girls and all your stuff down here," Willy said.

"So how long were you lying on the ground?"

"Not too long."

"Do you think it's daylight by now?"

Willy shook her head.

Vanessa went to check on her sisters.

Ellie didn't respond when Vanessa touched her shoulder. Vanessa kissed her forehead but didn't try to rouse her. Her semiconscious state was a blessing at this point.

Georgiana mumbled a bit when Vanessa stroked her face and arms. "Willy is here with us," she told her. "She's going to help me find a way out." Then she kissed her and told her to go back to sleep.

"With Vanessa holding the penlight, she and Willy inspected every inch of the walls, first in the area around the iron doors, then in the open area between the two passageways, and finally the pile of rocks that blocked the other end of the tunnel. Willy tried to move one of the boulders at the bottom and hopefully disrupt the entire pile, but she couldn't budge it.

"We need something to pry one of the lower boulders loose," Vanessa said.

"I wish there was some water," Willy said.

Vanessa didn't bother to answer. She wondered how long it would be before they passed out from dehydration. Already her tongue felt dry and swollen, but that probably was from the tainted wine.

With Willy following, Vanessa returned to the benches. They turned one of them over, and Vanessa stood on it while Willy struggled to work the legs loose. Once this had been accomplished, they dragged the bench top back to the pile of boulders, and Willy tried to use it as a wedge to loosen a pivotal boulder. Again and again, Willy tried, with Vanessa adding her weight, but to no avail.

They tried another boulder and another until Vanessa decided a change of tactics was needed. She returned to the row of luggage and removed Georgiana's tripod, which in its folded-up configuration was about the size of a small fireplace log.

Willy put one end of the board at the base of a boulder,

and Vanessa scooted the tripod under that end. Willy pushed down on the board using all of her substantial weight.

The board splintered.

Willy picked up the folded-up tripod and found a space between two boulders into which one end of the tripod would fit. Then she picked up a large rock and began pounding on the other end.

Again nothing happened.

She and Willy crawled up to the top of the pile and began displacing any rocks that were small enough to be moved. They did manage to open up a space large enough for Vanessa to put her forearm through.

Vanessa could feel exhaustion taking hold of her muscles. And Willy seemed to be sliding into resignation. "Maybe we should just try going to sleep and hope we never wake up," Willy said.

"No. We are going to get out of here," Vanessa insisted. She had to get out of here so she could finish raising Lily and Beth. So she and her sisters wouldn't have to die down here.

Maybe they could devise a sling of some sort and pull the boulders away.

Vanessa went back to the luggage and brought back two leather belts from Ellie's bag. She buckled them together into one long strip and put it around one of the smaller boulders next to the opening they had made. Then with Willy pulling one end and Vanessa the other, they were able to pull away two small boulders and open up a larger space.

"It just has to be large enough for me to crawl through," Vanessa said, shining the light on the opening, which would do nicely for a small dog.

Vanessa was exhausted. And she could tell Willy was, too. But what else could they do but keep trying?

She shone the penlight through the opening and could see that the tunnel with the pair of rails continued on the other side.

Willy pounded the tripod into the opening and pushed a rock down the other side. Then another.

"You're getting close," Vanessa told her. "Just a little bit more."

Willy put a leg through the opening and, with a loud grunt, pushed with all her might.

Vanessa could hear a dislodged rock rolling down the other side of the pile.

Willy slid down to the ground and lay there panting like an exhausted dog.

TWENTY-NINE

*V*ANESSA wormed her way through the opening, then scooted down the pile of rocks on the other side. She took several deep breaths, then investigated her surroundings with the narrow beam of light.

She thought of the men who had died in this mine so many years ago that there was no one left to grieve for them. She wondered what horrors they'd endured before they died and imagined the suffering of their families. "I'm sorry," she said out loud. "If your spirit still haunts this place, would you please guide my steps? I really need to find a way out so I can get help for my sisters. I'm sure you don't want anyone else to die down here."

Vanessa stumbled along following the iron rails, her step growing progressively more unsteady. The grade was downhill, which was discouraging. She was going deeper and getting wearier with each step. And scared. More scared than she had ever been in her life.

Periodically, she turned off the light to see if she was still surrounded by absolute darkness.

She was.

The tunnel had offshoots that burrowed steeply downward into the earth. She followed what appeared to be the main passageway. Like a robot, she put one foot in front of the other and kept walking.

The grade evened off for a time and then she realized she was going uphill. Which sapped her strength but could be a hopeful sign. Maybe she was climbing toward an entrance to the old mine, one that wasn't locked.

After an indefinite time she heard a rumbling sound. And wondered if a ghost train was coming down the tracks.

Or maybe her poor exhausted mind was playing tricks on her.

She walked on. Then she heard the sound again.

Thunder.

She turned off her light. The thick darkness had lessened.

She switched the light back on and kept walking. Around the next bend in the tunnel, boulders and loose earth were strewn all over the track. And there was a hole overhead with roots reaching down inside the tunnel. Light was coming through. Dawn's early light.

The opening looked large enough for her to climb through, but it was too high for her to reach. She tried to roll one of the loose boulders over so she could stand on it. But the boulder would not budge.

She called "Help!" several times, but her voice seemed lost in the subterranean space. She thought of the wilderness around Hattie's mountain. The chances of someone being close enough to that hole in the ground to hear her were infinitesimal. But not outside the realm of possibility. A hunter could be passing by. Or a hiker.

She called out again, then waited for a response.

Again and again she tried, until her calls were so feeble a person would have to be standing at the edge of the opening to hear her.

She tried jumping and grabbing hold of one of the exposed roots. She grabbed hold, but it pulled loose, bringing a cascade of dirt with it.

She backed up and tried a running jump. A second root pulled loose. But even if a root would hold, she did have the strength to hoist herself through the opening.

Maybe if she could sit on Willy's shoulders . . .

But Willy would not be able to get through the opening back at the rock slide. And they didn't have the strength to enlarge it.

Drops of rainwater were coming through the opening. She opened her mouth and caught what she could. Each drop felt precious.

She knew that dehydration would eventually set in. She wondered how long it took to die of it. A couple of days maybe of drifting in and out of consciousness. No one would be looking for them because no one knew where they were. And they weren't due back in New York until next week. By the time anyone realized they were missing, they'd be dead.

Maybe Georgiana had awakened from her drugged sleep, she told herself as she turned around and retraced her steps. Maybe the two of them could come back here and together they could push one of the boulders under the opening. Or she could hoist Georgiana on her shoulders.

They had to try.

And if their efforts didn't work, what then?

But Vanessa already knew the answer to that question. It would be as though they disappeared from the face of the earth. Their bodies would never be found.

She thought of Lily and Beth. Her precious daughters would never know what happened to their mother and aunts. Penelope would come home from France and hound the FBI and the state police in Montana. And in Colorado. Vanessa had mentioned to the clerk at the hotel in Helena that she and her sisters were going to the state.

And Ellie might have told Boone that they were heading to Colorado during the conversation she had with him on her cell phone before they boarded the plane. But Boone wasn't about to come looking for them.

Vanessa allowed herself to imagine such a scenario anyway. Boone couldn't reach Ellie on her cell phone and became desperate. He would call . . .

But even if Boone were the knight-on-a-white-charger type, he wouldn't know where in the state of Colorado the damsels in need of rescuing were located.

And Colorado was a big state.

She wondered if the pilots who flew them to Steamboat Springs even knew what their three passengers' final destination was.

If anyone did connect the missing sisters with Hattie, she would probably claim that they never arrived at her house. And how would anyone prove otherwise?

Vanessa looked longingly at the patch of sky overhead, then trudged on. With the tunnel so close to the surface, she was surely near to an exit.

She trudged on but soon was shining the light on a cave-in that completely blocked the way.

With one goal in mind—to be with her sisters—Vanessa turned around and retraced her steps. When she reached the pile of boulders, she dragged her unwilling body up to the opening, then squeezed her way through the hole she and Willy had made, then scooted down the other side, dislodging some smaller rocks.

With the penlight showing the way, Vanessa rounded the bend in the tunnel. Georgiana had moved closer to Ellie. She had risen up on an elbow and was staring blindly into the beam of light. "Who's there?" she called out.

"It's me," Vanessa answered.

"Thank God," Georgiana sobbed. "I thought I'd had a stroke or something and gone blind."

Vanessa knelt beside her baby sister and took her in her arms.

"Something's the matter with Ellie," Georgiana said. "She was moaning and crying out. Is someone coming to get us? We need an ambulance for her."

"I know, darling," Vanessa said, smoothing her hair.

"I'm thirsty," Georgiana said, clinging to Vanessa's neck, "and afraid. Really afraid. Oh, God, Vanessa, I'm so glad you're here. And where are we anyway?"

"We're in an old mine that's under Hattie's mountain," Vanessa explained, lowering Georgiana's body and turning her attention to Ellie. She felt warm and was either sleeping or unconscious. Vanessa did not try to wake her.

She stretched out between her two sisters.

"But *why* are we here?" Georgiana asked.

"Hattie was afraid that we would tell her secrets and locked us up down here."

"How long have we been here?"

"All night. The wine Willy served us was drugged. She carried us down here while we were unconscious. She dropped Ellie coming down the steps, and her leg is broken."

"If you were unconscious, how do you know what happened to Ellie?"

"Willy told me. Hattie locked her in here with us." Vanessa shined her light around, looking for Willy. She was where Vanessa had first spotted her, curled into an unmoving, shapeless lump, her face against the wall.

"Where have you been?" Georgiana asked. "Did you get help?"

"Not yet. I need to rest for a while, then maybe I can find a way out of here. I did find a place where I could see the sky, but I couldn't reach the opening. Maybe you can go with me and climb on my shoulders and crawl through."

But Vanessa had to rest first. Right now, she couldn't take another step, much less lift her sister on her shoulders. And Georgiana was too slight to lift her.

Or maybe with Willie and Georgiana both helping her, they might be able to enlarge the hole at the top of the pile of boulders and make it large enough for Willie to craw through. Then she and Willie could hoist Georgiana up to the opening in the tunnel roof. Hopefully a road or a house was nearby.

It was their only chance at rescue.

Vanessa stretched out between her sisters and shined the penlight upward—a pillar of light in the darkness.

She thought of her daughters. She wasn't giving up. Not yet.

She turned off the light and allowed her eyes to close. But if she allowed herself to go to sleep, she might never wake up.

"Georgiana?"

"Yes?"

"Can you stand up?"

"I don't know."

"Let's try." Vanessa turned the light back on and rolled onto her hands and knees, then pushed herself to a standing position.

She helped Georgiana to her feet. "My head hurts like hell," Georgiana said, "and I feel so dizzy. If I just had some water . . ."

Her weight sagged against Vanessa. Gently she helped

her back to the ground. "We'll try again in a little while," Vanessa said.

Vanessa stretched out again and allowed her thoughts to return to her daughters. How blessed she was to have such great kids.

A memory flitted through her mind. They were in Central Park. Beth was about six months old, lying on a blanket mesmerized by the swaying tree branches overhead. Lily was toddling around on sturdy little legs. Georgiana was a skinny high school girl with her hair in a bushy ponytail, and Ellie a college girl in jeans and a blazer. Vanessa had just spotted their parents coming down the sidewalk to join them. Hand in hand, her handsome parents were laughing about something. They waved when they spotted their waiting daughter and granddaughters and hastened their step. Together they all went to the zoo, then met Scott back at the apartment, where they ate pizza and played poker and drank beer at the dining room table. Vanessa could almost hear their voices. And the laughter.

She turned off the penlight and placed it in her pocket. Then she lay on her back and put her right hand on Ellie's arm, her left on Georgiana's.

She was beyond tired, Vanessa thought. Exhaustion was heaped on top of her like a pile of boulders. Only her mind was free.

"We're going to die down here, aren't we?" Georgiana asked.

"We'll both feel stronger after we rest," Vanessa said, "and I'll take you to the place where you can see the sky."

"Do you believe in heaven?"

"I'd like to think there is such a place."

"If there is a heaven and we don't get out of here, Daddy will be up there waiting for us."

With that lovely thought Vanessa closed her eyes. She imagined the three Wentworth sisters walking down a path between big old trees with their branches meeting overhead making a lovely green tunnel with dappled light on the path and her sisters' faces. At the end of the tunnel they could see a form silhouetted against the sunlight. It was their waiting father, his arms opened, ready to embrace them.

Her imagining was so real that Vanessa could almost feel the heavenly air softly caressing her face.

Air.

Vanessa opened her eyes, leaving the lovely green tunnel behind. Something was different. The air was different. And it was less dark. She could make out the benches against the wall.

She pulled the penlight from her pocket and shone it on Georgiana's face. Her eyes were closed. "I'm going to check on something," Vanessa said, touching her arm.

"You're coming back, aren't you?" Georgiana said without opening her eyes.

"Yes. I promise."

Vanessa walked slowly toward the curving passageway that led to the iron doors. Once she had rounded the curve, she stood there in wonder as she witnessed a miracle. One of the rusty iron doors was standing open.

She blinked her eyes. And again. Perhaps she was hallucinating.

She almost felt as though her mind had detached from her body, and she was floating above herself willing her body to take the next step. And the next.

She stepped through the opening into a cavern with rows of empty wine racks—the former wine cellar that Willy had mentioned. Daylight was streaming through an opened door at the top of a metal staircase.

She climbed the stairs and walked through the open door and found herself in the garage area below Hattie's mountain dwelling.

Vanessa remembered Willy saying that Hattie had fired the security officer, but just in case someone was in the office, she walked over to the concrete-block structure and tried the door. It was locked. And the windows were barred. She knocked anyway and kicked the door.

Then she punched the call button on the elevator but nothing happened. Which was probably just as well. She had no desire to face Hattie.

She tried a door on the Hummer, which was not locked. But there were no keys in the ignition. Or anyplace else. Probably they were locked inside the security office. But she did find an opened water bottle with a few inches of water left in it.

She sat on the running board and made a ceremony out of taking the first sip. Then she tried to decide if she had options and decided she did not. She would have to walk down to the road and flag down a passerby.

The bright sunlight hurt her eyes. Her watch said that it was five minutes after nine.

She reached the first security gate and wondered whether scooting under it or climbing over it would cost her weary body the greatest expenditure of energy.

She climbed over and kept walking.

And when she reached the second gate, she climbed over it. The road was just ahead. She could see a vehicle through the trees.

A dusty van with the words UNITED STATES POSTAL SERVICE on the side was parked by a large metal mailbox. Vanessa looked around for the mail carrier.

A path led from the mailbox. The mail carrier was standing by a high security fence.

A body was impaled facedown on the fence. A body with snowy white hair and dressed in black. The body of the woman who had given birth to Vanessa's father sixty-two years ago in the women's prison at Deer Lodge, Montana.

The mail carrier was staring at Vanessa. "Who are you?" he demanded.

Vanessa realized that he was taking in her filthy clothes. She touched her face, which was also covered with dirt.

The man was middle-aged. Not in uniform, but his billed hat bore the postal service logo.

"My sisters and I came here"—Vanessa paused—"to visit her." She nodded toward the body on the fence.

Vanessa stared up the face of a cliff. High above the path she could see a deck jutting outward. Just a deck. The rest of the house was not visible from this angle. She closed her eyes to deal with a bout of dizziness.

"Who are you?" the man called out again.

Who was she? She was the mother of Lily and Beth. She was the sister of Ellie and Georgiana and the daughter of Penelope and her dear departed father. She was the granddaughter of the woman whose dead body was on that fence, a woman who used to be named Hattie but now went by Myrna. Willy had told her Myrna's last name only hours ago, but she couldn't remember what it was. "My sisters need help," she told the man. "One of them has a broken leg, and the other one is very weak. Please, call an ambulance. Please."

Her legs felt as though they were made of rubber. They were no longer going to support her.

She sank to her knees. *I cannot lose consciousness. I cannot.*

The man took a few steps in her direction. Then stopped, fear in his eyes.

"My sisters are in an old mine," Vanessa told him, her tongue thick, her words slurred. "There's a stairway behind the security office. My sisters need help. They desperately need help."

"Who are you?" the mail carrier asked for the third time.

"Please," she sobbed as she collapsed on the gravel path. "It doesn't matter who I am. Just call an ambulance. Please."

THIRTY

HE county sheriff arrived first. Then the state police, followed by an ambulance. Ellie, still unconscious, and a limp Georgiana were placed on stretchers and carried out of the mine. A paramedic started IVs. Vanessa rode up front with the driver and sipped water from a plastic bottle. Her exhaustion was extreme, and she kept dozing off. Even with the siren blaring, she would fall asleep. The driver told her they were being taken to the closest hospital, which was sixty miles away in Steamboat Springs. He assured Vanessa that, since the town was a ski resort, it had lots of doctors with expertise in fixing badly broken legs.

When the ambulance arrived at the hospital, Ellie was administered to then sent to surgery. Georgiana, who was suffering from dehydration, dizziness, and an excruciating headache, was admitted. The doctor in the emergency room had wanted to admit Vanessa, but after drinking a Coke and eating a package of peanut butter crackers, she insisted she had to be with her sisters.

She hadn't realized just how filthy she was until she

drew curious stares in the elevator. Once she had arrived at surgery, she informed a woman at the nurses' station who she was. Ellie's surgery was under way, the woman told her. Then she provided Vanessa with a hospital gown, robe, and slippers; towels and a washcloth; and a packet of toiletries; then showed her to a bathroom with a shower. Vanessa stood under the shower for a long time, shampooing her hair, allowing the hot water to wash away the dirt from that dark place. But nothing would ever wash away the memory.

In oversize hospital attire, she went in search of Georgiana's room.

"Are you asleep?" Vanessa whispered.

"No," Georgiana said, opening her eyes. "Is Ellie okay?"

"She's in surgery."

"Was it a nightmare or did Hattie really lock us up in an old mine?"

"Yes, she really did, but don't think about that now. Get some rest."

"I love you, Nessa."

"I love you, too, honey."

"I wish Ellie didn't hate me."

"Shh," Vanessa said, smoothing the curls away from Georgiana's forehead. "We'll work things out when everyone is feeling better."

She stayed with Georgiana for a time then went back up to surgery. After begging more crackers and a carton of milk, she took a seat in the waiting room. She had dozed off when an authoritarian male voice said, "Mrs. Crowell?"

Vanessa opened her eyes expecting to see someone in hospital attire. Instead it was a burly man in a rumpled suit. He introduced himself as Detective Mike Lambert with the Colorado State Police and said he needed to talk to her about the death of Myrna Cunningham.

Vanessa tried to put him off, explaining that she was exhausted and worried about her sisters and asking if he would please come back another time.

The detective ignored her request, and Vanessa listened in disbelief while the man theorized how Myrna Cunningham ended up dead. As he saw it, Vanessa had taken the elevator up to Mrs. Cunningham's house, switched off the elevator so no one could follow her, and wrestled frail, elderly Mrs. Cunningham over the deck railing. Then Vanessa left the house via the path down the mountain and hid when she saw the postal van approaching.

Vanessa closed her eyes and drew in her breath. After all she had been through, the last thing she needed was to be accused of murder.

"What makes you think that Myrna Cunningham was murdered?" Vanessa asked the man, who was built like a prizefighter and was obviously accustomed to intimidating people.

"We consider all possibilities," he said, "but it's difficult to believe that a woman like her would commit suicide."

Vanessa couldn't take the man's words seriously. *A woman like her.* The detective had no idea what sort of a woman Myrna Cunningham was. He didn't even know her real name.

"Most likely it was an accident," she pointed out.

Briefly Vanessa told him that she and her sisters had come West in search of their father's birth mother, who was born Henrietta Worth, but after she killed a man in her hometown, she ran off and changed her name. As Hattie Polanski, she had been sent to prison for a killing a bank teller in Hayes, Montana. After giving birth to their father, she escaped from prison and ended up in Colorado. When Hattie/Myrna learned the daughters of the son she had given birth to in prison were looking for her, she invited them to her home, drugged them, had her oversize employee carry them down to the old mine, and left them all there to die. "Now unless you plan to arrest me, I need for you to leave. I am exhausted and worried and wish I'd never set foot in the state of Colorado and don't plan on saying another word to you or any other law enforcement officer until I have an attorney at my side."

When the detective left, Vanessa wanted more than anything to call her mother and daughters, but she knew she would be undone by the sound of their voices. And then she would have to explain why she was so upset. And she couldn't do that. Not now anyway. Mother would think she had to fly home. Lily and Beth, too. Their summer would be ruined.

She even thought of calling Scott. But what would she say to him? That she had almost died? That she missed him? That she would never forget the good years they had shared? And that she regretted the bad years, which were just as much her fault as his?

The orthopedic surgeon came to tell her that Ellie had come through the surgery just fine. Dr. Bernard was a chatty man with a Southern drawl and looked much too young to have all that medical training.

Vanessa stayed with Ellie in recovery, holding her hand and caressing her face. Ellie was pale as a ghost, her hair matted, her lips so cracked they were bleeding, but she was alive and her bones would mend.

It was almost seven o'clock when Vanessa followed as two aides wheeled Ellie—in a bed with her leg in traction and tubes in her arms—to a regular room. A nurse got Ellie situated, then turned a chair into a bed of sorts for Vanessa and provided her with a blanket and a pillow and a snack.

When the nurse left, Vanessa patted Ellie's cheek. "I'll be right here if you need anything."

Ellie mumbled something.

Vanessa leaned closer.

"Georgiana?" Ellie whispered in a raspy voice.

"She's in a room in another part of the hospital. She was dehydrated but is feeling better."

Just as Vanessa was about to settle into her makeshift bed, Dr. Bernard popped in to check on Ellie one last time before he called it a day. Vanessa watched while he leaned close to Ellie's face and asked, "How are you doin', Miss Ellie?"

Ellie managed another mumble.

"We got that leg bone of yours put back together," the youthful surgeon told her, "and it should be almost as good as new in a few months or so, and you'll be able to do all the things you were doin' before—like dancin' and runnin' away from the hordes of good-lookin' men who are courtin' your favor. Now, if your leg gets to hurtin', you have your sister call the nurse, and I'll be back to see you bright and early in the morning."

Vanessa wished she had brushed Ellie's hair and cleaned her up a bit. Ellie would hate for anyone, but most especially a handsome doctor, to see her looking her worst. Vanessa wanted to tell Dr. Bernard that her sister was really a beautiful woman and a fashion plate to boot. But that would be silly, she supposed.

The surgeon turned around and put a comforting arm around Vanessa's shoulders. "Get some rest," he said. "She's goin' to be just fine." Then he pointed at the makeshift bed, indicating that Vanessa should make use of it, and left.

. . .

When Vanessa awoke, daylight was peeking through the blinds. She went to Ellie's bedside and stroked her sister's forehead.

Ellie opened her eyes. "Hi."

Vanessa kissed her. "Hi. Do you know where you are?"

"Yeah. In a hospital. With my leg in traction." Ellie's voice was so hoarse that Vanessa realized it was painful for her to speak.

Ellie grabbed Vanessa's hand. "Why were we in that dark place?"

"It's a long story, honey. I'll tell you about it when you're feeling better."

"The pain was horrible."

"I know," Vanessa said. "You were very brave."

"Is Georgiana okay?"

"Yes. You both drank a lot of Hattie's wine, and it was drugged."

"What happened to my leg?"

"Later," Vanessa said.

Ellie reached for Vanessa's hand, her eyes filling with tears. "You know what the worst thing was?"

"What?"

"I was afraid that I was going to die before I could tell Georgiana that I was sorry."

Vanessa washed her face and brushed her teeth and combed the tangles from her hair before making her way to Georgiana's room.

Georgiana was still asleep. Vanessa stood watching her for a time. She wondered if Georgiana would ever look old. She still looked like a young girl. A sweet young girl. Vanessa wanted to wake her and tell her that Ellie was sorry, but maybe that should come from Ellie herself.

Vanessa kissed Georgiana's forehead, then went back to Ellie's room. Someone had left a bottle of orange juice and a newspaper on the dresser. She drank the juice, then returned the narrow bed back into its chair configuration. She wondered about breakfast. Did nonpatients receive food trays? If not, she was going to have to go begging for coffee and sustenance. Their luggage and handbags were still in police custody. She had no money. No clean clothes. No makeup.

She reached for the newspaper, and her heart skipped a beat when she saw the picture of Hattie on the front page. Actually it was a photograph of a painting of Hattie that portrayed a handsome, imperial-looking woman standing beside a large bronze sculpture of an eagle. The headline read "Founder of Aquila Industries Found Dead." Vanessa scanned the article, then went back and read it word for word. Basically it said that Myrna Cunningham, the reclusive founder of Aquila Industries, was found dead by a rural mail carrier yesterday morning near her mountain estate. A family member speculated that Cunningham fell to her death while taking a steep path with numerous switchbacks that led to her mailbox, a morning ritual for Cunningham, who was known to be remarkably physically fit for a woman her age. Law enforcement officers, however, had not ruled out the possibility of foul play. Cunningham's business interests in the state and beyond were vast and included Bitterroot Mines. She was the mother of U.S. representative Randall Cunningham—whose father was Myrna Cunningham's second husband and died of a heart attack when Randall was two years old. The boy was later adopted by Myrna's third husband, James Cunningham, an Olympic swimmer who died in a plane crash in 1989. Now serving his third term, the Colorado congressman was said to be exploring the possibility of entering the race for state governor and was thought by many political observers to have presidential ambitions. Myrna and James Cunningham had three other children: Carter, who was Aquila's CEO; Katherine, who ran the family's charitable foundation; and Rachel, who was a geology professor at the University of Colorado and served on the Aquila board of directors.

The article also listed the names of six grandchildren and concluded by saying that those present at the scene of the accident were Myrna Cunningham's longtime employee and companion, Wilhelmina Kiel, and three women who were believed to be guests in the home but whose names had not been released by law enforcement authorities.

Vanessa sat with the newspaper in her lap. She wondered if this was truly all the information the newspaper had on the recent events at the Cunningham home. How innocuous the article sounded. No mention was made of the "guests" being rescued from an abandoned mine underneath Myrna Cunningham's mountain home. Or Myrna Cunningham's plot to murder her "guests" with the help of Wilhelmina Kiel.

Vanessa tossed the newspaper back on the dresser and had just decided that she was going to have to go begging for breakfast and coffee when there was a knock at the door. Hospital personnel gave a perfunctory knock before pushing the door open, and Vanessa didn't bother to respond.

No one entered and there was a second knock.

She got up from the chair, retied the sash of her robe, and shuffled to the door in her cloth slippers.

A nice-looking, middle-aged man in a gray suit was waiting. "Vanessa Crowell?"

Another detective, Vanessa decided. This one was older and better dressed than the one from whom she had undergone the third degree yesterday, an experience that had left her feeling less than kindly toward law enforcement officers.

"I am she," she responded in as calm a voice as she could summon, her hand firmly on the door handle.

"I'm Randall Cunningham. Could we go someplace and talk?"

THIRTY-ONE

$\mathcal{I}$T took Vanessa a couple of heartbeats to realize she was looking at Hattie's congressman son. Or rather Myrna Cunningham's congressman son.

"I'm not sure I want to talk to you," Vanessa said, aware of curious stares from the nurses' station. Probably they wondered why a handsome, well-dressed man was talking to a woman in dire need of makeup and suitable attire.

"I'd really appreciate it if you would," Randall Cunningham said, his expression and voice imploring. "I flew in from Washington as soon as I learned of my mother's death. I talked to Willy and the detective in charge of the investigation, but there's a whole lot I don't understand."

"I'm sure there is," Vanessa said, her tone deliberately cool. She realized that Randall Cunningham had just suffered a loss, but she had no condolences to offer.

She took a step back into Ellie's room.

"Please," he said, grabbing hold of the door she was about to close. "I realize that you and your sisters have been through a bad time—"

"A bad time!" Vanessa interrupted in an angry whisper. "My sisters and I have been through hell!"

Randall Cunningham let go of the door and took a step back.

"Look," Vanessa said, lowering her voice still further. "I realize that probably none of what happened to me and my sisters is your fault—at least not directly so—but your mother had every intention of leaving us to die in that abandoned mine. And I was interrogated by a detective yesterday who seems bound and determined to blame me for your mother's death."

"Please," Cunningham said, his brow creasing. "I need to understand what happened out there at Eagles Nest."

"It's not a pretty story, and I doubt if you want to know the truth of it any more than that detective did." Then she added, carefully enunciating each word, "Your mother tried to murder my sisters and me."

The congressman ran a hand through his hair in a frustrated gesture that reminded Vanessa of her father. This man looked much like her father, with the same chin and wide brow and coloring, which shouldn't have been surprising. Randall Cunningham was her father's half brother. But her father had been raised an orphan, while this man had been raised to be president of the United States.

"The detective said that Willy was pretty much a zombie when the state police brought her up out of the mine," Randall Cunningham said. "They brought her here and she was admitted as a psychiatric patient. When I talked to her, she was half out of her mind and not making a whole lot of sense but kept saying what 'nice ladies' you and your sisters were, and that my mother was your grandmother because she had a baby that she gave away back when her name was Hattie, and that baby grew up to be your father. Willy also told me about the article that appeared in the Denver newspaper and how excited she was when my mother told her to call the sisters and invite them to Eagles Nest. I just finished reading that newspaper article, which left me more confused than ever. Apparently my mother felt very threatened by what you and your sisters had unearthed about her past, but what was in that newspaper story seemed innocuous. Mostly I learned that you and your sisters lived in New York and found a letter with a Montana postmark and launched a search for your father's birth mother. I gather that woman turned out to be my mother."

The newspaper story. Vanessa had bought a newspaper at a drugstore in Helena and read it on the way back to the hotel. Had that been just two days ago? Or was it three?

A wave of light-headedness came over her. She closed her eyes and leaned against the doorframe. "I need something to eat," she said, "and I have no money since the police have not seen fit to give me my purse. Or my luggage."

Randall Cunningham took her arm. "Food first. We'll sort out the rest later."

Vanessa glanced back at Ellie. She seemed to be sleeping peacefully in spite of her injured leg being in that ungodly contraption. Vanessa let the door close behind her. "I can't be gone long," she told him.

He pulled out his cell phone and gave a breakfast order to someone named Paul, then led her down the hall. Conscious of the curious stares of those around her, Vanessa hoped they weren't going far, because hunger and caffeine deprivation were about to get the best of her.

Randall Cunningham took her to the break room next to the nurses' station. Shortly a young man in suit and tie arrived carrying a tray laden with food from the hospital cafeteria—oatmeal, fresh fruit, bacon and eggs, and biscuits and honey. A young woman, also in a suit, followed with two large Styrofoam cups of coffee. The congressman thanked the two and dismissed them.

Cunningham sipped coffee while Vanessa ate everything in sight and asked for more coffee. She would remember this meal all her life, she realized, not because she was in the presence of a congressman or because the food was noteworthy, but because this was the breakfast she ate the day after she and her sisters were given a second chance at life.

Vanessa pushed away the tray. "Okay. The newspaper article. We didn't want to embarrass Hattie," she said, not bothering to keep the irony from her voice, "so we didn't tell the woman who interviewed us at the Hayes newspaper office anything about Hattie being in prison or having a child out of wedlock. We knew she had been an inmate at the women's prison in Deer Lodge, but we didn't know what crime she had committed. And we knew that she had a baby while she was incarcerated there, and that the baby was our father. The note in the Bible was from your mother thanking her aunt for taking in the baby. That note was postmarked Deer Lodge, and it was that postmark that launched our search."

Vanessa gave Randall Cunningham a condensed version of what his mother had told them during that surreal session in her office. She told him how and why his mother killed the son of the man who owned the mine where Hattie's father had worked. How Hattie met a boy named Josh Polanski while hitchhiking, and how she and Josh attempted to rob a bank in Hayes, Montana, and during the bank robbery one of the tellers shot and mortally wounded Josh, and Hattie killed a bank teller. How Hattie was sentenced to life in prison but after the baby was born managed to escape.

"Josh Polanski was the father of that child—of our father," Vanessa explained. "Hattie didn't tell us much about what happened after that. Or maybe she talked on after we drank the drugged wine that Willy served us and we lost consciousness. Apparently, though, your mother realized from the moment she saw the article in the Denver paper that her secrets were threatened. She feared our sleuthing might lead to a scandal that would end your political career and decided it was more important for you to run for president than for my sisters and me to go on living."

"Willy indicated something to that effect," the congressman acknowledged. "She also said that she didn't want to take you and your sisters down into that old mine, but she had always done what my mother told her to do because my mother had been good to her and she loved her more than anyone else in the whole world. And then Willy said that after she had carried all three of you down there, Mother locked the door with her still inside."

He folded his hands and placed them on the table, and a stern look settled onto his face. "It seems to me that since my mother apparently went back and opened the door, she must have been just trying to scare you and your sisters."

Vanessa shook her head. "I don't know who opened that door. But I am certain that your mother intended to get rid of us permanently, and I can't imagine her changing her mind. Your mother had a lot to hide."

Randall Cunningham was silent for a minute as though digesting Vanessa's words. He looked past her as he said, "The detective who spoke with you yesterday checked out some of the things you told him with Montana law enforcement agencies. He learned that a man named Edward Sedgwick, who was the son of the man who owned the Coal Town mine, disappeared back in the summer of 1945 and has never been heard from since. But the detective hasn't been able to verify that there was a bank robbery and trial in Hayes that same year."

Vanessa took another sip of her coffee, then said, "Edward Sedgwick and his car are at the bottom of a place your mother called Quarry Lake, which is located near a town east of Coal Town originally settled by Germans, and at one time all the signs on storefronts were written in German. Hattie knew about the lake because years before she and her parents and her little brother, Patrick, went there on a picnic. She shared a number of poignant memories about her family. I think they really loved each other, but life was never the same after Patrick died."

The congressman shook his head. "Mother *never* talked about her early life, and she had no photographs or keepsakes or mementos from her childhood. Not a one. We never made a trip back to her hometown, never visited her family's graves. My mother was the most private person I have ever known, and I find it extremely difficult to believe that she would tell total strangers things that she never told her own children."

"I guess she wanted to make sure she didn't say anything that would cause you and your siblings to snoop around in her past like my sisters and I did," Vanessa said with a shrug, "especially since she apparently planned great things for you from the day you were born. As for why your mother shared her deepest secrets with my sisters and me, I think she realized from the moment she saw that picture in the Denver newspaper that she was going to do away with us, so it didn't really matter what she said. She knew that if we kept sleuthing around, someone was bound to remember that Hattie Worth was the girl involved in the Hayes bank robbery. And then we might go back to the Hayes newspaper and give the editor a follow-up story that was a whole lot more sensational. Hattie apparently decided to make a game out of it. She was playing a sick game when she dredged up her past with us as captive listeners because all along she planned to make sure that we were never going to have a chance to repeat what she told us."

"That's my mother you're talking about," Cunningham said, anger in his voice. "She was a remarkable woman who instilled in her children a sense of duty and taught us the value of hard work and treating others with respect."

Vanessa shrugged. "That may very well be. But unless what your mother told me and my sisters was a pack of lies and she locked us up in an abandoned mine just for sport, your mother had a past that includes murder, bank robbery, and escaping from prison."

The congressman leaned back and regarded her with narrowed eyes. "If you hadn't come looking for her, she could have lived out her life in peace," he said, not trying to keep the bitterness from his voice.

"Yes, I suppose that's true. And in a few years she could have been standing there in front of the Capitol building in Washington, D.C., watching you sworn in as president of the United States of America and allowing the whole world to think that she was an admirable woman who had lived an exemplary life. Your mother was living a lie. A really *big* lie.

"We came looking for her," Vanessa continued, "because our mother wanted us to take a trip together. I imagined us finding a sweet old lady who would cry tears of joy when we found her. Instead we almost lost our lives. And now I have to deal with an ambitious detective who would just love to call your mother's death a murder and blame it on me."

Vanessa closed her eyes and put a hand to her forehead. Her sisters were alive. Her children still had a mother. She wanted to get on with her life and not have to hire an attorney to defend herself against trumped-up charges made by some law-enforcement officer who wanted to make a name for himself. She didn't kill that old woman, but she wasn't sorry that Hattie was dead. The woman had either killed herself or slipped and fell. Or maybe the security guard she'd fired came back to settle the score. Vanessa wondered if it was possible for anyone to know for sure.

"The police said that someone had wiped away all the fingerprints in the house," Randall Cunningham said in an accusatory tone.

Vanessa was surprised that a law enforcement officer had shared information about the investigation with him, but maybe a congressman who was the son of one of the state's wealthiest citizens had special privileges. "And you think that *I* did that?" Vanessa demanded, looking him directly in the eye.

Cunningham shrugged.

"The last memory I have of being in that house," she informed him, "was sitting at the conference table in your mother's office and realizing that I'd been drugged or poisoned."

When Cunningham tried to inject a comment, Vanessa held up a hand, indicating she had still more to say.

"I did try to go up to the house to find a phone and call for help, but the elevator didn't respond. So I walked down the drive and climbed over both security gates. When I got to the road, I saw the postal van and was overjoyed. Then I saw the mail carrier standing there by . . ." She paused, remembering the ghastly sight of Hattie's lifeless body impaled on the spikes atop a seven-foot iron fence.

She looked at the handsome face of Hattie's illustrious son. Did Congressman Randall Cunningham think that she was a murderer? "I did not push your mother off that deck or down that path," she said. "The last time I saw her was the night before in her office."

He stared down at his folded hands for a time, then

said with a resigned sigh, "I believe you, and I think I can promise you that the coroner will rule that her death was either suicide or an accident."

"Which do you think it is?"

"I can't imagine my mother committing suicide."

"And I can't imagine her unlocking those doors and allowing us to go free. Willy said your mother had dismissed the security officer before we arrived. Maybe he came back and opened the door, and Willy left the mine for a time. Your mother had been the center of Willy's life, and she had dutifully gone along with your mother's plan to get rid of my sisters and me even though she realized it was horribly wrong. Then after Willy had done her bidding, your mother abandoned her and left her to die along with us. Maybe Willy had a chance to settle the score and took advantage of it."

Cunningham shook his head. "I understand that Willy was still in the mine when the police and paramedics arrived."

"She could have left while I was searching for a way out. She probably knew how to get the elevator to work. Or maybe she climbed up to the house on that path."

But the congressman wasn't listening. There were tears in his eyes.

He had loved his mother, Vanessa realized, horrible person that she was. But Vanessa could not bring herself to express one iota of sympathy. She regretted Myrna Cunningham's death only because it meant that she would not spend the rest of her life in prison.

"It will all come out," Myrna Cunningham's son said with a deep sigh. "The remains of the man at the bottom of the quarry lake will be found. And someone will come forward with memories or old newspaper clippings showing that back when my mother was still Hattie Worth, she was convicted of murdering a bank teller."

"Is this going to ruin your life?" Vanessa asked.

"Maybe." Then he sagged back in his chair and slowly let out his breath. "Or maybe my wife and I will take a slow boat to no place. I never really wanted to go into politics. Now I'm off the hook. Ironic, isn't it?"

Vanessa nodded. Yes, it was ironic.

She stood and retied the sash on her robe. "What will happen to Willy?"

"My brother and sisters and I will see that she is taken care of—and has legal representation if it turns out that she needs it."

THIRTY-TWO

HE two women used flashlights to light the way as they climbed the narrow path. But already the darkness above the eastern horizon was fading.

Thanks to her weekend biking, Vanessa took the climb in stride and was only slightly winded when she reached the top of the hill. As was her mother.

"You come up here often, I take it," Vanessa said with admiration in her voice.

"Yes," Penelope said as she sat on a still intact section of an otherwise crumbling rock wall and patted a place beside her.

Vanessa seated herself and took in the predawn view from the top of the hill. Intermittent clusters of light from villages and farms floated in pools of darkness, and occasional beams from headlights wound their way through the countryside.

Vanessa used her flashlight to examine her immediate surroundings. The rock wall showed signs of having once encircled the crest of the hill. And standing sentinel atop a rocky crag were the ruins of an ancient tower that could be seen from the terrace of Jean Claude's farmhouse and that he referred to as "the Roman ruins."

The arbor-shaded terrace was used as a summer dining room. Since Vanessa and Georgiana had arrived three days ago, every meal had been eaten there, and each one had been lingered over and enjoyed. Which was nice. Maybe after a summer in France, Lily and Beth would occasionally be willing to forgo television and linger over a meal.

"It's time," Penelope said, putting a hand on her daughter's arm. "Turn off your flashlight."

Vanessa obliged, and they waited while the eastern sky became steadily lighter. Even though dawn had arrived every morning since the world began, Vanessa felt as though she were waiting for some auspicious event to take place, which it was, and a miraculous one, and for those last few seconds of anticipation she found herself holding her breath.

Just as the first rays burst over the horizon, a distant rooster began to crow. A second rooster joined him. And then a third chimed in at the precise instant a church bell began to peal.

And all around them, from a distance and close by, other roosters let the world know that they had awakened, and other church bells joined in to announce the new day. Their music was discordant yet incredibly beautiful and moving. It was a concert Vanessa would never forget.

"Thank you," she whispered to her mother.

"Food for the soul, isn't it?"

Vanessa nodded. "You should have insisted that Georgiana come."

"She wanted to sleep in, and I can bring her another morning. Besides, I wanted to share it with you first. You need it more."

For the longest time they sat there watching the golden light spread itself across the French countryside with its picturesque hamlets, patchwork of cultivated fields, wooded areas along a meandering creek, and vintage farmhouses with their cluster of outbuildings.

Other sounds came forth. A tractor coming to life. The lowing of cows. Barking dogs. Birds singing.

Beauty and peacefulness were a delightful combination, Vanessa realized. After a time her mother linked arms with her and said, "I thought this might be a good time for you to tell me what happened in Colorado. You've only told me bits and pieces. Georgiana and Ellie, too. I need to hear the whole thing from start to finish."

Vanessa sighed and shook her head. "I can't. Not yet, anyway."

"Yes, you can. Start by telling me exactly how Ellie's leg got broken."

Vanessa closed her eyes, remembering how she had shone the tiny beam of Georgiana's penlight on Ellie's leg and seen the jagged end of a bone jutting through flesh and recalling Ellie's pain and her own feeling of utter helplessness.

A shudder went through her entire body just as it had then.

To explain about Ellie's broken leg meant she would have to explain who Willy was and how they came to be locked away in an old mine and why the woman who had given birth to their father wished them dead. And how could she tell such a disturbing story in such a peaceful place? It would seem a sacrilege. She felt a wave of anger that her mother expected that of her.

Penelope pulled from the pocket of her jacket a bottle of water and two croissants wrapped in a cloth napkin. Vanessa took a bite of her croissant and drank some of the water.

"Is it what happened in Colorado that makes you so distant or is it because it pains you to see me with Jean Claude?" Penelope asked.

"Actually, being here with you and Jean Claude is easier than I thought it would be," Vanessa acknowledged. "I think the poor man is afraid of me. You must have told him tales about your ferocious oldest daughter."

"Let's just say he realizes that you're the daughter who's the least accepting of our relationship. He's a good man, Vanessa. I'll never love Jean Claude the way I loved your father, but I do love him, and my life with him is very satisfying."

Vanessa had wanted to not like her mother's lover, but Jean Claude was gentle and considerate and obviously adored Penelope. Adoration from a man was something Vanessa had never experienced. And probably never would, she thought with a sigh.

"Ah, another sigh," Penelope said. "So many sighs since you arrived. That's something new with you. You were incredibly sad when your father died, and you were angry and hurt when Scott left, but whatever happened in Colorado has made you distant. You were always my strong, sensible girl. I counted on you to look after your sisters, which you always did, and now you are looking after your own daughters. You will always be that sort of person—responsible and reliable—but now you seem to be operating by rote. You seem to have lost heart."

"It's like when Daddy first got sick, and I couldn't do anything to change the inevitable outcome," Vanessa said, and another sigh came unbidden. "Then Scott left, and no matter how many promises I made, he didn't come back, and my daughters have suffered because of that. Down there in that old mine, I felt the same way. I had tried everything I could think of to get us out of there and finally gave up. My sisters were going to die because I failed."

She waited for her mother to comment, but Penelope was silent.

Her mother's silences had always had more impact than her words. Vanessa closed her eyes. "The beginning was Hattie's letter, of course. The postmark was the first clue."

Once Vanessa started, it was as though the dam had broken. She felt the need to share every detail, to leave nothing out. She got misty-eyed when she told her mother about the elderly woman in the nursing home at Deer Lodge who had taken care of Hattie's baby until Vera arrived by train: "That was the sweet moment. It was downhill after that."

Then there was the yearbook picture. The newspaper article. The phone call from Willy. The flight to the middle of nowhere. The incredible house jutting out from the side of a Colorado mountain. And Hattie's incredible tale of murder and bank robbery that ended with their being served drugged wine.

Vanessa clung to her mother's hand while she told her of the horror of waking up in the abandoned mine and knowing that her sisters' lives depended on her finding a way out.

"I tried," Vanessa remembered. "I really tried. But finally I was ready to give up and curled up beside my sisters and began organizing my last thoughts. I thought about you and Daddy. And Ellie and Georgiana and I growing up together. My precious daughters. What hurt the most, of course, was the thought of leaving Lily and Beth.

"As to who opened the door to the old mine, I suppose I'll never know for sure," Vanessa said. "Maybe one of Hattie's children got wind of what their mother was up to and put a stop to it. Or the security guard she's fired came back for some of his possessions and snooped around a bit."

Vanessa closed her eyes, seeing the rusted iron door that could have barred them from living out the rest of their lives. "The more I think about it, though, the more it seems that Hattie herself had to have opened it—not because she wanted to save the daughters of the child she gave away but because she couldn't bear the thought of her poor Willy feeling abandoned and unloved in that old mine as she waited for death. Of course, their relationship would already have been damaged beyond repair. Hattie had revealed her evil side to the person who most loved her. Maybe that was what Hattie was thinking as she navigated the path down her mountain. The state police thought it was highly unlikely that she could have ended up impaled on that fence if she tumbled down the path, but maybe she didn't tumble. Maybe she spread her wings like an aging eagle and flew to her death."

"But we didn't die, and out of the nightmare Ellie found love." Vanessa had to smile. "Amazing, isn't it? Fashion-plate Ellie who never left home without full makeup and the perfect outfit and shining hair and was on a perpetual quest to find Mr. Right, and then Mr. Right turns out to be a Georgia-born orthopedic surgeon practicing in Steamboat Springs, Colorado, who happened to be on call that day and first sees Ellie when she is an unconscious, filthy, stinking mess with a bone sticking out of her leg."

"You should have called me sooner, Vanessa," Penelope said. "I would have flown to Colorado. And when you did call, you were so vague. Georgiana and Ellie were much more forthcoming, but they'd been unconscious and didn't know the whole story."

"I'd already been grilled by the police and by Hattie's son and didn't want to tell the whole damned story another time. And I didn't want you flying back to the States and interrupting the wonderful summer that you created for Lily and Beth, my wonderful daughters, who are . . ."

Vanessa searched for a word to describe the change in her daughters. "They are wiser. They understand that there's a world beyond their little circle of friends and their school, and that there are other cultures and other ways to think and live. In the town square last night watching them mingle with the friends they've made this summer and actually speaking some French, I was overwhelmed by the change in them."

"*Wiser.* That's a good word," Penelope observed. "And you will let them return next summer?"

Vanessa nodded.

"Okay, let's see now." Penelope held up her left hand. "Ellie is in love and bubbling over with happiness." She folded down her index finger. "Georgiana has given up hand and foot modeling and has been awarded a contract for a coffee-table book that will document the upcoming national tour of singer Trisha Bell and her band, of which Georgiana's own faithful Freddy is a member." She folded down her middle finger. "Lily and Beth are wiser," she said, folding down fingers three and four.

"And that leaves my firstborn child." She held up her thumb. "What's next for my darling Vanessa? What do we do about her melancholy, which began long before Scott left and the Hattie trip came along?"

"*Melancholy?* That's a word one doesn't hear very often. A literary-sounding word for 'sad.' But I'm not sad. Really I'm not."

"What are you then?"

"In a holding pattern, I guess," Vanessa said, making sure she didn't sigh, "and waiting for something or someone to come along to break me free. Sometimes I think I should be out there looking for a man, but I've learned to get along with myself on the weekends the girls are gone, and at this point in my life I just don't have the energy or the confidence or the desire to change my ways in order to accommodate a male presence in my life. Right now, I want to focus on my daughters."

"What about finding a new job? You've never really liked the one you have."

"Actually, I hate my job," Vanessa said with an emphatic nod, "but I have to think about benefits and retirement. I can't tell you how hard it was going back to work after that trip. Of course, no one knew that I'd been to hell and back, and I didn't enlighten them. But everything about my job seems inconsequential, and the years are flying by. All too soon my daughters will leave the nest. But what can I do except put one foot in front of the other and keep on trudging?"

"Why don't you write a book?"

"*Me?*"

"You have a degree in journalism. You write very well. You could write about what happened to you and your sisters on your trip—either a fictionalized version or true-to-life. You've got to admit it's quite a story."

"Yes, it's quite a story," Vanessa agreed. "Ellie had thought about writing a magazine piece about three New York sisters searching for their long-lost grandmother. But it was going to be heartwarming. Now *that* would have to be a work of fiction."

"I suspect Ellie's going to be much too busy for free-lance writing," Penelope said with a pleased smile. "I want you to think about creating something good out of a nightmare."

"I don't have the time," Vanessa protested.

"With my own writing," Penelope said, holding her fingers as though they were on a computer keyboard, "I find it very satisfying when I go to bed at night knowing that the lines I wrote that day, whether few or many, are not going away. So much of what we women do never stays done. The dishes and laundry we wash and the floors we mop just get dirty again, but in the morning the words I wrote the day before are waiting for me to add to and improve upon. They are my gift to myself. Think about it, dear."

"I will. Maybe I'll write a best seller and buy a second home in the south of France."

"Does that mean you forgive me for moving here?"

Vanessa put her head on her mother's shoulder. "I still wish that you lived in New York. And I wish that Daddy were still alive. And that Lily and Beth weren't growing up so fast. And that Scott and I had done a better job with our marriage. But those are things I can't change."

"Yes, my wise girl." Penelope planted a soft kiss on Vanessa's forehead. "So what can you change?"

"I want to enjoy life more. I want to be more like my mother, who chooses happiness over unhappiness." As Vanessa spoke the words, she realized how true they were.

And as she pondered that realization, she noticed three climbers on the path below. Georgiana, Lily, and Beth were climbing up the hill.

Vanessa jumped up and called to them and waved.

They waved back. Her daughters and her baby sister.

Vanessa wished Ellie were with them. But next summer they would all be here together. By then Ellie and her doctor would be married and maybe even have a baby or one on the way. This lovely, peaceful corner of the world would become the center of their family because this was where their mother was. They would come here each summer to renew their spirits and their family ties.

Vanessa turned and wrapped her arms around her mother and buried her face against her shoulder. She needed to cry a bit before her sister and daughters reached the top. Good tears, she realized. Tears because she was loved and loved in return, which is the greatest gift that life has to offer.

FAMILY SECRETS

THE suggested questions are intended to help your reading group find new and interesting angles and topics for discussion of *Family Secrets*. We hope that these ideas will enrich your conversation and increase your enjoyment of the book.

Many fine books from Simon & Schuster feature Readers Club Guides. For a complete listing, or to read the Guides online, visit http://www.BookClubReader.com

DISCUSSION POINTS

1. At the opening of the novel, Matthew Wentworth, father of the Wentworth sisters, has been dead almost a year. Which sister is struggling the most with his death? Do you think this affects their relationships with the men in their lives? If so, how?

2. Myrna reflects on her days as Hattie, and remembers her father after the mine accident, dying a slow death, with the scars on his back from the beatings he received at the hands of his father, and not a nickel to his name. She recalls the time her father sang the Christmas carol as a "moment of pure love, the sort of which does not come often in a lifetime, the sort of which one buries away because remembering is too painful." (p. 65) How did the death of Hattie's father impact her? How did her difficult childhood mold the adult she became?

3. Why do you think the girls, Vanessa in particular, had such a difficult time adjusting to their mother's news about renting the family apartment and moving to the south of France with her new boyfriend? Do you think that Penelope could have done a better job of informing her daughters about her decision?

4. From the very first sentence, we get a glimpse into Myrna's mercurial character: "As was her custom, Myrna had deliberately kept her visitor waiting for half an hour—a practice that established hierarchy." (p. 1) Why do you think Myrna chose to handle the arrival of her long-lost granddaughters in the manner that she did? What does this say about her character? What were her other options for dealing with her new-found family?

5. After Vanessa meets Randall Cunningham, Myrna's congressman son, he confides in her: "Mother never talked about her early life, and she had no photographs or keepsakes or mementos from her childhood. Not a one. We never made a trip back to her home town, never visited her family's graves. My mother was the most private person I

have ever known, and I find it extremely difficult to believe that she would tell total strangers things that she never told her own children." (p. 284) Were you surprised by Randall's reaction when he learns the truth about his mother from Vanessa? Do you get the sense that Randall was completely oblivious to his driven mother's ways? He then tells Vanessa that the door to the mine was open. Do you think Myrna came back to free them or did Willy escape to exact revenge on her employer?

6. Myrna reflects on her relationship with Willy: "Willy's entire life revolved around pleasing Myrna and her devotion to Myrna was absolute. . . . Already loneliness was seeping into Myrna's bones as she realized how adrift she was going to be without her Willy. Willy had cared more about her than anyone else in the entire world. More than her own children." (p. 240) Discuss Willy and Myrna's relationship. Do you think it ran deeper than just employer and friend? Was it reciprocal?

7. At the end, how has each of the sisters changed? How do you think they will approach relationships in the future? How will each sister take this incredible ordeal and relate it to their lives?

8. *Family Secrets* combines a touching family saga with thrilling action and intrigue. Were you surprised when the story took such a dangerous turn?

9. At the end, Vanessa has an emotional visit with her mother in France, where she breaks down in tears and realizes, "She needed to cry a bit before her sister and daughter reached the top. Good tears. . . . Tears because she was loved and

loved in return, which is the greatest gift that life has to offer." (p. 297) Love is a major theme in the novel. Discuss the different ways it is carried throughout. What are some of the other themes?

Q & A WITH JUDITH HENRY WALL

You had written eleven genre romances under the name "Anne Henry." What made you make the switch to mainstream fiction? Is your writing process any different?
It was easier to get a genre romance published than a mainstream novel, and romances provided a wonderful training ground for me. I learned about plotting and developing characters and about discipline and deadlines.

The writing is different in that genre romances have certain limitations. These books are about the obstacles that stand in the way of true love and how a man and woman overcome these obstacles. The story generally ends with the moment of commitment. With a mainstream novel, the author has a wide-open field.

In A Good Man, *you write about three old friends over the course of twenty-five years.* The Girlfriends Club *follows a year in the lives of four women who have been friends since childhood. You frequently write about relationships between women. What interests you about these kinds of relationships?*
Women befriending and sustaining other women is a staple in both fiction and real life. I suppose I write and read such books because it reflects the importance of women friends in my own life.

When working on a novel, what's your regime? Do you put any part of yourself into your characters?

Novels are about obstacles. If characters had clear sailing there wouldn't be a story. After I decide on the obstacles, I create a cast of characters and let them act out the story for me. Writing novels is like method acting. The writer has to crawl inside the skin of the characters and think their thoughts, feel what they feel, and react as they would.

Who are some authors that have influenced you?

The books that I remember most fondly are the ones I read when I was young—the Bronte Sisters, Daphne Du Maurier, Leon Uris, Taylor Caldwell, Pearl Buck, and Leo Tolstoy. Other favorites include Herman Wouk, Jane Smiley, Gail Godwin, and so many more.

Your novel, Mother Love, *was adapted into the 1995 television movie,* A Family Divided, *starring Faye Dunaway and Stephen Collins. If* Family Secrets *were to be adapted, who would you like to see star in it?*

I can see Brooke Shields as Vanessa, Cate Blanchett as Ellie, and *Hilary Duff* as Georgiana. As for Myrna/Hattie, Cloris Leechman would do a great job.

Have you ever addressed a book club that was reading one of your books? Is it helpful in your work as an author to hear feedback from your readers?

I've talked to many book clubs via chat rooms, through speaker phones, and in person and find it most gratifying after all those many months alone with my characters and their story to hear what readers think of them.

You once said that you wrote A Good Man *because your nephew once commented that "there were more jerks in (your) books than good guys." How much do friends and family influence your work?*

I used to write with a little censor bird sitting on my shoulder telling me what I could or could not write and asking me what my family and friends would think. I banished the censor bird years ago. Now I just write. A book takes on its own life.

What's the most gratifying part of writing a novel? The most grueling?

The most gratifying part is when an epiphany presents itself and the writing starts flowing like a fountain. The most grueling part is getting started in the morning. It's been said that the art of writing is the art of applying the seat of one's pants to the chair. I agree.

Have you always wanted to be a writer?

I always liked to make up stories. Whenever my first-grade teacher needed to leave the room, she would ask me to tell my classmates a story. And I used to tell my children stories on long road trips and thought I might write children's books someday. But when I began writing fiction, I realized children weren't the audience I wanted to reach. I enrolled in writing classes, went to writers' conferences, made friends with other would-be writers, and finally sold my fourth attempt.

1. Deer Lodge is an actual town in Montana known for its two largest contributions—mining and prisons. Deer Lodge was home to the Old Montana Prison, which is now a museum, and currently houses the main corrections facility in the state. You can learn more about the town here: http://www.bigskyfishing.com/Montana-Info/city-galleries/deer-lodge-mt.shtm

2. If your book club meets for dinner, why not assign a character to each member and have them bring a dish that their character would make or enjoy? For example, Ellie is sure to bring something elegant, sparse and chic, whereas Vanessa might opt for comfort food.

3. Learn more about the author Judith Henry Wall by visiting her official site: http://www.judithhenrywall.com